House of Grace

House of Grace

MARLENE CHASE

This book is dedicated to my two daughters, Evangeline and Laurel, whose grandmother—my mother—inspired this story. May their lives continue to resound with the beauty and grace that was hers.

Prologue

Summer 1980

The brooding sky unleashed its rage on the old Victorian house where Svetlana had taken refuge with her pregnant unmarried granddaughter. The house in the small northern Wisconsin town had offered her anonymity and granted a subtle peace—until Eliana died suddenly, leaving the pale, silent child huddled now in her lap.

"*Tishina, moy rebenok,*" the old lady whispered, though the baby had not uttered a sound to be hushed. When she felt her great-granddaughter's tight grasp on her fingers, she whispered, "Hush, my baby," this time in English, though she knew the child did not hear her.

Knotty branches scraped the window like sinister fingers. But Svetlana's fear was not for the storm. She bit her lip against the pain in her right arm, a warning that she would not long be able to care for the child. What would happen to Beatrice then? Who would care for a little deaf baby? She cuddled the child closer with her good arm. "*Tishina, tishina.*"

She had spoken only English since settling in the small American town, but lately, the language of her native Russia came more readily to her lips. With the words came the memories—the old nightmares that had tormented her for more than 70 years.

A blast of thunder shook the eaves, and Svetlana was thrust again into a dungeon where,e at the age of six, she clung to her mother, terrified by soldiers who clutched Nagant revolvers in their thick hands. The scene flooded back—Crack, crack, pop, pop! Bodies crumpled and dropped like dominoes on the hard earthen floor as she screamed in terror.

Tishina! Tishina! Svetlana's mother clapped her hand over her mouth and flung a cloak over the little girl's shoulders. "Run! Run!" she rasped into her ear. "You must stop for nothing. Ivan will go with you. Run! Run!"

Ivan—skinny, dull-haired, not yet ten years old, grabbed her hand, tears glistening on his blanched cheeks as guns flashed and exploded in the fetid darkness. He pulled her away. The cloak, still warm from Mama's body, bore down on her like a lead weight.

"*Nyet*, Mama. *Nyet*! No! No! I do not want to leave you!"

"You go now! And you must not take off the cloak until it is safe. Then you must hide it. There is no more time. Go now!"

And with Ivan yanking her roughly by the wrist, she had pushed through the falling bodies into the dark forest.

Svetlana pressed her fists against her eyes, blocking out the past. *How is it that after all these years, I still see it all? Still feel the weight of the cloak. Still taste the fear!* Lightning illuminated the garden and the little carriage house beyond the thick hedge through the high garret window. The eyes of the child in her arms shone with fright; a guttural cry escaped her lips.

"It is only light in the sky," she comforted the baby and held it tighter to her chest. But her heart was hammering a warning. *Soon. Soon. Beatrice, my sweet detka. Soon I will leave you, my sweet baby. Who will keep you safe when God takes me home?*

Alexei was her only hope. He must take her; he must guard her. At first light, she would share the secret of the cloak with him. "Alexei will keep you safe, little one," she whispered. A bolt of thunder seemed to pierce her chest, and she gasped with pain. "Soon, my sweet *detka*! Soon, I must leave you."

Chapter 1

Summer 2000

Anne Westin stepped onto the porch and drew in her breath, surprised by the coolness of the evening bereft of the day's heat. A lone cricket chirped a tentative evensong, then stopped as though sensing a predator. In the distance, a freight train wailed. Passenger service had long since been discontinued. On the outskirts of the small town, few cars passed. She shivered, aware of a bewildering sense of detachment.

But this is what she had wanted. Peace and an ordinary society of friends where, as George Eliot put it, "If one had a "keen vision and feeling of all ordinary life, it would be like hearing the grass grow and the squirrel's heartbeat ... and we should die of that roar which lies on the other side of silence."

These country sounds were hers now, as was this house with its expansive grounds and woods, the moon-silvered trees fronting the two-story 19th-century house with its charming cupola. Hydrangea bushes nestled close along the wrap-around porch as though to guard its long-ago secrets.

Beyond lay the private woods, hushed in the enveloping night. The woods inspired the name she gave the stately brick house that now belonged to her. Grace Arbor. She and Richard had found it on a recent summer visit and begun preparing for the day when, with family grown and gone, they would share a less stressful life. Richard would continue his work as a science editor, and she could give herself to her poetry and occasional work-from-home editing assignments. They were still young and eager for new experiences—for a time to grow yet closer to each other.

But she was alone as she moved toward the woods that seemed to beckon with an unseen hand. Her husband's absence stung with fresh pain as the heels of her expensive Italian shoes sank into the moist ground. They were the last pair Richard had bought her before his fatal heart attack at the tender age of 50.

Buying her shoes was an odd quirk of his. Odder still, she'd never had to return a single pair because they didn't fit or because she didn't like them. It was hard to believe she must live without him for the rest of her days. "Life must go on," Sara Teasdale's plaintive observation rang. "I'm not sure just why."

Suddenly, a blue jay swooped low overhead and let out a wail. It paused in mid-flight, veered, and flapped away toward a grove of elderberry bushes. As though dissatisfied, it rose again with a raucous screech and flew toward her. She could smell its wild bird odor as its wings fanned her face, and it dove into a clump of sumac bushes.

Puzzled, she pulled back a low-hanging bough and took a step forward. Her foot touched something hard, and she stumbled into a tangle of bushes. Leaves and prickly branches scraped her legs and snagged the flannel fabric of Richard's shirt that she'd slipped over her dress. Thrust onto her hands and knees, she gasped at the face beside her.

Eyes like burned-out fuses loomed from bony sockets below a shock of white hair. An old face like wrinkled leather but softened by moonlight. Inches from her fingertips, a shovel protruded from a mound of dirt, its scarred handle as worn as the man's face. She scrambled up, heart hammering in her ears, and ran to the edge of the clearing. She looked back at the shadowy woods. Nothing moved, not even the night wind. A host of crickets rasped a mocking song.

Gingerly, she returned to the site and forced herself to look again. It was no dream. The man lay face up in the bracken as if he'd fallen asleep there. And then she recognized him—her neighbor, Alexei Popov. He was dead.

She had seen him on previous summers trudging across the property adjoining Grace Arbor with a shovel slung over his back and a gentle, crooked grin on his face. Now, he looked almost peaceful. Resigned or knowing, as though he had a secret no one else knew, or as though it was the most natural thing in the world to die in a clump of sumac bushes with a blue jay weeping over his demise.

She huddled inside the flannel shirt. What had happened? Why was Alexei Popov in her private woods at night, his shovel stuck in the ground? Virtual death on television or video was one thing, but this! Trembling, she raced back to the sheltering arms of the house.

All the warnings from friends came back in a rush as she ran. "Do you know how cold it gets up there in winter? How will you manage alone in that big house far from the city?"

It wasn't all that far, and as for cold, she was used to the biting winds of Lake Michigan. The house, over a century old but beautifully restored, was an enviable place for their children to visit—and for grandchildren in some hoped-for future. Still, moving in without Richard was a big step. She was a widow alone in a town she knew little about. Now, one of its citizens lay dead on her property. She flung open the screen door and paused to catch her breath. From inside came a loud scuffling, then a thud. And she remembered. Her son was arranging the furniture that had been shipped that morning.

How ironic that the down payment had been made on the house only weeks before Richard's death. Friends urged her not to finalize the purchase, but she had not heeded their advice; she had gone ahead with the move.

"Not there. No, that's all wrong." An insistent voice fell on the air like a whine. Jennifer Stratton, Peter's girlfriend who had come to help with the move, had definite ideas about where everything should go. Interior decorating was, after all, her specialty. "Honestly," Anne heard her quip with exaggerated dismay, "moving out to the sticks in this wilderness and at her age!"

Anne swallowed. You'd think she was 80 instead of 50. She hesitated at the door and willed her breath to return to a more measured pace.

"Where'd you say you want this?" Peter stuck his head around the corner, holding her Austrian lamp with the crystal base. "Jen thinks we should put it on the table by the bay window, but that might block the natural light." He braced the lamp against the table with his thigh and, seeing her, paled. "What is it, Mom? What's wrong?"

She pushed past him and reached for the phone with stiff fingers, grateful that she had arranged its installation before her arrival. She could barely focus on the keypad. What irony that after living for decades in the wicked city, her first call to 911 would be in a sleepy town most people had never heard of. A town with quaint, old-world shops and houses bounded by lakes and pines and deciduous trees of every variety.

"Mom?" Peter rushed toward her, frowning through anxious eyes. His glasses had slipped down the bridge of his nose, and the effect was comical even as his nearness comforted her.

She tried to stop trembling as she spoke into the receiver. "Please," she said, "there's a man in the woods—and he's dead." She dropped down on a chair and took a steadying breath. "My name is Anne Westin. I'm at the Grainger place off Highway 8," she whispered, panic rising. "Please come. Please come right away."

Assured that help was on the way, she set the phone in its cradle but continued to grip its cool contour, struck by a strange sense of *déjà vu*. It was as though she had made this call before using the same words. A sweet sing-song phrase hammered in her brain. *Welcome home. Welcome home!*

Jennifer flounced into the kitchen dressed more for a benefit luncheon than for moving furniture. "What's happened?" Not a hair of her fashionable wedge budged as she moved closer, brows furrowed like pale caterpillars, green eyes as cool as they were beautiful. "Are you all right?"

"She's had a shock," Peter said. "What's happened, Mom?"

Anne, anxious for solitude moments earlier, was glad she wasn't alone. But Peter and Jennifer would head back in the morning after getting all her things moved in. Then what? She looked from one to the other, searching for words and finding her mouth as dry as cardboard. She was sweating under the shirt she had hastily drawn over her dress. If only he were here. He would know what to do.

But Richard wasn't here. He would never be here with that everything-will-be-fine aura that had always surrounded him.

"Mom?"

Anne took a breath and steadied herself. "I was just walking along the wooded border," she said, motioning to the window where the black night yawned wide and glassy without the benefit of curtains or drapes. "I followed a bird into a clump of bushes. It was hurt or something. And then I saw him—Alexei Popov, the old man from next door." She paused, horrified anew by his vacant eyes. "He's dead."

"Dead?" Jennifer's eyes flashed in their delicately boned sockets. "How do you know?"

Anne waited a few seconds before responding. "I'm quite sure." She hesitated. She had known the moment she saw him. "He must have been digging…"

"Digging? Digging for what, for heaven's sake," Jennifer quipped.

Anne sighed. She doubted Jennifer Stratton had ever given heaven or its Ruler a serious thought unless to suggest that the celestial city might need new draperies. "I've no idea," she replied, suddenly weary and desperate to erase the image of the dead man. "We saw him walking across the yard last summer. He didn't say much, just gave a funny little smile and nodded, not seeming to care that he was on private property. I don't know much about him, except he's Latvian or Russian."

A series of gold bracelets chinked on Jennifer's delicate wrists as she braced herself against an oversized trunk. Peter shifted from one foot to the other in agitation. "Some welcome," he said, folding his arms across his chest and eyeing his mother with concern. "I'm sorry, Mom. Are you all right?"

But flashing lights streaking into the kitchen cut off any response she might have made. A car was climbing up the long driveway with a lone occupant inside. No sirens, no screeching of brakes. Just one policeman. There were probably few emergencies in small towns like this one. Strange how different the real drama was from television's nightly fare.

She led the way to the spot where she had found Mr. Popov. The policeman walked around the body, touching nothing. The coroner would probably arrive soon, and eventually, poor old Alexei would be carried away. Someone would tag the shovel and anything else they found to identify a victim or determine a cause of death. Ordinary things. That death could be ordinary seemed to her suddenly ludicrous, a terrible betrayal of life.

"You found the body?" The 40-something officer with a sheriff's badge scrutinized Anne through shrewd but not unkind eyes. In rumpled khaki pants and an equally wrinkled polo shirt, he had not been prepared for official duty. Perhaps he'd been settled on his couch after supper when the call came. He ran a hand through his blond buzz cut and pulled a pen from his shirt pocket. "Sheriff Dan Mackowitz," he said, introducing himself.

"Anne Westin." She gestured to Peter. "My son—and his friend, Jennifer Stratton."

"I heard someone finally bought this old place. Mind you, in its day, it must have been a grand one. Been a trickle of renters from time to time, but…" Mackowitz left off, continuing to appraise Anne with quick, dark eyes. His lips looked cracked and sore, perhaps from too much sun and wind. "

"I just moved in today," Anne said. The damp ground soaked through her muddy pumps that she should have exchanged for sneakers before walking in the woods.

The sheriff eyed the small group. "Is your husband here?"

"No. I'm alone. My husband passed away earlier his year." She gestured toward Peter and Jennifer, feeling her throat constrict. "But—my son is here to help me move in."

She had looked forward to her first day—the beginning of a new life, a new challenge. She'd always wanted to be part of a small community like this, and the house was perfect—remote but near enough to town to avoid isolation. Even after the down payment, Richard had left her with enough money for comfort. There would be time to read and garden, to volunteer, and to be useful.

Peter was among those who had questioned her plan to move so far north. "I know you and Dad loved it as a vacation spot, but maybe now that he's…" He had turned away, his mouth a grim line. His death had been hard on Peter, who had found no acceptance or closure. Now, he faced another reminder of his father's death and his mother's vulnerability.

"It must have been quite a shock, Ma'am," the Sheriff broke in. "What exactly happened?"

She retold the account, wondering about Alexei Popov's family. Were they nestled quietly in that small house beyond the lilac hedge, unaware that their loved one was never coming home again? Perhaps they hadn't missed him yet, expecting any moment to hear his footfall on the steps. She framed the question nagging her. "Do you have any idea why he was digging on my property?"

Mackowitz shrugged one broad shoulder. "Popov was crazy as an old hoot owl, but he was harmless. He came here—oh, twenty years ago or so." He tucked a pen behind a sunburned ear and regarded her closely through eyes fringed by lashes so pale they disappeared. "The old Russian was always digging a hole somewhere. He was a bit childlike. No one paid him much mind."

Anne hadn't thought Alexei's expression in death had the earmarks of madness. Or did death end all flaws, make one suddenly whole again?

"He had some fool notion about a treasure," Mackowitz continued. "Used to babble on about finding it." He scratched his ear, dislodging the pen, and fumbled to catch it. "Old Alexei immigrated from some Eastern country—Russia maybe. Quite the storyteller he was—always going on about life in the old country and some treasure he had to guard. Folks say he started believing his own tales. Well, maybe that's what unhinged him."

Anne tried to recall the man as he had appeared the summer before—tanned and leathery, with dreamy eyes that seemed always searching. She hadn't been afraid of him, but she had been glad for the hedge of lilacs that separated their properties.

"He worked at the lumber yard before the accident—before his mind started to slip, and he began prattling about buried treasure and toting that shovel everywhere."

A second official car arrived, and seconds later, the coroner's long, low vehicle. Two men came toward them, cameras flashing. Anne glanced up at the sheriff.

"What about Mr. Popov's family? Who looked after him if he was—as you say— mentally unstable?"

"Lives with a sister—a big clout of a woman who raises chickens and sells eggs and vegetables around town. Probably gets welfare. I couldn't say. Then, there's that retarded kid they call Beatrice."

A sad picture framed in Anne's mind—a downtrodden family without enough money or the ability to earn it. Or the inclination? The country was full of people cared for by the state, many of them doomed to repeat an established family cycle of dependence. What would Mr. Popov's family do now? How would they react to the news when it came? She searched her memory, recalling a grim woman who wore peasant babushkas. But she hadn't seen a young person around Alexei's place. *That retarded kid they call Beatrice.*

Mackowitz rubbed his jaw with thick fingers. "We all wondered when the old guy would just keel over. He was too old for all that digging and fretting. People said he would *pop off* and die one of these days." It was a crude reference to "Popov," a common Russian name. "No offense," Mackowitz quickly added, but a bright spot appeared on his cheek.

Of course, the coroner would have to determine the cause of death. One couldn't simply assume. Shocked anew by the strange ease with which they talked over the inert body, she grieved for Alexei Popov. Who was the man behind those mysterious eyes?

Life was fragile, short, and often brutal, she knew. Why hadn't she and Richard tried to befriend the man—a foreigner who was probably looked on with suspicion? Busy with plans for their future home, they had enjoyed a summer of industry mixed with pleasure. They had been absorbed in their private concerns and didn't mind if the old man cut through private property to the road. A Russian immigrant? What did they really know about Russia?

They knew about the country's failing economy and the unprecedented resignation of Boris Yeltsin. Suspicion ran high in most American minds that recalled the Cold War, and the West might well perceive the elevation of Vladimir Putin with trepidation.

"The family's a case, all right," Mackowitz said, pausing. "Don't expect the welcome wagon from them. The sister and that kid don't mix well with folks around here." He stopped, perhaps aware that his words sounded derogatory, and rubbed a hand through his short, straw-colored hair. "Well, Mrs. Westin, I'm sorry this had to happen at your place, especially on your first day here. We won't know anything more until we get the coroner's report. Sure sorry, ma'am."

He turned and called over his shoulder to a younger officer. "Anyone talked to the sister or the kid yet?" At the negative shake of the deputy's head, Mackowitz looked back at Anne. He raised a shaggy eyebrow. "You'll be around if we need you?"

She nodded, feeling a shiver pass through her again. She had hoped to feel close to Richard in this house they had planned to enjoy together. Here, she would keep all the goodness, the love, the honor that had marked their life together. She would hold him in her heart and live their dream at Grace Arbor. But now he seemed a phantom—ethereal, unreal. What if she couldn't handle living here alone?

"I told you she should never have come to this hick town," Jennifer was saying into Peter's ear. She had lowered her voice, but Anne, hearing her quite clearly, winced at the criticism. "She's never going to fit in, and you can see how unstable these people are. And this house is positively Victorian."

Peter took hold of his mother's hand. "Come on, Mom. It's been a long night; you should get some rest."

She let him lead her back to the house to the wary hum of crickets whose chirping cadence seemed to mock her. "Welcome home, welcome home."

Chapter 2

Vera Popov shifted an ungainly straw basket to her left arm and flinched. Time was when she could heft a load six times that heavy and not bat an eye. Now she felt every one of her years. How many years? She used to joke about not knowing, but it made her sad. Thinking of the past always did.

She approached the last few stops on her delivery run, weary to the bone. It seemed to her that making her deliveries took far too long. If she'd learned to drive it would be so much easier, but she'd never been good at reading. Besides, all those cars and trucks moving at the same time were scary. And she was getting older.

She felt a sharp catch in her hip. Maybe she was more than the 68 or 70 she thought she might be. Maybe she was a hundred. She pushed out her lower lip and drew it in again, thinking how Alexei might pat her shoulder and tell her that she would always be his *little* sister.

She paused to rest. Alexei didn't remember much of anything these days, let alone birthdays. She'd had to keep things going on her own since he'd gone daft—and no thanks to Beatrice, who should have stayed to help with the chores instead of going off to that school. What did a girl like her need it for anyway? It wouldn't change what she was, what everyone knew she was.

Things hadn't been too good between them since Beatrice came back. Vera swatted a fly buzzing around her sweaty face.

It was all that stuff they were teaching her, putting ideas in her head. She pushed up her tattered red scarf and wiped her forehead. *We never should have taken her in. We were too old, and Beatrice isn't right.* It had been Alexei's idea, and once her brother got something in his head, there was no changing his mind.

"She's all alone," he had said, "and I promised Svetlana. The child can be help to us later." Twenty years had passed since they'd taken in the baby named Beatrice. *What Russian girl ever had such a name?* Vera set her jaw and turned into a gravel drive-way. She winced as she felt the stones beneath her thin-soled shoes.

If Alexei ever found what he was looking for, she might have new shoes every month and flaky *pirozhok* to eat whenever she wanted. *And pretty jewelry.* She put a hand to the brooch that lay against her heart, caressed it, feeling something like peace. It was the only pretty thing she owned.

She turned into Clyde Cutter's driveway and huffed to the house where the old farmer waited on his slanted porch, an ancient dog with a stumpy tail at his feet. It rolled watery eyes at her but declined to get up. Vera handed Cutter two cartons of eggs.

He lifted the lid with grimy fingers. "These ain't as big as usual. You change the feed or something?" He frowned, took the eggs, and set them on the rickety porch swing from which he'd just risen.

"Same as always," she grunted. "You want 'em or not?" She didn't like Clyde. Not since she'd overheard him talking to Mr. Barnes in the hardware store. *That Rusky is two yolks short of a double egg, but she knows a good 'un when she hatches it!*

Big-mouthed know-nothing! She was a foreigner. So, what? There were lots of immigrants in America. She and Alexei had been born in the old country but left it behind more years ago than she could count. *Alexei.* She liked the sound of his name. She had chosen to call herself "Vera." It was a name no one questioned and carried no meaning that she knew of.

She seldom thought about her childhood. She had few good memories to recall and many that hung over her like black clouds. She looked away from the aged farmer who no longer farmed. She wanted to tell Clyde Cutter what she thought of him. Still, he'd been buying her eggs for years, and customers didn't grow on trees. Most folks settled for the cheap ones they could pick up at the market. Best not to dicker with those who prefer eggs from free-range chickens.

The old man in overalls and faded red shirt picked up an egg and held it close to one rheumy eye. He drew a scratchy breath. "I guess I'll take 'em."

Vera took the four bills from his hand and stuffed them into her pocket. He knew she had the best eggs around. She nodded, which was as close to sociability as she could muster.

He looked up, casting his gaze beyond her. "Say, what's going on down your way?"

She frowned. Was it any of his business? People should mind their own affairs like she did.

"Saw the police car and some folks from town driving up. Might be that big house over your way. I heard some rich city woman finally bought the place." Cutter spat in the time-honored way of old farmers at work in their fields. But Cutter had settled in town, tinkering with old cars and a tractor he no longer needed.

Vera peered beyond the hill. She could see activity near the woods, a car parked on the road near it. It looked like someone was walking away from her door. If the goings-on were at the Grainger's place, what did they want from her? She didn't like people coming around. She could feel the ache in her bones deepen, a sure sign something bad was brewing.

She walked on, closing the gap between the Cutter place and hers. The man she had seen at her door was leaning against a post by her chicken coop, clearly waiting for her. She pursed her lower lip. "Town people," she muttered. She didn't like them, never had. If she could just sneak in her back door and not have to talk to him. Sore feet aching, she hurried away from her neighbor's porch.

"Ms. Popov?" The voice stopped her before she could turn in at the rear door, which Alexei had never gotten around to fixing.

She paused with her hand on the broken latch and saw the badge, an officer with dark, messy hair—the officer who worked with Sheriff Mackowitz. She swallowed, set her basket on the ledge, and peered at him suspiciously.

"I'm sorry, but I have to talk to you," the young man said in a low voice, his eyes cloudy through tinted glasses. "Can we go inside?" He was skinny and leaned sideways like he hadn't been built straight. His pants were too short, making his feet look too big for the rest of him. She'd seen him in town, driving one of those police cars. He glanced in the direction of the woods, then back at her. "Please."

A small cluster of people mingled in the woods beyond them. *Those are private woods, part of the Grainger place*, she thought, her mind a perplexing muddle. "We talk here," she said. "What is it?" She grasped the green brooch on her dress and felt calmer.

"Ms. Popov?" The voice softened, and he spoke slowly as though to a child who needed comfort. He hesitated and looked at her fingers stroking the brooch. "It's pretty, ma'am."

She liked it when people noticed the gem so glittery and fine. It made her feel proud. She didn't like taking it off, even at night.

Sister, you must put in safe place, Alexei would say when he saw her wearing it. Then, when his mind had begun to slip, he seemed to notice nothing. He would walk away, mumbling thick accented fantasies.

The deputy's voice broke in. She heard it as though from a long way off. "I'm sorry to have to tell you. There's been an accident." He paused, shifted his feet, and then went on. "It's your brother, ma'am. We found him in the woods." He looked at her with sad eyes. "We need you to identify the … him."

She pulled her sweater over the brooch, over the coldness that gripped her. "Alexei? What you say about Alexei?"

"I'm sorry, ma'am. I'm afraid he's dead." He held out his hand to steady her. "Please, you have to come with me."

An accident! She couldn't move her arms, so she let them hang down over her hips and walked stiffly after him. She knew it would happen one day, the way a person knows that it is summer when leaves shine on the trees. That in winter, everything grows cold and dies. But it was summer, and Alexei shouldn't die.

The cluster of people moved aside as she and the deputy approached, leaving the figure on the ground in full view. She looked down at his face. Peaceful, utterly serene. Free from pain, from the struggle to make enough money to live, free from the taunts of people. Free from—her. She caught her lower lip in her teeth, aware of a rising panic. She should cry or something; he was her brother, but he had left her. She was alone, truly alone now. She groped with trembling fingers for the brooch.

"Is it your brother, ma'am?" the low voice prodded. She jerked as though someone had awakened her from sleep. She nodded dully and willed her feet to move. She didn't want to look at him anymore. Not like this. He'd gone, and she was left behind, just like before.

She heard the sound behind her—someone running on light feet in a kind of wild dance. Beatrice! Someone must have given her a ride home since there was no sign of her bicycle. She stopped at the edge of the woods and advanced slowly, her gaze fixed on the figure on the ground. When she dropped down beside Alexei, her sobs broke the air like bones shattering.

Alexei had been the light of her life from the moment Svetlana put her in his arms twenty years before. Now, the light had gone out. Beatrice would be not only deaf but helpless without him. Something in Vera stirred. She should comfort the girl, but she couldn't move or even hold out a hand.

The skinny lawman with big feet pulled Beatrice back gently, turning her from the scene. He looked at Vera. "Ma'am, can you talk to her?"

She could "talk" to her, but what could she understand? Beatrice lived in the silent world she had inhabited all her life. She needed comfort, to know everything would be all right. But would anything ever be all right again?

Beatrice continued to sob. She looked up at her aunt, her face wet with tears.

"Don't do no good to cry," Vera said, unable to soften the hard edge in her voice. "Don't do no good."

Beatrice looked like she had been slapped, and Vera was sorry she hadn't been kinder. Beatrice had loved Alexei. The two were thicker than thieves, she thought wildly as the girl flung herself against Vera's chest like a wild bird beating its wings in defense of itself.

Vera's arms felt like dead tree trunks. She could give no comfort. She felt only anger and terrible fear. Alexei was gone, just like he had left her before. It took 18 years before he had taken her to his house and later to America with Svetlana.

"You must be kind to Svetlana," Alexei had said many times. "She suffers; she can never forget what happens when she was little girl."

Vera groaned. Svetlana hadn't suffered—not like she suffered. Svetlana had escaped from those soldiers and their guns, hadn't she? And she was lucky enough to serve in a royal house where she had food and shelter. She had got rich enough to come to America and buy the big house beyond the lilac hedge. As Svetlana's hired servant, Vera cleaned that house and did her bidding as Alexei had ordered. Then Svetlana died, leaving a deaf baby behind for her and Alexei to raise. Vera felt a thickening around her heart. She was alone now—truly alone. Maybe if she'd been smarter, life would be different. *Two yolks short of a double egg. Oh, Alexei!*

She was smart enough to know you couldn't bring back the dead. You could cry all night, and nothing would be different in the morning. She pushed Beatrice away so that the girl could read her lips. She must be firm; she must make her understand. "Alexei is dead. We leave him to rest. You go home now."

Beatrice shook her head so fiercely that thick strands of her hair slapped against Vera's face. "No! No!" She pushed past Vera and the startled deputy to kneel again beside Alexei, to press her cheek against his leathery one. After a long moment, she grew calm but remained beside the body of the man who had been like a father to her.

Vera looked away. She knew she was not part of the bond that had drawn them together. She was left out—always the one left out. She fidgeted in her dusty tennis shoes and pressed her fingers firmly into Beatrice's soft shoulder to make her know it was time to go.

The girl got up and sprang away. Vera laid her palm over the gem that burned beneath her sweater and housedress and clutched it all the way back to the little shambling house. She clung to the strange comfort in its beautiful green depths.

Near the house, chickens strutted and pecked around her feet, cackling a greeting or a plea for grain. She knew them by name. They were her friends; they depended on her. To them, she was not dumb old Vera, two yokes short of a double egg. But tonight, she had no heart even for them.

She had no appetite for supper either. Later, she saw Beatrice looking into the little sun porch that had been Alexei's bedroom. The girl leaned her forehead against the doorframe for a long time before tiptoeing away.

Vera lay down, fully dressed. The officer said the new owner of the Grainger house had found Alexei. She swallowed something sour that rose in her throat. *The woman shouldn't be there. It isn't her place!* She should go back where she belonged and leave them in peace. Maybe people like Shane Eldridge would stop talking about things they knew nothing about. She rubbed her hand over the swell of her stomach, feeling the ache there. But what if the gossip was true? Now Alexei could never find it.

She pictured him trudging off with his old shovel over his shoulder like some medieval hunter jabbering on endlessly about finding Svetlana's treasure. He got worse after Beatrice left for the school that taught the deaf to speak. Lately, he hadn't made any sense at all.

Where was he now? What happened when you died? If she were smarter, she'd know. Vera tried to imagine her brother smiling and strong. She pulled her sweater tighter against the night chill and remembered a lifetime in the old country when they were children.

She remembered the day they took her to the orphanage after the accident that killed their mother and father. She could never forget the dark, the cold rooms and nameless children lined up on hard little cots. She remembered how hard it was to sleep when you were hungry.

Eventually, as with all orphans who reached 16, she was turned out to forage for herself on the streets of Moscow. Girls like her had little chance of earning their bread without selling themselves. So long ago—another country—another era. She hadn't thought about those days for a long time.

Alexei had been luckier. He had not been taken to the orphanage but apprenticed to a wealthy cabinet maker who had married Svetlana. Years passed until Alexei found her in the brothel and begged Svetlana to take her in. She and Alexei had served her well enough that Svetlana had brought them along when she and her daughter Eliana came to America.

Vera turned on the lamp by her bed. She always slept with the light on so she could feel its heat warming her face. There must be no more dark corridors where hungry children slept. *Never again! Please God—if you really are God—never again!*

A shadow passed behind her curtained doorway. Beatrice appeared, red hair spilling over her shoulders and shining in the lamplight. Tall in her long blue robe, she was no longer a child but a woman. She crept like a cat on velvety feet. Vera's nerves jumped.

Beatrice would likely leave her, too. It had been "Uncle Alexei" she loved, even though he wasn't her real uncle, any more than she, Vera, was her aunt. "What you want?" she asked, raising her head from the pillow. Her voice sounded as hard and bitter as she felt. Beatrice would go away too—leave her in peace. But there was no peace, only a hard lump where her heart should be.

"Are you okay?" came the unaccustomed voice. It still surprised Vera that Beatrice had learned to speak at that fancy school. Shadows circled the girl's eyes. She held a tissue to her nose that was red from weeping. She lifted her shoulders. "I brought you tea."

Vera glanced at the tray with a mug and a little pile of crackers. It still shocked her to hear Beatrice speak. She should thank her and say she was sorry about Alexei, but she couldn't bring herself to speak. She rolled away toward the wall.

A light clink on the dresser and the soft rustle of the curtain meant Beatrice had gone, leaving the tray behind. Gone without comfort from the one who should provide it. Vera thumped the mattress with her fists. She was angry at Beatrice, at Alexei, at Clyde Cutter, at the smug neighbor who now owned Svetlana's house—at the whole unfair cup of life. After a while, she slept with her fingers coiled around the green brooch.

Chapter 3

The sun broke through the haze above the ridge and ruffled the rose-patterned curtain. Anne woke confused, but quickly, the previous day's events came into startling focus.

Voices drifted up the stairs. Having helped unload trunks and crates, Peter and Jennifer would leave after breakfast. Peter, who always viewed the natural world with fascination, had likely been up before dawn exploring. He had probably analyzed a dozen local wildlife specimens and taken a morning run through the woods. She chuckled despite the previous evening's debacle.

Jennifer, an interior decorator of some note, would be anxious to return to her world of bright chintzes and social fund raisers. Her voice rose over Peter's as she pointed out the house's imperfections, waxing eloquently about the uneven cornice over the hall windows. "Didn't they use a level or ruler to restore this old place?"

Anne sighed. There were more problems than crooked cornices in a house a century old. Something tragic had happened right here on her property. Her next-door neighbor was dead, and she hadn't the faintest idea what had happened or why. The sense of uncertainty lay over her like a pall. She had looked forward to coming here, but what would life really be like?

She put on jeans and one of Richard's oversized shirts and went downstairs to the aroma of coffee, pausing in mid-flight.

She imagined what it would be like if Richard was here, a tender smile working its way from his eyes to the gentle curve of his mouth. If she could only put out her hand and find his there. Gripping the banister, she forced away the sweet nostalgia.

At the counter, Peter fiddled with the coffeemaker, and Anne was struck by how little he had changed since he was eight or nine years old. His glasses still slipped down the narrow bridge of his nose, and his hands still moved with busy intensity. Gentle and inquisitive, he had always been interested in everything. Perhaps that's why it had been difficult for him to settle down. Something always drew his attention. Anne was glad that, despite his angst, he hadn't lost interest in life's wonders.

Even the perfectly cosmopolitan Jennifer couldn't change Peter's love of nature and passion for science. They had been going together for a year or so, but the subject of marriage hadn't surfaced. A good thing, Anne thought. Peter needed more time to heal after Richard's death. Something had broken in him when his father had been taken so suddenly. He never spoke of it, but she couldn't help thinking that it festered beneath the surface.

"Morning, Mom," Peter said, peering over his glasses." He looked rested after their strange night, but something in his too-wide smile betrayed unease. He was filling a thick, garish mug pulled from among a box she had labeled *ESCATOS*.

There should be some humor in packing up to move, so she had written the Greek term for "last things." She smiled as she wrapped her hands around the mug, averting her gaze from the muddy newspaper by the back door—a grim reminder that yesterday, Alexei Popov had died on her property.

Jennifer dropped a suitcase inside the kitchen door and shuffled to a chair. "I hope you slept better than I did," she said dramatically, reaching for a cup of coffee. "I must say I'm not sorry we're leaving today." She gave Anne a sheepish look. "You ought to come back with us too, you know."

Anne let the comment go unanswered. She had made it clear that she had no intention of leaving her new home. She would stay at Grace Arbor. She held out a plate of buttered toast. "Have some breakfast. You two have a long ride ahead of you."

"What kind of town is this anyway?" Jennifer asked after a few seconds of silence. She took a bite of toast and chewed daintily.

"I'm told Ladystone was named for the young bride of an eighteenth-century statesman who carved out a homestead from acres of raw wilderness."

"Wilderness," Jennifer said wryly. "I can believe that."

Anne ignored the comment and continued. "After designing a log home for his new bride, he built a paper mill in the heart of lumber country and began a thriving town." Anne paused. "Unfortunately, he died when he was still a young man. The mill never really flourished after that."

"They kept the town going, though," Peter added. "Even during the 30s when the Depression decimated other little towns."

"Well, I can't imagine what one does to keep from total boredom here," Jennifer said. She placed her dishes on the counter and raised her pale eyebrows.

"Finding a dead man on your property is hardly boring," Anne said.

Jennifer laughed and cast Peter a wry look. "For my part, I'd rather cope with the Dan Ryan expressway at rush hour."

"I think Jennifer will always be a city girl, Mom," he said, shrugging his shoulders. "Like they say, 'you can take the girl out of the city, but you can't take the city out of the girl.'"

Anne sighed. She was a city girl, too, but the hectic pace had left her longing for a quieter life. *The grass growing … the squirrel's heartbeat ... the roar on the other side of silence.* She drew a breath. "I plan to enjoy the rivers and woods and get to know this house and my neighbors." After last night's terror, maintaining a restful spirit might be a challenge.

She swallowed a lump in her throat as Peter and Jennifer rinsed their dishes and checked tags on their luggage. Once they were on their way, she would be alone. Really alone, as she had never been before.

Peter squeezed his mother's shoulder playfully, but his eyes remained solemn. "It's going to be different living in the boondocks, you know," he said quietly. "I hope you know what you're getting into."

She savored the feel of his hand on her shoulder. He had been such a comfort after Richard's death. "This is hardly the boondocks, but thanks, dear. I'm only a few miles from town." She winked. "And I'm already well known to the local police."

"How about I leave you my cell phone?" Peter had been pressuring her to get one, and she had resolutely refused. One more baffling electronic gismo; another disruptive annoyance in restaurants or on the street. Cell phones were downright invasive. She had decided to be the last woman on the planet to get one. By the end of the 80s, they had become much more affordable but were still bulky and powered by plugging into the car cigarette lighter. Nokia models sold for $400 at full price.

She placed her cup in the sink and curved her left arm around Peter's waist. "Thank you, dear, but no." She smiled at the disapproving shake of his head. "Come back soon. You know I'll miss you," she said, meaning it. But she couldn't deny a certain eagerness as she considered her need for solitude, time to settle her thoughts.

She waved until they were halfway down the road toward the state highway. And whether from excitement or fear, Anne felt chilly enough to grab her sweater from the back of a chair. A good long walk was just what she needed. It would give her a feel for the neighborhood again and the opportunity to see if the blackberry bushes along the northern ridge had ripened. One of the things she and Richard had looked forward to on their last summer vacation together was homegrown blackberry pie.

Their brief summer in the small town had been rejuvenating. They had taken in the local sights and sometimes did nothing but sit in the sun. In the evening, they might go out for dinner or to the local root beer stand. Once, they took in the county fair and brought back a teddy bear the size of Mt. Rushmore. She embraced the sweet memories, letting them renew her joy.

As she walked along, a pale sun shone on grass still wet with dew. The breeze was so fresh it might be edible. Lacy bridal wreath and blue cornflower glistened in pastoral contrast to her earlier fears. She reveled in the beauty of the world as she recalled lines from Hopkins' poem:

> Oh, morning, at the brown brink eastward, springs —
> Because the Holy Ghost over the bent
> World broods with warm breast and with ah! bright wings.

She passed her neighbor's house. Margaret Edgerton had driven up to Grace Arbor one afternoon last summer in an ancient Oldsmobile, offering tomatoes from her garden. They had spent an hour of enjoyable camaraderie. Now, Margaret's old house, faded from sun and wind, appeared to lean as though too tired to stand upright. The roof was patchy with ill-matching shingles, and one black shutter hung loose, making the window look like a sad little face. Grass grew high along the foundation, and dandelions dotted the lawn in buttery profusion.

Margaret had taught elementary school to two generations of the town's citizens. Known for her firm hand and kind heart, she was said to be a pillar of the community and her property a landmark. But Anne saw that the driveway now was strewn with weeds and pebbles. Here and there, a tree limb lay abandoned after a storm. A rusted tractor leaned against a weather-bleached shed. Perhaps Margaret was unable to keep up with the repairs now. Or maybe she had left, and someone else had moved in.

Anne sighed. Would she be like Margaret in a few years? Old and alone, comforted only by memories? She stopped to lean against a slender tree—a rare white birch. Experts predicted that within a few years, the species might die out altogether. The thought did little to brighten her mood.

Richard would not approve of this morose preoccupation. He had always refused to be consumed by dark thoughts. If only he were with her now. Daydreaming and looking back were pastimes of the old, weren't they? She was still young, and besides, wasn't 50 the new 40? She shook herself mentally. She would check on Margaret Edgerton soon, but it was time to go home. Time to face the sealed boxes and empty rooms.

As she approached, she was surprised to see a young woman in her yard standing with arms outstretched as though to embrace the house. In jeans and a blouse of sky blue, she rocked from left to right in a kind of slow dance as copper hair billowed around her like a gilded cloud.

Anne walked on, closing the distance between them steadily. When she reached the top of her driveway, she paused. Why didn't the dancer turn to greet her? What was she doing, swaying like a woodland sprite? Was she meditating? Practicing Yoga techniques? "Hello!" she called.

Only a few feet from the porch, the young woman did not turn around. Presently, she lowered her arms and wrapped them around herself as if she were cold or in pain.

"May I help you?" Anne asked, stopping beside her.

The young woman jumped, nearly losing her footing, and stared out of wide eyes so deeply blue they were almost violet. Her hands flew to her mouth as she began inching backward.

"Wait!" Anne called.

But she leaped away behind the house and scrambled through the thick hedge, leaving branches quivering in her wake.

Who was this intruder? And why had she been staring at Grace Arbor with such a look of awe? Why had she run like a frightened animal when confronted?

Anne went inside the unsettled kitchen that retained the evening's damp chill. She pushed the button on the coffee maker, disturbed by the incident and feeling desperately alone. Finding Alexei Popov dead on her property had been horrifying. Now, someone was loitering near her house. Could the lovely young woman be Alexei's girl? The one Mackowitz had called "a case"? Anne bristled against the demeaning label.

"Retarded," he had said. But the wide violet eyes had been intelligent, alive. Maybe she had simply wanted to be closer to the place where Alexei Popov had died. Anne shivered. She ought to walk over to her neighbor's house, knock on the door, and say she was sorry for their loss. But it had only been hours since the death. In the throes of new grief, the family would hardly embrace a visitor.

She knew what it was like. When Richard died, she had felt like Millay's "little brown pool, dying inward from the edge." No, she wouldn't call on the Popovs yet. Better to wait. If they were really "rude and antisocial," as the police chief said, they would probably not welcome her intrusion.

She poured herself a cup of coffee and climbed the stairs to the east bedroom. She would begin unpacking and turn that bedroom into her study. Work was good medicine for the aching heart, wasn't it? The wedding band on her finger suddenly blurred with unexpected tears.

Peter had hooked up her computer and printer, turning the snake pit of cords into one neat coil behind the desk. The intricacies of electrical and mechanical engineering would have to be learned like a new language. She sighed, remembering the hours it had taken her to put a microwave cart together, which Richard could have done in 20 minutes.

The morning slipped away. Well into the afternoon, Anne remembered the documents she was to take to the real estate agent handling the purchase of the house. Richard had come to trust the realtor, turning to him after a brief association with another agent, a man with the memorable name of Joe Lair. It was rumored that he might have been aptly named. Richard's choice of the well-respected, straight-talking Lance Crane had proved providential.

She tucked the papers into her briefcase. Richard and the realtor had become friends in the process of locating a retirement house. They were approximately the same age and loved the river. They had fished together, returning from a local restaurant with sunburned foreheads, sheepish faces, and fried chicken. So much for their fishing prowess.

Now, she found herself looking forward to seeing Lance. She wanted to hear a friendly voice. It was still early enough; she'd drop by and hope he was in. She left everything in its disordered state and went to shut the windows. A cool breeze wafted through the old sheet she had hastily affixed for privacy. The summery fragrance gave her heart. Thank God there were still silver maples and sunshine and honeysuckle—Emily Dickinson's "old sophistries of June."

Suddenly, a darting movement through the lilac hedge caught her eye. A flash of blue fabric and red hair gleaming in the sun. She drew in her breath. The girl was back. Maybe she was just curious to see who had moved in. Or was she watching her?

Anne set her jaw and gave the latch a final snap. She had come here for privacy and peace, but the neighbors behind the high hedge were unsettling her nerves. She jerked the curtain closed and, snatching her briefcase, made her way downstairs to the door.

Chapter 4

*B*eatrice peered over the thick hedge that separated the Grainger estate from the house where she lived with Alexei and Vera. *Only Vera*, she corrected herself, wiping away a fresh tear. The day Alexei died, she had stayed in her hiding place a long time, sharing her grief with the brooding pines and scampering creatures unmoved by the death of the one she loved the most in the world.

She had paused as she stepped out of the sheltering woods, seeing the Grainger house beyond and a tall man with heavily-rimmed glasses behind dark eyes that seemed tinged with amber, perhaps from the sun that gleamed on his brown hair. The stranger was talking to the new owner, and watching his lips from behind a shrub, she knew he loved her. His mother, perhaps? *What would it be like to have a mother?*

Another stranger stood nearby, clutching her arms against herself and tapping one foot impatiently. She wore a bright magenta blouse with gold chains around her neck and bangles at her wrists. After a few moments, she unfolded her arms and clutched at the man's sleeve, saying something she couldn't read. Beatrice watched the two climb into a car and speed away, the new owner waving from the porch.

Had it only been two days since Alexei had died alone in the dark woods? Time seemed to have stopped, and she wondered how it could possibly continue. But here she was, once more peering over the lilac hedge that separated her from the Grainger House. Her muscles ached from trying to see without being seen, from the sorrow that wrapped around her. As she watched, the new owner suddenly emerged from the house and walked around the path to where her late-model car was parked. She got into it and, after a few moments, started down the long drive-way. Beatrice raised herself on tiptoe as the car moved away. Silence descended. The grand house, left to its solace, seemed relieved, too, as the new owner disappeared.

Please, let her keep driving and never come back. Her thoughts might be a prayer—if she knew how to pray.

She stepped out from behind the hedge. How she loved this house with its cupola and mysterious windows. As a child, she used to pretend it was hers. She would play along the wind-ing creek, catch tadpoles, and climb the trees. Despite repairs and updates, the house had remained vacant for a long time. Occasionally, people came, walked around the perimeter, strok-ing their jaws, and talked among themselves. Then they'd go away, leaving the house at peace.

As a teenager, she liked to bring her books and sit under a tree hidden from the road. Where no one would point or nod or speak into their hands. Where she could not see them smile sadly over the fate of Alexei Popov's poor dumb girl who lived in the rundown house behind the property.

She crept around from the back of the house and checked the hydrangeas and the graceful spiraea sprays with hundreds of tiny white flowers on a single branch. She had looked after the perennials at the great house since she was little. She had learned their names and preferences for shade or sunlight. Uncle Alexei knew how she loved being here in this secret garden. She imag-ined his smile and eyebrows that looked like cricket legs arched over his eyes. She thought about the tuft of beard, white in his sun-weathered face.

She pulled an errant weed from among the ferns that grew on the shady side of the house. No one had tended them while she was away, and weeds had spread, choking the tender fronds. In the few weeks since her return, she had nurtured them with fierce intensity. Then, the city lady had come, putting an end to her gardening.

She had learned that there were 12,000 species of ferns, which had no seeds or flowers but reproduced by spores. Uncle Alexei had listened patiently when she told him about the ferns. She talked to him, even when he began to mumble and fidget and when his eyes went vacant, the trivia no longer registering in his brain.

Beatrice knew she shouldn't come here. The house belonged to someone else now. Someone who could come back at any moment and surprise her the way she had that morning.

She paused at a low window and frowned at her reflection, the long copper hair curling in wisps around her face. She inspected her high cheekbones and wide eyes, which were too deep to be blue. Alexei used to say they were dark as purple verbena. She wondered about the lady who had hung on the young man's arm. What color were her eyes? She was shapely and beautiful; Beatrice saw herself as skinny and awkward. The man with the kind eyes wouldn't look twice at a girl like her.

She turned away from her image. In a few days. she would be twenty-one. Not that anyone would remember. No one ever remembered except Uncle Alexei; in the last few years, he had forgotten, too. He'd given her a hat from the "Nearly New" shop on her twentieth birthday. It was green with gauzy ribbons and enormous red poppies. "For you, my little *lapushka,*" he had said.

"Why do you call me that?" she had wanted to know.

"It means little cat in my country. And it is only for someone special like you." With an elaborate gesture, he placed the hat on her head and watched as she whirled around in an exaggerated dance just for him.

"Poor old Alexei." That's what everyone called him—a pathetic figure picking up scrap metal and telling wild stories to delight children and annoy grown-ups. A slow tear slid down her cheek. She rubbed it away, tasting its salt. A toad hopped onto a flat rock and blinked at her. She could see its small body expand and contract and wondered what it thought about. Did toads think? Or just sit in the sunshine like grumpy old men?

Beatrice laughed at herself, at her toad thoughts and silly wonderings. Would she never grow up? Everyone grew up; everything changed. It was the way of life. She'd known someone would buy this house one day. Her house. She liked to think of it that way. But she was just the girl who lived behind it and who loved this house for a reason she could not explain.

You are a silly girl, she told herself and dropped again to her knees. She drew in the delicate fragrance of sweet peas that grew among the ferns. What hand had made them so beautiful? Had that same hand made her? And why had He made her as she was?

Suddenly, she became aware that she was not alone. She glanced to her left. Large feet encased in dirty tennis shoes stopped just inches from her. An unmistakable odor of talcum powder and onions identified the interloper.

"I told you, you ain't got no business here," Aunt Vera said. "This house belong to new lady now." Her heavy arms flapped as she signed, thick fingers beating the air. Furry caterpillar brows crawled over stormy eyes as black as her short hair, which at seventy gave no sign of graying.

"I'm sorry!" Beatrice signed. She rose to her full height to face her aunt. Taller by a head, her gaze fell on the elegant brooch that always hung on her aunt's flowered housedress. No pants for Vera; she was old school. Facets of the green stone matched the sparks from her angry eyes. Then as suddenly as light changes the color of a gem, the old woman's face went slack. She dropped her arms to her sides.

"We got things to do. No time to waste here." Vera turned away, stumbling over the pail Beatrice used for weeds.

"I know. I just wanted to check on the flowers," she signed. But Vera had turned her back.

Beatrice dusted off her jeans and squared her shoulders. Things would change now that Alexei was gone. There would be few words. Uncle Alexei had formed them for her silent ears in his funny, patient way. He would take her hand in his when they walked through the meadow on a warm afternoon. Her throat tightened.

Vera turned and squinted through small black eyes—flat, as though the life had gone out of them. "Why you come to 'dis house?" Anger brought out her thick Russian accent. "Why you tend flowers in garden don't belong to us?"

Beatrice turned away. She could not have told why being here with the earth under her fingers felt so good, so natural. She could not explain why she needed to be here. She felt the tears come again. She and Uncle Alexei had taken care of her; they must have loved her. Didn't they? Who would love her now?

Maybe she would never know about her real mother and father, except that both were dead. Her grandmother, too, had been very old by the time she was born. Alexei would say only that her grandmother had been born in Russia and that her life had been hard.

She followed Vera back through the lilac hedge where clusters of tiny flowers had dried up on the bushes. She felt as used and old as they. She had a sudden longing to run after Aunt Vera and grab her large hand. But she would be chided for being foolish. Slowly, she followed her through the lilac hedge, leaving the garden she loved behind.

She saw him waiting outside their house. Shane Eldridge, dark hair gleaming in the sunlight, leaned against his car. He was handsome in a white shirt and dark sunglasses—like a character from a novel or a movie. She felt her stomach flutter. Boys had seldom come around, but since she'd returned and gotten a job at the hospital, Shane had started paying attention to her. Her breath caught.

"Hello there, little Bea."

She smiled and looked down at her sandaled feet, dusty from the garden. She must look a sight in her soiled clothes and wind-blown hair. She wished he wouldn't come by unannounced, catching her off guard. He was so sophisticated, so cool. He had once lived in New York, he told her. It seemed like the other side of the world—some magical world she would never see.

"Come for a spin with me," he said, forming his words much more slowly than necessary, for she had become very good at reading lips. "A ride," he clarified, as though she didn't know what a spin was. It stung. She should be used to people thinking she didn't know anything. Being deaf didn't mean being dumb. How could people still think that way?

She could smell the heady fragrance of Brut After-Shave and see the rippling muscles in his biceps as he strode confidently toward her, hands riding loosely in his pockets. Vera reached him first and planted both hands on her large hips. She glared at Shane. "Vat you vant?" she growled.

Shane smiled. "Ms. Popov, you don't mind if I take this lovely creature off your hands for a little while," he said smoothly and cocked his head at Beatrice in a pleading little-boy gesture. He peeled off a ten-dollar bill from his wallet and handed it to Vera. "And I need two dozen of your best eggs. You know, those free-range kinds from chickens that haven't been all caged up."

Vera frowned but wadded the money into her fist. "Eggs ain't ready yet. You pick up tomorrow." She looked curiously like a disturbed bullfrog as she hunched her shoulders and turned from Shane with a finger pointed at Beatrice. "You come back one hour."

Shane nodded politely, not losing his charming easiness as he opened the passenger door of a maroon Jeep. He gestured for Beatrice to get in, and they sped down the dusty road. Wind streamed in the windows and flattened their summer shirts against their bodies. Beatrice studied him from the corner of her eye. The curly hair on his forearms and the strong set of his hands on the wheel made her a little dizzy.

His skin was smooth and tanned except for rims of pale skin behind his ears, where the sun didn't reach. She was surprised by an urge to brush back the resistant tendrils that dipped over his forehead. Her stomach tightened like a bowstring. Did he like her? He'd begun coming around her house a few weeks ago to see Uncle Alexei. They talked, Alexei in his strange, disjointed way and Shane with a patient smile. He was one of the few people who bothered to talk to her uncle. She owed him something for that.

Shane ordered two large chocolate cones when they stopped at the Dairy Queen and licked a drip from the edge of one before handing it to her. The intimacy of the gesture made her nervous, but she took it and licked the ice cream gingerly. After a while, he leaned toward her. "I'm sorry about your Uncle."

She looked down, touched by his sympathy. There had been no one to talk to about the ache inside her and the fear about what would happen next.

"He was my friend," he continued, his face a study in concern. "I'm very sorry, my little Bea."

Her tears fell. She couldn't stop them. He pulled her into a warm embrace, and she felt his hands moving over her back and through her hair. She could feel the soft vibrations in his throat and his warm breath. His lips moved against her ear, and she could no longer see his mouth. She wished she knew what he was saying.

His hand traveled slowly up from her waist, rising higher. Breathless, she squirmed out of his arms. "I'm all right now," she signed, angry for being afraid and forgetting that Shane did not know sign language. She wanted him to find her attractive, to see that she was like other girls and could be witty, smart, and fun.

She wasn't the backward deaf girl anymore. She had grown up and had a job in the data processing department of the hospital. But at this moment, she felt vulnerable and alone. If she could only speak clearly, make people understand. But forming words was hard, and she could only guess if she made them correctly. He was watching her, an odd gleam in his eyes.

"I have to go home now," she said, careful to keep her hands rigid at her sides and not to sign.

"Sure, sure," he said. Then his eyes softened. "You should speak more often. You have such pretty lips." Was he laughing at her? Talk came so easily to Shane. It wasn't easy for her. Nothing about coming back home had been easy. Everyone still regarded her as "that poor little retarded girl of Alexei's who couldn't talk." But everything was changing. What she had learned at the school for the Deaf had changed her. Sometimes, she felt as though she was waking from a long sleep. She wished she could talk to Alexei about it.

"I'm coming to the funeral, Bea," Shane said with exaggeration.

People often did that, thinking that if they shouted loud enough, the deaf could hear them. At the school, she had been taught not to think of herself differently than hearing people and not to be afraid. But just that morning, she had run like a scared rabbit from Anne Westin.

Shane touched her face. "I can drive you home after the funeral, and we can talk." He squeezed her shoulders, his hands hot against her skin.

She looked down at her hands. She didn't want to think about tomorrow. About that final goodbye to the only one who had ever loved her. Did Shane love her? She liked it when he touched her, but sometimes she was afraid. There had been a boy once—when she was eleven—an older boy who had liked her. But then she had seen him and another boy together. She had read his lips and learned what he wanted from her.

But Shane was only trying to comfort her, wasn't he? "Thank you," she said once more, this time not caring whether the words came out right and feeling almost happy.

"Okay," Shane said, brushing a stray curl off her forehead. "Tomorrow then."

She jumped out and ran to her house, her heart beating fast.

She had no right to feel happy, not even for one moment. Uncle Alexei was dead, and she would never see him again.

Chapter 5

A woman in oversized glasses and hair piled on her head in the fashion of a bygone era ushered Anne into the realty office.

Lance Crane stood, quick recognition in his face, and came around a desk strewn with papers and books. "Anne! I heard you were back. It's great to see you!"

Surprise and pleasure beamed in eyes bluer than she remembered. They'd been in touch over the phone, but she'd forgotten how formidable he was in person. His hair had silvered completely in stunning contrast to his deeply tanned skin. He wore a white shirt with a crimson necktie loosened at his throat.

"Hello, Lance." She took his outstretched hand, which was sinewy, tan as his face, and strong. The previous summer's memories streamed back—having coffee with him and Richard. Both outdoor enthusiasts, he and her husband had quickly become friends. "It's good to see you too," she said, recalling their fishing caps hanging on pegs, their fishing poles balanced against the cabin door.

She gathered her wits and stammered, "I got busy unpacking and almost forgot about these." She pulled a sheaf of papers from her purse and held them out.

"Please, sit down," he said, pulling out a chair for her and sweeping a mound of papers to one side of his desk. "Can I get you some coffee?"

"No, I'm fine. Late lunch..." She watched his face as he leaned back in his chair and rifled through the small stack of paper. Had the news about Alexei Popov traveled? What did he think of the welcome she'd received? He tapped his pen meditatively on the arm of his chair and, after a long moment, looked up intently. "How have you been, Anne? I mean, since Richard—" He drew his brows together in quick embarrassment.

Anne dropped her gaze to a thin layer of dust on the windowsill. "It's been hard, but Richard and I had good years together." She drew in her breath and let it out in what probably sounded like a sigh. Most people avoided the mention of her husband's name, fearing it might launch her into melancholy. Lance's straightforward concern was refreshing. "I miss him," she said. "We'd planned to grow old together here." She looked up, cheered by his familiar face. "But now... well, I have my memories."

"The children—are they well, Anne?" His voice had deepened, whether from concern or some remembrance that troubled him. She smiled. It was good to be with someone Richard had called "friend," someone who might be her friend too in this new setting that had taken on such alien proportions.

"They're fine, too," she said. "Peter's a microbiologist— still single—married to his work. He just left this morning after helping me get settled. And Dawn is in college and working at a children's camp this summer. She's a counselor for underprivileged children. She was always good with children." She stopped herself. It would be easy to ramble on about the children.

"But what about you?" she asked, meeting his gaze. His wife had died of cancer several years before; there had been no children—no one with whom to indulge his nostalgia, no son or daughter to look out for him when he got old. A glance at his left hand indicated that he had probably not remarried.

He began to weave his fingers together as though something had come unraveled. "Well, I'm still here," he said with a lift of silver eyebrows. "Selling a little real estate, getting my boat out on the water from time to time." He shrugged. "Things are okay." Lance pushed in the end of a ballpoint pen, released it, and pressed it again. The lines in his forehead deepened, and a little muscle in his jaw tensed. "I heard about what happened. I'm sorry," he said. "It's a tragedy, but finding him must have been hard."

"It was pretty upsetting," she said, shaking her head to dispel the image imprinted there. "Chief Mackowitz said he probably had a heart attack, maybe from the exertion of digging. I understand he did that a lot." She paused. "Did you know Alexei Popov?"

"Everyone knew Alexei," he said. "I've only been here a few years, but I found out what a colorful character he is. People say he lived here a long time."

"They say he wasn't quite right in his mind."

"He was attacked on his way home from work—beaten up and left in a ditch. But that was long before Rose and I moved here." Lance hesitated, setting the pen down with deliberation as though the mention of his wife had derailed his thoughts. After a pause, he continued. "Never was well after that, they say—wasn't able to work, just scoured the countryside for bits of tin and aluminum and other junk he brought home."

"That's terrible," she said. "How long have he and his sister lived in that old place behind mine?"

"Long as I've been here," he said. "It wasn't always so run down, though. Alexei was good with his hands; he was quite a craftsman until his accident." He leaned back against a leather chair worn at the armrests. "Their house was actually built on your property before it was re-zoned."

"Really?" She realized she knew little about the house. Richard had handled the details.

"Alexei and his sister used to work for the former owner," he continued. "An elderly European lady with a lot of mystery surrounding her. Odd tales about her." He paused and cleared his throat. "Small towns thrive on gossip—especially when it comes to exotic places and eccentric people."

"I understand they were from Eastern Europe—Russia?"

He shrugged. "A part of the world that Americans don't readily embrace. The Cold War and all that spy stuff still puts people on edge. The "perestroika" and "glasnost" of the 80's didn't do much to improve our perception."

Had Richard checked into the background of the property? It had not occurred to her to ask. The house and grounds were lovely and available, and they were in a beautiful location in Northern Wisconsin, where they'd always wanted to live. As for gossip, she'd never put any stock in it.

"Finding Alexei there must have been pretty scary for you, Anne."

Hearing him say her name touched her somehow. She nodded and picked up the thread of her story. "He was digging up the ground in the woods on the north end of my property." She looked at him and saw confirmation in his face. "When I found him, he was lying there with his shovel by his head." She paused, remembering the staring eyes and rigid body.

"It must have been a terrible shock." A silence followed until, at length, he said, "It's a wonder you didn't just pack up and go home."

"My son thought I should. And his girlfriend thinks I've lost my mind. But Richard and I were smitten with the property the first time we saw it." She broke off imagining Richard listening from beyond the grave with indulgent attention. She shook herself mentally.

"I've named it Grace Arbor because of all the trees around it." She laughed. "I'm not sure why. Naming your house is something the British do—and usually with a lot more ingenuity and creativity. But I still feel the house is right for me, even though I'm alone now. I want to make it my home. I'm grateful for all you've done to secure it." She felt suddenly awkward. She had given a lengthy rationale he hadn't asked for. She couldn't have explained, in any case, the sense of rightness she felt about the house. Well, until finding Popov.

"Well, if you're still intent on it, Anne, I'll take care of the details." He looked down at the documents on his desk, picked up the pen again, and tapped it on his desk. "There are other houses, other properties, though. I could help you locate something else. It's not too late." His voice had taken on a surprising urgency.

She looked up, startled. The deal was already sealed, and she had moved in lock, stock, and barrel. Would he return their initial investment and put the house back on the market? She searched his face. "I wouldn't think of it," she said firmly.

He gave his pen a final tap and leaned back in his chair. "Then it's settled." He took a deep breath as though in resignation. "I'd like to come out and see the property. The boundary lines need to be re-checked to make sure they agree with the assessment on the finalized deed."

"Certainly," she said.

"It should have been done before now," he continued, squaring a stack of papers with studied concentration. "My surveyor kind of dropped the ball." He rose and came around the desk, extended his hand. "I hope you'll allow me to assist you personally."

"Of course." She studied him briefly, still surprised by his quick suggestion of giving up Grace Arbor. "Now is as good a time as any," she said. "If I'm not keeping you from something."

She had planned an afternoon of shopping and reacquainting herself with the town, but that could be put off until tomorrow to solidify necessary legal matters. "If I'm not messing up your schedule ... "

"Schedules can be rearranged, especially for friends who turn up after too long an absence." He buttoned his coat at a still-trim waist and pressed the intercom button. "Joyce, I'll be gone the rest of the day. Tell Shane I'll see him in the morning." Turning to her, he added, "Let's take my car. After the walk-through, I'll bring you back to finalize the deal."

She hesitated, torn between irritation at his taking command and relief at having a decision made for her.

The sun on green fields yielded a soporific glow as they rode out of town—a glow she'd missed on the way in. Cornflowers and Queen Anne's lace danced across the meadow like grand ladies at a green and gold ball. She loved wildflowers—nothing fancy or contrived about them. Lance must have arranged for the careful landscaping around Grace Arbor, and silently, she blessed him for it.

When the distinctive house came into view at the crest of the hill, Lance said, "You probably haven't had much time to meet folks yet."

"Not really. Richard and I didn't get to know much about our neighbors." She thought about the young intruder she'd seen and Lance's comment about the incomplete survey. "I don't suppose your surveyor would be the young woman with red hair I saw this morning," she said.

"No," he said, "My surveyor is ... " He broke off, and the lines at the corners of his mouth turned down slightly. He shrugged. "Tell me about this young woman with red hair."

"She was watching the house today—staring at it as though she was hypnotized." She paused when he said nothing. "The first time it happened, I was practically on top of her before she leaped away like a scared rabbit. When I said hello, she ignored me, and just this afternoon when I was closing the window in my study, I saw her again. She's quite attractive—long coppery hair and the most amazing eyes. She ran away behind the hedge."

"Sounds like Alexei's girl—his niece. I heard she's back in town." Lance stroked his chin slowly. I don't think she's his real niece, but they say she's lived with the Popovs since she was a child. Beatrice is deaf."

"Oh!" Anne said, understanding dawning.

"The Popovs are Russian immigrants who've lived here for 20 years or so, but I think they left Russia much earlier...maybe as long as 50 years ago. They don't have much money, and from the look of that old place of theirs, they've spent nothing on its upkeep. Someone must have sponsored the girl who went off to a specialized school. She just came back, I hear."

Lance rounded the bend that took them past Tanner Falls and onto the highway. "Beatrice never was much for mixing," he said after a brief silence. "There aren't many deaf people in the area, and folks often find it hard to embrace people who are different."

Of course! No wonder there had been no response to her greeting from the road. What would it be like to live in a world where lips moved, thunder crashed, lovers wooed, and you never heard a sound? Never heard a Beethoven sonata or a lark's bright trill in the meadow. No wonder Beatrice had run. She must have been frightened when she'd turned to see someone so close behind her.

Reaching Anne's property, Lance steered his jeep up the long driveway. Trees formed a leafy canopy like greeters at a wedding. "Who are the Graingers?" she asked, wishing she hadn't waited until now to be curious about the house's history.

"The last renters lived in it only a few years and died in an automobile accident." He helped her from the car, and they walked toward the porch on the east side of the house. "People often hesitate to buy a house of someone who has died," he said, then gave a low whistle as he looked around. "But this is a gorgeous property."

"I think the Graingers must have been very good tenants, or perhaps it's my realtor I should be thanking. I could hardly believe how well cared-for everything looks."

He followed her gaze to the well-weeded ferns, oriental lilies, and irises blooming along the perimeter of the house. "That's the glory of perennials, I guess. They spring up year after year and take care of themselves."

"No," she said firmly. "Someone has been taking care of them. You must have arranged for a landscaper to keep things up since last year."

He shook his head. "Landscaping doesn't go with the contract." He stood with his hands in his pockets. "It seems you have a mystery gardener."

He walked around the house, examining the invisible boundary lines, and then circled it once more. She followed him past the green lawns and toward the strip of woods on the other side of the driveway. Anne pondered the mystery of her flowers and shrubs while they drew closer to where she'd found the body. A chill crept through her despite the summer day. She'd be glad to pass through the narrow line of trees to the other side.

Suddenly, they both stopped in mid-stride. The area had been marked off with a low roping of some sort, and Chief Mackowitz stood peering down at the ground. Anne grasped Lance's sleeve, her breath catching in her throat. It wasn't so surprising, her inner logic reasoned. It would be standard procedure to review the scene where someone had died—but she'd thought the authorities had done that yesterday.

"Pardon the intrusion, Mrs. Westin," Mackowitz said, turning. "I phoned to tell you we'd be coming, but you weren't home. We're just gathering some routine information. Shouldn't take too long."

Gone were the wrinkled khakis and careless sport shirt Mackowitz had worn the day before. In their place was a blue uniform shirt with a badge and navy pants. Anne could hear the strains of a Bach fugue coming from his nearby car. She stared in the direction of the sound.

"There's nothing better than Bach on a summer day, don't you think?" Mackowitz rubbed a hand over his jaw. "Crane," he said, acknowledging Lance. He continued to pace, peering at the ground through narrowed eyes.

Anne could have expected country hoedown music from this small-town sheriff—but Bach? This community was full of surprises. "Did you find anything unusual?" she asked tremulously.

He placed one gloved hand on a gnarled tree limb and wiped at his chapped lips with the other. If he heard the question, he gave no indication. "Be through here soon."

"Is all this necessary?" Lance asked, a curt edge to his voice. "Mrs. Westin has only just moved in. You can see how upsetting this is for her."

For answer, Mackowitz peered down at an outline at the base of the tree. Crude chalk lines marked the place where Alexei's body had lain. He directed his attention to Anne. "You sure you didn't see anyone that night?"

"No one," she said, feeling suddenly wary. Did they do this with everyone who died—or was there something suspicious about this death? She crept closer to Lance, glad she wasn't alone. "What are you looking for?" she asked, frowning severely at Mackowitz. "What's this all about?"

"Maybe nothing, Mrs. Westin." Mackowitz tapped a tree limb with a finger encased in a transparent rubber glove. "The blood on this branch might simply mean that Alexei hit his head when he fell—but there are signs of a struggle. See the way the ground is scuffed up there? And then there's the wound to Mr. Popov's head. He seems to have been hit by something pretty hard."

Anne gasped. "You mean … "

"Don't mean anything for certain sure, Ma'am, except … " He broke off and rubbed a hand over his stubbly hair before looking at her directly.

An owl gave a mournful cry from a nearby tree as though announcing some portent of doom.

Mackowitz stood back a little and studied Anne's face. "The thing is … " He paused and crossed his arms over his chest. "We don't think Alexei was alone out here."

Chapter 6

"What are you saying?" Anne stared at Sheriff Mackowitz, noticing at this oddest of moments that his crew cut was uneven on the left side. She felt Lance's arm grow rigid.

"Just that there are indications that someone else might have been with him," Mackowitz said. "Won't know much until the coroner's report comes in."

Anne felt a shiver race through her.

Mackowitz stuffed a small notebook into his jacket pocket and scrubbed a hand across his jaw. "Well, I don't need to bother you folks anymore today." He glanced fleetingly at Anne. "We may have some more questions later. You'll be available?"

She nodded as a second squad car drew up near the wooded spot. Mackowitz strode toward it, boots soundless on the soft earth. *More questions later?* Her privacy had been invaded, and threats of more intrusions were likely. This was her home, her property. Still, if someone had caused a man's death...

"Are you all right, Anne?" Lance's voice—low and anxious.

She nodded, but her thumping heart told her she was not all right with this beginning to her life at Grace Arbor. Not all right at all.

"I'm sorry," Lance said, looking down at his shoes, which were wet and stained from dirt and underbrush. In the stillness left by the departure of the police cars, she could hear his slightly unsteady breathing.

She drew in her breath and exhaled sharply. If only Richard were here. He would know what to do. He'd make sense of it all, and things would be normal again. But Richard wasn't here and never would be again. She swallowed and squared her shoulders. "I'll be fine." She stepped away from Lance and braced herself against a tree a few feet from the oak where Alexei had apparently hit his head. *Or where someone had...* She stopped herself. There would be more investigations and more people tramping over her property. More questions, rumors.

"Anne, maybe you should consider spending some time in town," Lance suggested, closing the gap between them and placing a protective hand on her arm. "I can arrange it for you—until this is over. Or I could show you another property. Nothing's signed in stone. Maybe this isn't the right house for you."

She shook her head vigorously. If she left now, she would be admitting she couldn't cope without Richard or her children. She would fail before she began. No, she would weather this storm. And she wouldn't turn to Lance or any man to handle things for her.

"No. I'll stay here. The investigation can't last much longer. Besides..." She paused. "It's not like there's been a murder or anything." She stopped, shocked by the word 'murder'. "I'd like to pick up my car now."

"All right," he said slowly. "I can finish the rest of the survey another time." He dug his hands in his pockets and kicked at a stone in his path. "I'm sorry..." He floundered, seemingly unable to find the right words to comfort her. "Look, let's get you out of here for a little while. There's a great Italian restaurant in town. You haven't had supper; I haven't either. You need a break from all this."

She looked from Lance to the outline on the ground. "Well, I ... that is, there's so much to be done," she began, confused but touched by his concern. His eyes were focused on his shoes as he waited for her decision. He was, after all, being quite gallant, and despite her jangled nerves, she was hungry. Her car was back in town anyway.

"Well, all right, " she said, sidestepping the area as though it could contaminate them and taking his arm. "I love Italian." Gesturing dismissively at the police barrier, she added, "And I hate this!"

The restaurant turned out to be another surprise. She had expected a family diner or a small mom-and-pop cafeteria but found herself inside a restaurant that rivaled an upscale city establishment.

"They just opened a few months ago," Lance said as they approached the gleaming glass doors with ornamental shrubs bordering the entrance. The windows, set in tawny brick, boasted fashionable wrought iron grills and flower boxes with annuals in vibrant colors. Green and white awnings were drawn against the waning sun, and candles had been lit for the approaching evening hours.

It was nearly seven, and the tuna on rye she'd had for lunch had worn off hours ago. Anne realized that, despite everything, she was hungry. A middle-aged host with a green bowtie and a comic mustache directed them to a table. Anne turned to Lance with a skeptical glance.

"I know," he said, laughing. "The mustache is a bit over the top, but they're going for an authentic Old-World feel."

The patrons were a mix of young and old in assorted fashions, from jeans and tee shirts to dressier styles. Anne smoothed the ruffles of her white blouse and brushed the front of her lime-hued skirt.

Wordy menus offered a variety of entrees, both Italian and American. She chose spaghetti bolognaise in affirmation of her growing appetite, and Lance ordered lasagna.

"You come here often?" she asked.

"Been here once or twice. They do a great lasagna, but I don't mind getting dirty in the kitchen myself. I'm a fair cook." He smiled then, his blue gaze reflecting the light from the candle. A drizzled maze of colorful wax cascaded from the ornamental wine bottle in the center of the table.

"This is so charming," she said, admiring the crimson cloth napkins. "And real linen, too. As I recall, the going business last summer was the new Dairy Queen with a brazier."

"Progress," he said. "This town has needed something to jumpstart the economy. He bit into a breadstick, and a shadow passed over his face. "A lot of folks have pinned their financial hopes on the copper mine. I hope they're not disappointed." He brightened as though from concerted effort and changed the subject. "What are your plans now that you've come to live here?"

"I haven't decided for sure. I plan to take it slowly, not rush into anything. I'm working on a few editing projects. I could expand all that, but I need to get my bearings and get to know the community." She might have added that she needed to find out who she was now that Richard was dead, her children were grown, and the path ahead lay unmarked.

"I hoped this would be the right setting for you." He took a quick drink of his Perrier water. "But it doesn't seem to be turning out that way." He paused and searched her eyes. "I wouldn't blame you if you changed your mind."

We've already had this conversation, she thought, vaguely uncomfortable with the number of times he had suggested that she consider other properties. He was merely looking out for her welfare, wasn't he? Was he feeling in some way responsible for her because he had handled her purchase? Because Richard was his friend?

She had been enjoying the evening. It was the first time she'd gone anywhere with a man since she'd been widowed. She was even finding herself concerned about her hair and clothes, and that hadn't happened in a while. She spread her napkin on her lap with intense concentration and studied the man across the table, working to do so unobserved. There was strength in his features. Silver hair heightened the deep tan of his face and the blue of his eyes. But they were restless eyes that suggested anxiety or vulnerability. What had life been like for him since Rose had died?

"And what about you, Lance?" she asked. "Do you enjoy working in real estate?"

"Business isn't booming, but it's enough to keep me out of trouble. I teach at the junior college, too, during the season. Most of my students are over 40. It's surprising how many people decide on second, even third careers."

"You still follow the Cubs?" It was another thing Lance and Richard had in common.

"Of course. Once a Cubs fan, you're hooked for life— whether they win or not. I guess it's our claim to fame. Or to failure!" He laughed and took another drink of his Perrier. "I reserve time to take the boat out, of course. That's what keeps me sane."

She liked the way his smile started slowly and deepened. "I remember how you and Richard looked forward to those fishing forays last summer. I still have a box full of hooks and lures I don't know what to do with." She laughed. "I'm not much for baiting hooks and sitting in agonized hope hour after hour that some hapless fish will come along and bite."

"And I don't think sitting in front of a computer for hours on end would be much to *my* liking," he countered good-naturedly, watching her over the rim of his glass.

"Editing isn't very glamorous, to be sure." She took a slow sip of water before continuing. "But it's satisfying when the right word or phrase transforms an idea and makes it come alive."

"I didn't expect you to settle here after … " He stopped, fingers poised over his water glass. "I thought you would stay where all your family is, your memories." An odd shadow crossed his face.

"You're wondering why I didn't get a cat and rent a quiet apartment in the city," she said, laughing but quickly sobering. "Or move in with my kids. No, I think there's something more for me to do now at this time in my life, and I don't want to miss it." She felt her spirit rising. "I want to … What was it George Eliot wrote—something about hearing the squirrel's heartbeat and the roar that lives on 'the other side of silence?'"

"That's quite beautiful. I haven't heard those classic lines in a long time."

The waiter brought their entrees, and dinner progressed in easy camaraderie. She liked the soft rustle of laughter, the muted conversation, and the chink of china. But voices suddenly broke the cordial atmosphere. Two men were being ushered into the restaurant by the mustachioed waiter. One man laughed at something the waiter said. Dark and stout in a gray silk suit, he walked with what could only be termed a swagger, elbowing his companion and laughing as he moved.

Something was oddly familiar about his voice. Anne knew that face! There was no mistaking Joe Lair, the realtor Richard had not hired after an initial consultation. He was coming toward them, a few steps ahead of the young man with him. She remembered Lair's swarthy good looks, smooth speech, and manner.

So, Lair was still prowling around, she thought with metaphoric irony and settled back to her spaghetti. The way people talked about him, it was surprising that he hadn't left town and moved on to a more amiable community. But she had heard that he had something to do with the copper mine. Perhaps he'd earned some respect by contributing positively to the local economy.

At least he has good taste in restaurants, she thought. She glanced across at Lance and saw that his expression had darkened. He was watching Lair's companion, the young man dressed in a black shirt and low-slung jeans. Arresting gray eyes were fringed by lashes most girls would die for, and swirls of dark hair broached a high forehead. Anne watched a circular pendant sway from a silver chain on his chest as he neared.

Lair stopped abruptly at the table where Anne and Lance were seated. A startled lift of his thick eyebrows signaled that he recognized her. A gold tooth gleamed in the overhead light. "Mrs. Westin," he said politely, inclining his head and stretching a hand to Lance.

Lance did not extend his hand, and an awkward pause followed, during which Anne struggled to discern the silent interplay. Seconds later, Lair cocked his head and shrugged. "Good seeing you too, Crane." He strolled past them, the younger man following at his heels.

Lance attacked his lasagna, knuckles white on his fork. Anne waited for him to say something, but he kept his eyes on his plate, his dark expression forbidding any question. Why had Crane been so rude? And were they doomed to finish their meal in this strained silence?

When a waiter approached, Lance looked up. "Excuse me," he said politely. "May I have another Perrier? For the lady as well." As quickly as the sun breaks through cloud, all hint of annoyance disappeared from his face. "Now, Anne, I was telling you about my boat. I call it the Rosie-O."

She struggled to catch up and get from point A to point B. "Yes, I remember Richard enjoyed fishing from your boat."

"She's a dependable old girl, the Rosie-O," he hurried on—a little too brightly. "Still gives me a pretty good run on the river. I had to refinish the bulkhead and replace the propeller last spring when I hit a sand bar, but she runs good as new now." He pushed his lasagna plate to one side and snapped up a menu. "How about some dessert?" Suddenly chatty and gregarious, he asked, "What do you say to Manola's famous cheesecake with raspberry sauce?"

"Sure," she said. "I'll try it, but I'm going to make a quick trip to the ladies' room first."

She needed time to organize her thoughts, not just about Lance's behavior with Joe Lair, but about everything. She'd begun a new life in a new home, trying to come to grips with the loss of her husband and her widowhood. She'd looked forward to peace, serenity, and getting to know her neighbors, but nothing was happening as expected.

When she returned, Lance was not at the table. She glanced around and discovered him at the far end of the restaurant—at Joe Lair's booth. She stepped behind a Fichus tree to watch unobserved. Lance was saying something to the young man who accompanied Lair. She watched the handsome features—his half smile as he leaned back, arms folded rigidly across his chest.

What did Lance have to do with this young man? And with Joe Lair, for that matter? And why had he waited to speak to them until she left the room? She returned to her chair and carefully smoothed the napkin over her knees.

"Sorry," he said, returning seconds later. "Just a little business to tend to." He attempted a smile, but his eyes held no humor. "Are you ready for coffee? I've asked the waiter to bring us some fresh."

He seemed he wasn't about to discuss his business with the two men. Nor did he mention it when dinner was over, and he'd shaken her hand and said good night. Anne knew it was silly to feel excluded. Why should she expect him to confide in her—if there was anything to confide about?

Chapter 7

Lance pressed the "brew" button on the coffee maker, frowning at the mess of dishes and drying bread on the counter. Shane had come in very late, made a sandwich, and left food residue and soiled dishes behind. Lance had heard the screen door slap in its frame well after midnight. The Saturday before, it had been two in the morning when he came home.

Lance released a weary breath. He had taken his nephew in only a few months before but quickly regretted his impulsive promise to his sister. Jane's headstrong son had always been difficult, but after cancer struck, she had despaired of finding a way to help Shane.

"Maybe you can talk some sense into him," she had appealed. "He's always looked up to you."

Perhaps he had at once, but now Shane debunked every value he and his family members had tried to foster in him. When he began associating with a rough crowd, and Jane's illness grew worse, she pleaded for help. When she passed away, there was no one to watch out for Shane. It had been all right initially, but he grew restless and easily bored with real estate work. *Work of any kind*, Lance thought sadly.

He scraped the dishes and threw the bread crusts into the trash. Shane was no longer a boy; at 21, he was not pulling his weight. Nor had he found anything to attract his interest. Until he hooked up with Joseph P. Lair, entrepreneur, investment specialist, and opportunist. Lance swallowed hard, the coffee bitter in his throat. When he'd seen Shane with him at Manola's, he couldn't bring himself to introduce him to Anne. What would she have thought? He'd declined to shake the hand of a man he deeply distrusted. He'd been rude, he knew, but Lair brought out the worst in him.

Grabbing his mug of coffee, he pushed open the sliding doors to the patio and made his way down the rock-hewn steps to the runabout rocking gently in the water. Its glistening hull beckoned him like a sea siren. He pushed off with one hand and settled in the comforting hold, eager to feel the sun on his aching shoulders. He'd never thought fifty-five was old, but today, he felt like a candidate for the front porch rocker.

He traced the polished edges of the Rosie-O, named for his wife, whom he had married one cold February morning, changing the course of his entire life. For her he had designed the house, the deck, and private boating dock. For her, he would have given the moon, the sun, and all the stars put together.

But one summer morning, she slipped quietly away, the disease having run its deadly course. He drew in his breath as the sun burned through his skin to the deadness beneath it. Other men sustained losses as great as his and went on with their lives. Why couldn't he shake this cowardly depression? He couldn't even dredge up the strength to stop Shane in his downward spiral.

In a little while, the river would be alive with boats, fishermen, and vacationers. But now, a stillness pervaded. It was his favorite time of day when the sky was a sun-washed blue with gulls crying overhead. He reached into the tackle box for crusts he kept for the birds that Shane had quickly dubbed "rats with wings."

He tossed the bread into the air and thought about the previous night's visit with Anne Westin. He'd been nervous; he didn't really know how to talk to a woman anymore, at least not a woman like Anne. She hadn't changed much. Still the same graceful figure, quick mind, and eyes that could change from brown to green and back again in a flash. She was beautiful, but there was something more—something that shone from inside.

He tried to remember the lines she'd quoted. It had affected him deeply, for it took courage to listen for "the roar that lives on the other side." He'd chosen the safe silence where no roar could disturb him.

Why had he talked so much, prattling on about his morning rides and some nonsense about the river and his sanity? He'd also mentioned teaching real estate law to middle-aged men at the junior college, but not about the pain that kept him at a distance from his students, his friends, and even the God he had been taught to honor.

Then Lair had come into the restaurant with Shane. How could he have introduced the young man to a woman like Anne? He cringed. *I'm ashamed of him. Truly ashamed.* And, though he hated himself for it, he couldn't shake his fierce wish for Shane to go away and leave him to his tenuous peace. *I don't even have the courage to care about my sister's son.*

Anne would be ashamed of him if she knew. Her eyes had narrowed with injured surprise when he'd suggested again that she might find another house without the cloud that shrouded the old Grainger place—the house she had renamed "Grace Arbor." Decade-old rumors had died down to some degree, though a few townsfolk still believed the house haunted or cursed. Dark tales of Russian intrigue hadn't died with the advent of Perestroika.

She had stated her decision with a firm thrust of her chin. "I have no intention of leaving." How could he explain that it would be better for all concerned if she chose otherwise?

They'd parted with a handshake—quick, professional— though he'd wanted to prolong it. No doubt he'd turned her off. It was probably for the best. He wouldn't be good company for her. Lance returned to the dock and tossed the tie rope over the post.

Skipping lunch he had no taste for, Lance loaded the lawn mower on the back of his truck and headed for his elderly neighbor's house. For most of the summer, Margaret Morris had been unable to handle chores at home. She needed help; he could at least mow her yard for her.

He mowed with a vengeance, eager to assuage his anxious mind with manual labor. He finished quickly and began putting away his equipment. But Margaret, sitting in a chair by the window, waved him inside. She wore a plain brown dress too big for her and a gray sweater that hung shapelessly from her narrow shoulders. Her hair, usually wound in a neat coil, flared like a dust mop around a face grown shockingly thin. The lady he remembered had been careful about her appearance, and her home had once been neat and tidy.

"Mr. Crane, you gladden an old woman's heart," she said huskily when he was seated near her worn lounge chair. "I don't see many folks these days. And you're a dear to come."

"Glad to help," he said. "Are you all right?"

She dropped her head onto the natty gray sweater, and Lance wondered if she would fall asleep. But after a moment, she looked up, her eyes misty. "I guess you heard. Alexei is gone."

"I'm sorry," he said, a picture forming in his mind—Alexei with his battered hat in his lap with Margaret in her ancient porch swing. Lance suspected that the two might have married long ago if the accident hadn't happened—if Alexei hadn't lost some of his mental faculties. And if Vera hadn't done her best to keep them apart. Now Alexei was gone, and Margaret was alone. After so many years of dedicated service to the community, Margaret Morris deserved better than this.

"Forgive me for not getting up," she said, interrupting his thoughts. "I should have lemonade and cookies for you..."

"No need, Mrs. Morris," Lance said.

"Sad way to treat my favorite neighbor," she said with a hint of a smile that made her look years younger. She must have been a lovely woman once before loneliness and sickness had taken their toll.

"You've had a rough go of it this winter," Lance said, shaken by her shrunken figure.

She swept a hand through the air as though batting a pesky fly. "At my age, a person can't expect to feel too perky, but I'm all right." She was silent for a few seconds, then looked at Lance through puzzled eyes. "I saw your nephew the other day. Is he doing some work for you?"

"I hired him to do some surveying and odd jobs for me," he said slowly, wondering what Margaret was thinking of him.

"He was here yesterday," she said, the furrows in her forehead deepening. "He said he was supposed to test my property for metals."

Test her property for metals? Lance knew the copper mine had excavated a lot of uncultivated land in the county, but were they tinkering with private property now? He had no answer and waited for her to say more.

"He was here last night," she continued. "Spent a good bit of time in the dark out there. I was watching from the window." A shy grin passed over her lips. "Old women watch at windows, you know." Her watery eyes flashed in a sudden burst of spirit.

Not knowing how to respond, he stared at her in embarrassment.

"Still, it gives a woman a start to find a man nosing around on her property." She paused as though sensitive to his embarrassment. "But no harm done. There's nothing but black dirt and weeds out there anyhow. I'm sure he was mightily disappointed."

Anger rising, Lance drove home after promising to check into the matter and assuring Margaret Morris that Shane wouldn't bother her further. What was he doing going over Margaret's property with his ridiculous Geiger counter—or whatever metal enthusiasts used these days. You'd think he was an avaricious ten-year-old determined to get rich.

He parked the truck and headed to the house, slowing his steps when he saw Shane sitting on the porch with a can of beer in his hand.

He was slumped in a deck chair, bare feet propped up on the wrought-iron table. He looked younger than his 21 years in cut-off jeans and no shirt—more like a boy playing hooky. But something far more serious was pulling him farther down to some unreachable impasse.

Be patient, he counseled himself as he approached Shane but felt his temper rise.

Shane looked up with an innocent grin. "Morning, Uncle."

"You didn't show up at the Creighton place yesterday," Lance began, pushing down his anger.

The muscles in Shane's neck tensed, and his light gray eyes grew dull. He shrugged, bare shoulders rolling nonchalantly. "Sorry. I'll do it on Monday. I went to see Bea. She needed me." He took a swallow of his beer and waited several seconds. "You heard about her old man dying. Tough break. She was pretty close to the old guy."

Lance pushed a hand through his hair. He'd seen Shane with Beatrice Popov. She wasn't his kind of girl. And what was the fascination with her aged uncle? Shane had been acting like he and Popov were best buddies—hanging around him when he trudged through town, saving beer cans for him to trade in. Surely, he didn't believe that foolish story of buried treasure, the idle gossip of a few locals old enough to remember it. Shane was bright, wily even—not the type to be taken in by such nonsense.

Shane lifted his head, drained the last of his beer, then flashed a cocky grin. "Crazy old coot. He didn't know which end of the shovel to dig with."

Quick anger pulsed in Lance's temples. "Your mother taught you better than to talk like that. The man's dead!"

"Merely making an observation," Shane sputtered.

The young man's flippant attitude was nothing new. Still, Lance was startled by his insolence. He drew in his breath, willing himself to stay calm. "Look," he began. "We've got to get some things straight. You've been coming home at all hours of the night and dissing the survey work you're supposed to be doing for me. *And messing around on private property.* We're falling farther and farther behind."

Tension rippled in Shane's jaw. "No sweat. I'll get the Creighton survey done tomorrow. What's the big rush anyway?" He pushed his chair back and got up, glaring at his uncle.

Lance pressed his lips together in grim restraint. They were even in height and could peer directly into each other's eyes. Their builds were so similar that someone observing might even take them for father and son. "What were you doing with Lair?" he demanded.

"I told you," Shane said, grabbing his can. "They've been shorthanded at the copper mine, and I've been helping out. Lair says it's only a matter of time, and the ore will put this town on the map."

"The only thing Lair is going to do for this town is create disaster," Lance said evenly. "And if you're fool enough to get tangled up in his schemes, God only knows where it will end."

Defiance lit the pale eyes as Lance stared tight-lipped at him. After a few seconds, he held up his hands in a gesture of surrender. "Look, I just give him a hand now and then at the mine. I'm going to get your work done. It's no big deal. As for last night,

Lair and I just ran into each other, and he invited me for dinner. That's all."

Lance knew about the grunt work Shane had been doing at the fledgling mine south of town, but why Lair would bother with a kid like Shane, he couldn't figure. "The fact is you haven't been doing the job you were hired for," Lance said, "not to mention that up until now, you've been getting free room and board."

Shane took a step back. The muscles in his jaw twitched as though he tried to contain his temper. "Look, I promise to be at the office at seven every day next week. Scout's honor." He crushed his beer can with one hand. "Can I go now?" Without waiting for a response, he turned and walked away, shoulders slumped like a petulant adolescent's.

Lance shook his head, mystified by his ineptness where Shane was concerned. He was handling everything wrong. He should make things clear—either he would pull his weight or move out. He wasn't a kid; he was 21 and still freeloading. But he was Jane's only son. What would become of him if he kicked him out?

They said you needed tough love to raise kids these days. But Lance could feel only bone weariness. Love was, after all, for the very courageous or the faithful. He was neither. He'd sheltered his sister's son but failed to reach him utterly. And now Shane was taking up with the likes of Joe Lair.

Feeling more tired than a healthy man his age should, he rose and followed Shane into the house. There was still the matter of Margaret Morris to be discussed. But once inside the front door, Lance heard the back door slam and, a moment later, the roar of the pickup. Lance had agreed to let him use it to get back and forth to work, but Shane seemed to have claimed it for his personal use whenever he felt like it. He even left empty beer cans in the truck bed. Lance shoved his hands into his pockets. What was he going to do? Things were roaring out of control.

Drained and angry, he watched the truck rumble up the road. Why couldn't he do something, say something that would alter the mess Shane was making of his life? Indeed, why couldn't he do something about his own?

Chapter 8

Anne woke to brooding clouds on the day Alexei was to be buried. The rain that had fallen through the night continued its relentless grieving as she took in the gloomy landscape. Wind whipped the trees in the wooded area at the far boundary, reminding her that no quick resolution had been forthcoming. The circumstances surrounding Alexei Popov's death remained a mystery.

She tackled the stacks of packing boxes and crates that lined the walls. Familiar things helped establish a connection to a new place, but she knew feeling at home at Grace Arbor would be no easy undertaking while the investigation remained open. She pushed up her shirt sleeves and slit the first box, labeled "fragile," and felt akin to it.

The first bubble-wrapped package contained the delicate pianist, a golden-haired girl in billowy skirts that had been a birthday gift from her daughter. The figurine's finely crafted features and cherubic face reminded her of Dawn and how much she missed her. When she telephoned the week before, she had been her buoyant self, full of exciting details of her job as a camp counselor for refugee children.

Dawn had always marched to the beat of a different drummer since she was a child. As a teen, she'd shown little interest in things most girls favored: clothes, boys, and personal image.

She had to be prodded to buy something new and tended to be overweight. At a size 14 petite, she seemed unconcerned about such matters. There was so much in life she wanted to do.

With a sigh, she placed the piano girl on the table and reached for a doe with her fawn in a forest of ceramic trees—a gift from Peter given the year thrill seekers shot three deer—one a pregnant doe—at a local park. The national media carried the story for days. It was like Peter to memorialize such an event. She put both figurines in the curio cabinet. Side by side, they represented the beautiful and the reprehensible, and Anne was reminded of the incessant war between good and evil.

At the bottom of the box was the mountain man, features skillfully carved into fine wood, that she and Richard had bought on a trip to the Allegany Mountains. The figure was a bent reed of a man hardened by wind and rain; a pack and shovel hung over his shoulder. She gasped, startled at the resemblance to Alexei Popov.

Lance had said that Alexei had been a skilled craftsman until the accident, which left him childlike and forgetful. Why, she wondered, must some people endure painful loss while others seemingly breezed through life hale and healthy? Tenderly, she placed the figure on the mantel, struck by the death of a harmless old man and wanting to believe that his life in the next world would make up for the struggles of this one.

She and Lance had talked about other things at dinner, too. She had found his company more than agreeable, she realized in reflection. Being with him, she had felt almost young again in the comfortable ambiance of the upscale restaurant—until Joe Lair had shown up.

It disturbed her that Lance might have some connection to the disreputable Lair, or did that conversation at Lair's table have more to do with the handsome young man with pale gray eyes?

Another question plagued her. Why had Lance been so quick to suggest changing her mind and finding something "more suitable for her needs"? He was only trying to help, wasn't he? She sighed deeply. Would her property recover its charm for her after all this business was settled?

Feeling suddenly warm in the cluttered kitchen, she forged a path through the boxes and went to the seldom-used front entrance. The back door was much more convenient and a quick few steps to her car. But a good cross breeze might refresh her for the rest of her tasks. She flipped the deadbolt and opened the paneled oak door.

Something wedged between the screen and front door fluttered to the ground. Probably an advertising circular. She turned it over idly and was startled to find a black-crayoned message crawling uphill on a piece of white paper. "Go Home."

She dropped it as though it were hot or might explode in her hands. Someone had written the warning and left it at her front door. *Who would do such a thing?*

She looked around, but only the morning landscape greeted her—no sign of people around. Hurt and resentment flared as she read and re-read the note. But no amount of scrutiny yielded a logical reason for the message.

Mind aflame, she returned to the kitchen. How silly and childish. Who cared if she lived here or not? Surely Beatrice and Alexei's sister couldn't be guilty of such behavior, could they? What had she done to them? She'd hardly had time to incur their displeasure, and the more she thought about it, the more ludicrous it seemed. She wadded the note into a tight ball and threw it across the room just as the telephone rang.

"Mom? You okay?"

Peter's mellow voice brought surprising tears. She forced them back. "I'm fine, Peter," she said huskily. "I've just been busy putting things away, getting settled."

"You sound out of breath. Are you trying to beat the Guinness world record for unpacking? You don't have to do it all in one day."

She laughed. "There *is* an awful lot to do, but I'm pacing myself, I promise." The crayoned message swam before her eyes. What would Peter think about it? She longed to tell him, but why worry him over a silly prank?

"I'll be up Saturday," Peter said. "I should get there by early afternoon if I can finish my work. I've been swamped this week." His chatter, full of boyish enthusiasm, gave her time to compose her thoughts.

"I'm looking forward to it, Peter," she said, meaning it. "There's a water show in town. Maybe we can picnic in the park and take it in. Is Jennifer coming with you?"

"Nope. Just me this time."

When they rang off, Anne sat with the receiver in her hand. Had she made a mistake coming here to live? She watched raindrops collect in little rivulets on the window and felt overwhelming disappointment. *Go home!* The message swam before her eyes. She had expected neighbors wanting to lend a hand, offers of friendship, and recipes shared. She swallowed the lump in her throat. So much for the welcome wagon.

No one was clamoring for her friendship, she thought wryly, and the childish warning at her door had probably been left by Beatrice or Vera. But this was no time for self-pity. A neighbor had died. She should pay her respects; she owed that much to Alexei, regardless of how his family treated her.

The funeral was set for eleven. She dropped the wadded note into the waste basket and went upstairs to change into her black dress—the one worn for Richard's funeral. The familiar pain tugged at her even after so many months had passed. She closed her eyes and whispered a prayer for calm.

Before leaving the house, she switched on the oven timer. The casserole would be ready to deliver to the Popovs when she returned. Preparing food for the family of a deceased neighbor was decidedly old-fashioned, but some traditions should never die. "No pun intended," she said out loud, eager for a human voice—even her own. "Anne Westin," she muttered. "You're positively Victorian!"

She found the funeral chapel at the north end of First Street and made her way inside. Heavy oak seats, dark and ponderous, held the mourners, and as heads turned toward her, she felt an overwhelming desire to escape. No one would miss her or expect her to be there. After all, she was a newcomer to town; she hardly knew Alexei. She sat rigidly, feeling as wooden as the pew.

Had she overdressed? She looked down at her ebony slingback heels with their tiny ornamental buckles. Probably. But Richard had bought them for her, and she'd worn them to his funeral. She felt herself embracing the familiar Richard-size ache that pressed in.

Why had she come? Something in Alexei Popov's face as he lay under the pine tree had pleaded for something. She looked around for Margaret Morris. She might be able to tell her something about the Popovs—something that might explain the note. But Margaret was not among the mourners.

She took a seat in the middle of the chapel and bowed her head. When she raised it, she saw Beatrice in the family row, slender in a simple black sheathe reminiscent of the legendary Audrey Hepburn. Next to her in a button-down dress more purple than black was Vera. Her arms were folded over her formidable breast, and her hair was slicked back to the nape of her neck.

Anne looked from one to the other as though she could see through the backs of their heads to their minds. Had one of them left the note on her front door? Beatrice or Vera? Or neither one?

A man in a striped suit sat in the row just ahead of her, lantern jaw set. Was he a relative, a former colleague? Two older women sat next to him, occasionally nodding to each other. On the other side was a mother with two little boys who tugged on their mother's dress and pointed with fat fingers.

She inhaled sharply when she saw a young man in khaki pants, the sleeves of his shirt rolled up to his elbows, revealing a snake-like tattoo. No jacket or tie, resistant strands of dark hair tousled over a broad forehead. She remembered him; he'd been in the restaurant with Joe Lair. Her pulse quickened as she studied him from the corner of her eye. She saw him working his knuckles and staring ahead. Pungent cologne swept toward her, and she suppressed the need to sneeze.

The officiating minister was a dry kestrel of a man with a tight voice that wound down mechanically as the minutes passed. It was a short service, over in little more than half an hour. Beatrice and Vera were the first to be ushered out. Then, an older man rose stiffly and stumbled after two women who gave each other embarrassed nods. Anne stepped into the aisle after the young man with the tattoo and saw that his eyes, fringed by lashes most women would die for, were glued on Beatrice.

Feeling utterly out of place, she got in line behind the hearse and followed to the cemetery. No one had greeted her or spoken. *But funerals are hardly the place for socializing,* she told herself. Mercifully, the drive was short. The coffin was placed on rails over the grave, and the little crowd circled the canopied spot. The prayer, then, "Ashes to ashes; dust to dust," and it was over. So little ceremony for one who had lived so long.

The tattooed man put a protective arm around Beatrice and looked down at her with studied intimacy while she stared straight ahead. Vera turned to glare at him until he stepped aside a little and dropped his arm from the young woman's shoulders.

Beatrice moved away from the grave site, her hair floating behind her like an amber cloud. A dislodged wave grazed her left eye. *Like a wounded swan on a blue lagoon,* Anne thought. It was hard to imagine the vulnerable young woman leaving a crude message at her door with a threatening message, and yet it was possible.

Vera labored after Beatrice toward the hearse that would return them to the funeral home, her eyes darting restlessly left and right. When they reached the edge of the little circle, Anne stepped out hesitantly. It was now or never.

"I'm Anne Westin," she began, extending a hand. *As if you didn't know!* Beatrice stopped and looked up through red-rimmed eyes, then stepped back, her lower lip trembling.

"I'm so sorry for your loss," Anne said gently, careful to face her directly, knowing that Beatrice could only hear by reading lips. "If there's anything I can do to help, I'm just a short distance away." The words sounded trite and banal in her ears, and Anne struggled to find better ones. Were there ever any right words for a time like this?

Beatrice looked at Vera, her eyes deep violet pools, then down at her sandals.

"I've made a casserole for you," Anne continued. "I'll bring it over later."

Beatrice gave no sign that she understood. Her eyes were fixed on the gravesite, yards away now, and Anne felt a wave of sympathy. She wanted to say, "I'm sure Alexei was a good man. I know you'll miss him very much." Grieving people were better off with few words. Sometimes, a touch was best, but these mourners were not likely to welcome it.

Beatrice turned abruptly with an expression that might have been anger or distrust or disappointment and followed Vera to the hearse. Anne stood alone. Even the young man with the tattoo had disappeared. She leaned against a tree, not caring about her dress or the fact that her elegant heels were sinking into the rain-softened sod. Car doors slammed; motors hummed. Soon, Alexei would be lowered into the ground and covered up. It took only moments to bury years. She raised her eyes to a small ray of sunlight creeping through the leafy expanse above her.

Thank God there was another reality! She clung to it as her thoughts went to Richard. His body also lay beneath the grass, but his soul was alive in a new and eternal dimension, and she would see him again. Did Alexei's little family have that assurance about their loved one?

Suddenly, she caught sight of someone hovering near the canopy—a woman in a dark dress, head bowed, hands folded as if in prayer. A few wispy tendrils of silver hair escaped her black pill-box hat. Anne recognized Margaret Morris, the wiry teacher who, it was said, cowed many a mischievous student in her day. Now, she stood unsteadily over the gravesite when everyone else had gone.

"Margaret?" she asked softly.

The elderly lady raised moist eyes that might once have been blue but now were washed of all color. "Anne Westin, isn't it?"

"Yes." Anne took the woman's hand. She had changed since the summer they had met, and her pallor and thinness struck Anne. "I'm so sorry about Alexei."

Taking Anne's arm, Margaret stepped back, leaving narrow shoe prints in the soft ground. She drew a white handkerchief from the folds of her dress and blew her nose. "I'm glad you came. I heard you were in town. I…" She paused and frowned, uncertain what to say next.

"It's good to see you, Margaret," Anne said softly. "I'm sorry we have to meet like this." She hesitated. "Are you all right?"

"I haven't been out of the house in days," she began. "But I had to come today." She pressed her lips firmly together, but Anne could see they were trembling.

She looked around for an idling car or someone waiting nearby. "How did you get here?"

"The seniors bus brought me most of the way," she said with a little lift of her chin. "But I'd be grateful for a ride home if you're going my way."

"Of course." Anne kicked herself mentally. She should have offered her a ride to the funeral. When Margaret stepped away hesitantly from the canopy, Anne walked her to her car and helped her inside, closing the passenger door carefully. The rain had intensified, and the wipers fanned furiously as they left the cemetery. It had to be more than a mile to Margaret's place. Quite a trek to say goodbye to a neighbor, especially when she was clearly not well.

When they were parked in the driveway of her house, Margaret turned to look at Anne. "Alexei used to be so full of life and energy. And he was smart—very smart." Fresh tears fell.

Anne recalled Lance telling her about Alexei. How boys from a neighboring town had attacked him, been caught and punished, but the damage they'd inflicted had remained. "You've known Alexei a long time?" she asked, touched by Margaret's sorrow.

"Sometimes it seems I have always known him," she began, her eyes fixed on some unreachable spot. "He and Vera came here with Svetlana and her baby granddaughter." She paused, and her tone was soft, almost reverent when she spoke. "The baby is grown now—Beatrice. She was here today." She pressed her lips together, and a long moment passed before she continued. "Her mother was Russian, but Russian names at that time only brought trouble. Svetlana was wise to give her a German name instead. Poor Beatrice. Little lost baby with no mother or father. Then Svetlana died, too." The words drifted off into silence.

Anne swallowed. Lance had told her about a woman who had left Russia and settled somewhere in the Eastern United

States and of a daughter who grew up and married. At some point, they came to live in the house now Grace Arbor. After the daughter died, Svetlana supposedly gave her granddaughter to the care of her trusted servants. Had there been a legal transaction? An adoption?

Margaret touched a hanky to her nose and continued. "Alexei was happy to take Beatrice in. He loved her, but Vera..." She stopped, clearly editing her thoughts. "Vera won't let anyone get close. She keeps a fierce hold on things she claims as her own." She leaned back with a low sigh. "God knows she deeply resented Alexei's friendship with me."

Margaret rocked slowly in her seat, twisting a handkerchief in her lap. A picture emerged in Anne's mind—Vera with a black crayon held in thick fingers.

Suddenly, Margaret's demeanor changed. She turned in her seat and faced Anne like a schoolteacher about to test a student. "What do you know about Russian history?"

The question startled her. Of course, Russian history continued to fascinate well into the 21st century. "I've read about the tsars, the political assassinations, shootings of the innocent, partisan intrigues." She paused, recalling much that was dark and frightening. "Worker strikes, mass uprisings, and everyone knows about the revolution and bloody civil war."

"And regicide," Margaret said, drawing a long breath. "The murders—secret executions in the middle of the night of the last ruling Romanov family. Even their servants and their pets were shot to death in the cellar of the 'House of Special Purpose' in the heart of Russia's Urals."

Anne felt her pulse quicken. "Are you saying that this Svetlana was involved?"

Margaret looked intently into Anne's startled face. Her eyes grew wide and dark. "Svetlana was there. A child of one of the Romanov servants—and one of very few who escaped the awful execution." She clasped her arms over her chest and drew a halting breath. "Svetlana told me what it was like, how she begged her mother not to make her leave her. When she was dying, those terrible moments in the dark cellar became so real to her."

"How awful," Anne whispered.

Margaret coughed and put a handkerchief to her lips. "I need to go in now. I'm very tired." She reached for the door handle.

Anne made to get out of the car and come around to help, but Margaret had already stepped out. "I'm really quite all right now. Thank you for bringing me home. It was most kind." She climbed onto the sagging porch as the rain continued to fall, her steps slow and deliberate.

Bewildered, Anne watched Margaret pass safely inside her door. What terrors had the woman named Svetlana experienced? What had plagued her memories as she lay dying in the house that was now Grace Arbor? Her house! Was the tale accurate? Margaret must have learned about Svetlana from Alexei, but was it all the aberration of a deranged mind?

Chapter 9

Peter Westin steered his Toyota along Highway 10, where trees arched over the road like a cathedral dome. Conifers and deciduous trees grew in a tangle of color from pale lime to emerald to a deep forest green. He had driven through this countryside only a week ago to bring his mother to her new home. Jen had complained that the trees made her feel claustrophobic.

He had met Jennifer Stratton at a regional science fair where she was commissioned to design aesthetic backdrops for technical displays. She was outgoing and beautiful while he tended toward reserve, but something in each of them had connected. She had taken the edge off the loss of his best friend from childhood and, more lately, the death of his father.

She was fun to be with and sophisticated, but they had drifted apart lately. Maybe he had expected too much from her. Their growing estrangement saddened him on one level, but on another, it confirmed that maybe there just wasn't enough between them to build a life on.

He realized now that he was tired—maybe too tired to work at relationships. His job at Rotak Industries, a company that researched environmentally safe products, involved long hours of experimentation and study. He liked his work. He was good at it, but he could feel the tension from the sustained concentration, the minutiae of exacting equations.

The late 80s had ushered in a heightened environmental awareness, leading to grassroots revitalization. For the first time in history, activists were beginning to confront powerful institutions as equals. All of this brought increasing pressure to bear on industries like Rotak. Peter sighed. A few days with his Mom in quiet surroundings might be just what the doctor ordered.

He adjusted his glasses and relaxed against the seat. He'd been working too hard, but it was rewarding to pour his energies into formulas and percentages, solid figures that added up and made sense. Life often did not.

There had to be an answer to the catastrophic problems of a world out of control. He admired the Huxleys, Emerson, and Skinner, who didn't look to romantic theories or pie-in-the-sky answers. As scientific rationalists, they sought solutions to life's perplexing problems in history and the sciences.

He liked looking for answers to life's puzzles and enjoyed analyzing nature's wonders and terrors. He'd studied hard as a child, often taking first place in his science projects. His parents had nurtured his early fascination with all living creatures and let him bring home the class gerbil over the summer—the rabbits and turtles. Dad had even spent a week with him at Palmer's Creek studying the insects that thrived there.

His parents had believed that a sustaining, governing Creator had everything under control and that He would eventually restore things to their proper order and beauty. People of faith must endure the temporary agony of a fallen universe and wait for a new earth to arise. Peter drew in a deep breath and sped up around a curve.

Perhaps there was some merit to the "Design" theory, but it didn't answer the persistent questions—like why his best friend had taken a hunting gun out of its case and shot his father. Peter shuddered. It had been a time of utter hopelessness and confusion. He had stayed in his room, unable to talk or eat, while his parents exchanged concerned glances and no doubt prayed for him. It had been comforting in a way to know they prayed, but he could not believe in a personal God—Creator or not—who allowed innocent people to suffer.

How could God allow a young boy to go so wrong or let a father die in his prime? If only he could talk to his dad again. Fifty was far too young to die. It shouldn't have happened. He turned onto the county road that led to his mother's new home and steeled himself against a surge of emotion.

The county road wound through rocky outcroppings and acres of forest where trees bent in green profusion over creek beds and winding streams. Cattails, milk pods, sumac, and wild-flowers formed a cornucopia of color. Fields of wheat, alfalfa, and corn stretched beneath endless reaches of sky with barely a cloud to ruffle the serene beauty.

He'd stopped at a florist in town and bought a box of yel-low roses—Mom's favorite. After the miserable welcome she'd gotten on her first night in this town, she needed some TLC, and he determined to see she got it. He hoped the matter of the neighbor's death had been cleared up. She didn't need any more reminders of death. He grasped the wheel tighter. Mom had to be lonely without Dad. Still young and beautiful, she should have someone to share a life with, but she wasn't likely to find such a person in the slumbering town she'd adopted.

He ran a hand through his light brown hair and glanced in the overhead mirror. He didn't want to give her cause to worry about him. At least he'd taken time to cut his hair, which he often forgot to do until it began curling on his collar or when Jen threatened to play barber. He'd gotten a decent shave, too, but his eyes were circled in shadow. "Windows of the soul," people said. What did they see when they looked into his eyes? Life could be a lonely, perplexing ordeal. In Thomas Hobbes' philosophy, it was "nasty, brutish and short." He thumped the steering wheel, disgusted with his self-absorption, and focused on the expansive countryside.

The road narrowed and became primitive—trees and bushes twisting and tangling along the river as water rushed frothy and white from high cliffs. He slowed to watch as he drove along the upper bank, stunned by the beauty and power of the scene.

Suddenly, a bright flash caught his eye. A girl in a yellow jacket ran along the bank, her long copper hair flaring out over her jacket. Her movements were erratic, frantic. Something was wrong; she was afraid of something. He stopped and pulled the emergency brake. Pocketing his keys, he climbed out and raced toward her.

She ran along the rocky bank where the ground sloped dangerously toward the creek below, then began to claw her way down. She clung to knotted tree limbs and protruding branches, the hood of her jacket bobbing like a fisherman's buoy. Suddenly, he saw the object of her attention—a deer thrashing about in the shallow water at the bottom, its front legs and torso caught in the branches. One of the animal's legs stuck out oddly from its tawny body.

Peter straddled the ridge. "Hey! Be careful," he yelled. "This gorge is dangerous!"

But he might have been addressing the wind. She did not respond or turn at the sound of his voice. She was a few feet away from the trapped fawn now, a slender form in blue jeans and tennis shoes turning one way, then another, hands fluttering in bewildered agitation. Suddenly, she turned toward him and began to run, arms flailing. As the distance narrowed, he realized that she was saying something in sign language. She was deaf.

Drawing on his memory of simple signs he'd learned in undergraduate school, he said, "Let me help you. Careful now!" He came alongside the thrashing animal while the girl stepped back, pressing her hands over her mouth.

"There, fellow, take it easy," he crooned, bending over the young deer, a fawn still sporting its white markings. The summer he'd spent as a forest ranger's assistant had taught him something about animals, but his pulse quickened as he grasped the fawn's slippery body. He felt the fast beating of its heart and recognized the panic in its eyes. He pinned the animal's body with his leg to keep it still and carefully began to free it from the tangled brush.

The fawn broke free. Peter grasped it and held it firmly, careful of its front foreleg, which was most likely broken. "There's a blanket in my car," he said to the girl, hoping she could read his lips since both arms were busy with the animal. "In the back seat."

As she scrambled up the bank, he followed, awkwardly balancing the weight of the thrashing animal. When he reached the top, he saw that she was unfolding the blanket with trembling hands.

"He's in shock," he said. "We'll have to wrap him up." Tenderly, Peter secured the blanket around the fawn, speaking to it softly as he worked. The leg would have to be set.

When the animal's thrashing was under control, he introduced himself. "My name's Peter Westin. My mother just moved into the old Grainger place about a week ago. I'm on my way there."

She nodded and wiped her cheek with the sleeve of her jacket. A frown creased her forehead, and an angry scratch marred the creamy surface. "Beatrice," she said shyly, giving only her first name and clutching her jacket over her chest. "Will he be all right?"

She unlocked her arms, and a thick strand of bright hair dipped over one eye, an eye so deeply blue that it appeared almost purple. She moved her fingers rapidly, searching his face. "I was taking a walk. I saw it down there. He was trapped." She paused and watched his eyes for assurance that he had understood. "I didn't know what to do."

He estimated that she was in her early 20s, with finely cut features and an aura of innocence that touched him. "I'm glad I could help," he stammered. "But we need to get him fixed up. My mother's place is nearby. We could take him there."

She looked away as though distracted or nervous. She was wise to be cautious about getting in a car with a stranger—even here, far from the city. "Don't worry. I won't hurt you," Peter said, hefting the fawn and placing it in the young woman's arms.

It was only a short distance before the house came into view. On the porch, his mother was waiting as she used to wait for him to come home from school. Beatrice eased out of the car with her blanketed burden but held back shyly against the car. He beckoned for her to come, but she took the barest step forward.

His mother hurried down the steps to greet them and stared at the trembling animal, her features wreathed in confusion. "Are you all right, Beatrice?"

Peter was taken aback. Mom knew this young woman's name. When Beatrice didn't respond, he said, "We're both a little wet, but we're okay."

Anne hesitated only briefly. "Bring him around back. He'll be comfortable in the shed."

Peter followed his mother, leaving Beatrice several paces behind. The door swung open, and Anne switched on the lights. "Put him in the stall behind that bench. A confined space will make him less fearful."

"We need something for a splint and some bandages," Peter said, placing the animal onto a rumpled canvas. He gently set the deer's leg as best as possible when the needed materials were found while his mother held it still, speaking softly.

Beatrice watched from the door, her forehead furrowed, then crept closer, eyes fixed on the fawn. Her chin trembled as she glanced at Anne. "Can you keep him here?" she asked in sign language. "My aunt won't..." She broke off, her eyes frantic.

"Sure," Peter said before Anne could speak. "He can stay in the shed. My mother loves animals. She's taken in gerbils, guinea pigs, parakeets, and all the other critters I used to bring home. He'll be fine."

When Anne brought a rubber glove filled with milk, the fawn began to suck hungrily. Beatrice knelt in the straw and watched with wonder in her eyes. Peter handed the glove to her and felt oddly elated as he watched her feed the little fawn. It was strangely comforting and disturbing at the same time, and he wondered if he would ever see her again. If she were to take responsibility for the deer, she'd have to come back, wouldn't she?

He touched her arm to get her attention. "Someone will have to look after him until he's stronger. Will you come back tomorrow to feed him?"

She dropped her eyes but nodded as she ran her hand gently over the fawn's back. She got up and began to move away. "I have to go..."

"Wait," Peter said. "Let me take you home. You're wet. You'll catch cold."

Her eyes filled with worry, fear, or some emotion he couldn't name. She shook her head. "I can walk. I—" She backed hurriedly away without finishing the sentence.

Anne put out a hand to detain her. "The fawn will need you," she said, looking steadily at Beatrice. "Please come and see to her care. You're always welcome here."

Beatrice pushed past her without responding. It was rude, Peter thought, but who could know what it was like to live in a silent world? "Let me drive you," he called, but she ran away, her hair gleaming in the sun.

"Never mind, Peter," Anne said, taking his arm. "She just lives over there—behind us."

"There? Is she—?"

"Yes, she's the girl Alexei and his sister raised."

"But she's—" Peter gasped. From the description he had heard of Beatrice Popov, he had expected someone quite different. He searched his mother's face, puzzled that he had been drawn so quickly to her vulnerable young neighbor. He latched the shed door and brushed off his muddy jeans. "Are there any normal welcomes here?"

Anne hooked her arm through his. "Apparently not, Peter. Nothing's been normal here. It's been a strange week."

"She risked her neck for that animal," he said, looking over his shoulder in the direction Beatrice had taken. "That rocky slope was treacherous."

"She's lucky you came along."

"It was weird," he said. "I thought she was in trouble, that somebody might be chasing her. Then, of course, I realized she was deaf when she didn't respond when I called."

His mother stopped and rested her hand on a tree near the driveway. "Yes, I learned that when I came home and found her staring at the house."

"This house?"

"Yes, just staring, and later, I found her spying on me from the hedge."

He frowned and waited for her to explain.

"Actually," his mother continued, "she might even have left a ..." She let her sentence fall away.

"What?"

She shrugged. A frown creased her forehead, but she laughed and shrugged her shoulders. "She hasn't been very friendly, but she seems to think you're all right. Come on, I've got coffee brewing. I'll fill you in on what's been happening."

"Oh, I almost forgot," Peter said, breaking away. He clambered back to his car for the roses.

"Oh, Peter," she said when he thrust the huge bouquet into her arms. "Yellow roses! They are magnificent!" She buried her face in them. "You remembered."

"Of course. Favorite flowers for my favorite Mom." He thought he saw a tear in her eye and was glad he'd brought them. "Well," he hurried on, "the place looks great. You must have hired a landscaper already."

"Another mystery," she said, raising her eyebrows. "I don't know how it happened, but I'm glad the place wasn't left to the dandelions."

"A very attentive realtor," he mused. "Or maybe your neighbors did it as a gesture of goodwill." When she said nothing in response, he looked at her more closely and saw the shadow of trouble lingering there. So, things had not gotten better. It was a good thing he'd decided to come back so soon.

But even as he worried about his Mom's entry into the new world of Grace Arbor, he marveled at how the mysterious young woman with the old-fashioned name could so quickly have captured his imagination and roused his deep sympathy.

Chapter 10

*A*nne pulled on jeans and a sweatshirt and padded into the kitchen, careful not to disturb Peter. Hopefully, he would sleep in after his drive from Chicago yesterday. She had noticed the dark circles under his eyes and the tired lines around his mouth. He'd no doubt been working too hard. But he was here now, and she could offer some TLC. Strangely, he had encountered Beatrice and the injured fawn—a rescue operation that forced Beatrice Popov to face her neighbor for the first time.

The young woman had not wanted the confrontation; she had hung back by Peter's car. Guilty conscience, perhaps? Why couldn't she say what she had against her instead of hiding behind bushes, spying on her house, or sending cryptic notes?

Anne stood hesitant in a beam of early sunlight, thinking of the young woman's brooding behavior. She had accepted her offer to keep the deer in her shed but without a thank you or even a nod. Peter was taken with her, but was she as sweet and innocent as she seemed?

Anne sighed. It wasn't fun being *persona non grata* in your neighborhood. Or was she being too hard on Beatrice? After all, it must be difficult being deaf. *If I could not hear, would I react to people with the kind of suspicion she shows?*

Did Beatrice know what her grandmother had experienced as a child? If what Margaret had said was true. Anne shuddered as she recalled the frightening revelation about a secret execution in the middle of the night when members of the last ruling family—the Romanovs— were murdered along with their servants and pets. Did Beatrice know about that?

For many years, there were no bodies to prove that those long-ago deaths really occurred. The lack of detailed information gave rise to numerous rumors of conspiracies and various survivors, not just in Russia but also in the West. Claims of affiliation with the last Russian dynasty had cropped up in movies, cartoons, and books based on the alleged survival of the most famous of all imperial daughters, Grand Duchess Anastasia. All of this helped reignite interest in the Romanov family in the 21st century. But had a child of a former servant once lived at Grace Arbor?

Everyone knew Margaret had been ill; perhaps her mind was going. Anne shook her head. It was a bizarre story. Did it really have anything to do with Beatrice? Perhaps with Alexei? A quick shiver passed through her. But it was a beautiful day, and Peter was here. She hadn't drawn the blinds before retiring, and the sun streamed into the kitchen. Her strong son was in the downstairs guest room—just a few feet away. Night sounds hadn't disturbed her, nor had she imagined intruders on her property; she'd slept soundly.

Opening the patio door, she inhaled the early air. Finches with voices light as the stems of lilies gentled the clamor of crows. *This is the best time of the day*, she thought, and began to hum the strains of an old hymn: *This is my Father's world ... all nature sings and round me rings.* She surveyed the flowers and shrubs around the house with appreciation. Why had someone maintained a garden on her property? Had some prior arrangement been made with a local landscaper? Would she receive a hefty bill in the mail one of these days?

The sound of a truck revving its motor ended her speculation about the flowers. She looked in the direction of the sound, absently at first, ears pre-programmed to ignore the traffic noise. But she wasn't in the big city anymore, and it was early for traffic of any kind in this quiet end of town. And suddenly, she realized that the noise had come from the base of her driveway. She strained her eyes to see. A blue pickup was zooming away too fast to get a good look or make out a license plate.

Perhaps whoever was driving the truck had used her driveway to make a U-turn. Or had he sped away when he realized she was watching? Images flashed in her mind—Alexei's lusterless eyes, the strange tale Margaret Morris had told, and hostile neighbors who resented her presence. She shivered as she went inside, latching the screen door after her.

Gathering ingredients for waffles, she plugged in the old griddle. There was nothing like a leisurely Saturday breakfast to calm the nerves. Still, as she methodically cracked eggs and measured oil for the batter, her mind searched for logical sequence. Where had she seen a truck like that? Had its driver been watching her house? Was she getting paranoid?

The note had been real enough, but it had seemed like a silly prank, something a child might have done. A child like Beatrice? If she told Peter about it, he might try to convince her to move back to the city, thinking his mother was no match for this remote place with its troubled neighbors.

She poured orange juice into tumblers when she heard Peter's step in the hall. She wasn't ready to admit defeat. Nor would she let anything spoil the short time they had together. Their relationship had changed since Richard's death. They were tentative with each other, as though they couldn't quite manage the rhythm of life without Richard, who had anchored them both.

"I'd almost forgotten how good that smells," Peter said, pulling up a chair. "It's good to be here." He leaned over and kissed her cheek.

She searched his face as though it could reveal a hidden secret. The dark under-eye circles of the night before had faded. He'd slept well. His hair curled slightly at his neck, evoking a boyish charm that stirred her protective instincts. "You know, you're my first guest," she said, smiling. She paused at the irony. He was at least the first *invited* guest. "The house isn't quite ready for inspection and isn't much like the home you grew up in."

"Home is wherever you are," he said, giving her the wink that always melted her. "Besides, the place is taking shape. You're doing wonders with it."

She smiled, touched by the studied light in his brown eyes. He always seemed to be reading people, trying to see what lay behind their words and actions.

"So, tell me. What's the scoop from the local sheriff?" Absently, he moved the curtain back from the kitchen window. "I see the tape around the area hasn't been removed."

"They're still investigating," she said with a sigh. "The autopsy showed more trauma to the head than would have been sustained through a simple fall. It may be tied up with this whole matter of some lost treasure people around here have been gossiping about." She stirred her coffee with deliberate strokes. "An idle tale that's been bandied about for a long time, I understand."

There was a measured silence as Peter poured syrup over his waffle, methodically filling each little square. "Do they have any suspects?" he asked, not looking up.

"If they have, they're not saying. Actually, no one's saying much to me at all. Even at the funeral, it seems I was off limits to everyone."

Peter glanced up sharply. "You went to the funeral?"

She shrugged. "Alexei was my neighbor, Peter. I only met him a year ago when your father and I spent the summer here, but I thought I should support the family. Besides, Alexei didn't have many friends." *Except perhaps Margaret Morris*, she thought, recalling the elderly teacher's sad vigil under the cemetery canopy.

What should she say to her son about the events of the past few days? Maybe Beatrice had scrawled the crayoned message in a moment of grief or anger. After all, her grandmother had once lived in this house. If she told Peter about it, would he confront her or report it to the police? Had the authorities considered that Beatrice might have a motive to do away with her uncle? But that was ludicrous. Wasn't it?

Peter leaned forward and wrapped his hands around his coffee mug. "I hear that her grandmother was from Russia," he said.

Anne nodded. "Her name was Svetlana Grainger. According to Margaret, she came to America and settled somewhere on the East Coast 50 years ago or more. When her husband passed away, she came here to live in this house with her daughter Eliana and Alexei, who was a trusted servant. Eliana died shortly after giving birth to Beatrice. Svetlana took care of her, but shortly before she died, she turned the baby over to Alexei."

"That's quite a story." Peter nodded slowly. "And that gossip about buried treasure—where did that come from?"

"An elderly schoolteacher from the area—Margaret Morris. She may not be reliable, but Alexei was her friend and apparently told her about Svetlana—and an escape from Russia after the Revolution of 1918. I understand it's been the local story for many years—cropping up, fizzling, then reigniting when someone or something stirs it up again."

She pressed her lips together, aware of Peter's studied gaze. There had been little time to analyze what Margaret Morris had told her, let alone to look for confirmation. She must ask Lance what he knew about Svetlana Grainger and her past.

With a sudden jolt, Anne remembered where she had seen the blue pick-up truck that had raced away from her driveway.

She had seen it only a few days before parked in front of Lance's realty office!

"If there really were jewels buried on the property, where are they now?" Peter asked.

Anne swallowed, too distracted to respond. Why would Lance idle his truck in her driveway? Why not come in or wave or something? She was sure it was his pick-up. He grabbed sunglasses from the sedan's visor when they visited the Italian restaurant.

"What happened to the jewels?" Peter asked again.

She was so stunned by the truck that she barely heard. "Sorry."

"I asked, 'What happened to the jewels?' And if her grandmother was wealthy, why is Beatrice living in that falling-down house? Wasn't something left for her future?"

"I don't know," she said quietly. What had Alexei known, and what had he been doing when he died? "It's all so bizarre," she said wistfully, "but let's not waste a beautiful day. "I'll just finish here, and you can check on our four-footed guest in the shed."

When he had gone, she tackled the dishes, glad for practical work to relieve the tension of unexplained riddles. Sun shone through the window over the sink as she worked. Presently, she saw Peter near the shed with Beatrice beside him. The girl looked up at him with a shy smile that transformed her somber features. Apparently, she had passed judgment on her son and found him trustworthy.

But was she plotting against *her* to entice her to leave? Did she have some distorted idea about Grace Arbor's ownership? Before she could think about it further, she saw Mackowitz drive up. She dried her hands and hurried onto the back deck to greet him.

"Hello, Mrs. Westin. I'm looking for Beatrice. Her aunt said she might be here." He fumbled for something in his pocket while shifting his considerable bulk from one dusty foot to another.

Anne was about to answer when Peter and Beatrice emerged from the shed, carrying an assortment of towels, bottles, and jars.

"Morning," Mackowitz said dully, nodding to Peter, but his eyes were trained on Beatrice. Speaking slowly and distinctly, he addressed her. "I'd like you to come with me to answer a few questions."

The young woman's face turned ashen. She began to gesture, her fingers making anxious pleas in the air. She looked from Peter to Mackowitz, eyes wide with confusion.

Peter stepped in front of Beatrice, demanding the sheriff's attention. "I'm Peter Westin. We met the night my mother first arrived."

"Westin," he acknowledged with a quick tilt of his head. "We need to speak to this young woman. An interpreter is coming down from Taylorville. She'll meet us at my office." He turned to Beatrice and spoke loudly and slowly. "Do you understand?"

Peter dropped a bucket to the ground and stood with arms crossed in front of him. "I'm sure she understands. There's nothing wrong with her mind," he said defensively, "only her ears."

Mackowitz ignored the mild rebuke and inclined his stubbly head to Beatrice. "There's no need for alarm. We need to clarify some things—about your uncle. And we can communicate better in town. You'll have to come with me."

Beatrice's hands flew up and began gesturing wildly. With each movement, her cloud of copper hair flew from side to side like red-gold wings.

Mackowitz seemed to be considering something. Then he reached into his pocket and drew out a necklace. "Does this belong to you?" He held up a thin chain with a delicately engraved heart that flashed golden in the sunlight. Anne could see the fear in the girl's luminous eyes and feel her pulse racing as she pressed closer to the little group on the lawn. She stepped in next to Peter, eyes fixed on the necklace in the sheriff's big hand.

Beatrice reached for it, but Mackowitz quickly withdrew it. "Sorry. It's evidence."

Her fingers flew in agitation. "Where did you—? How did you—?" She was stammering in a high, strained voice, her speech reduced to monosyllables.

Peter drew a protective arm around her shoulder and turned to Mackowitz. "What does that necklace have to do with anything?"

"It was found under some leaves near the body."

"She lives just beyond the woods," Anne protested. "She walks through them all the time. Losing a locket doesn't mean..."

"It may not mean anything, ma'am," he said patiently before turning again to Beatrice. "I'm just asking you to come to the office to talk. Mr. Westin here can come with you. Your aunt can come along, too." He shrugged and pocketed the necklace, pursing his cracked lips.

"I'll go with you," Peter said urgently, grasping one of Beatrice's fluttering hands.

She clutched his hand fiercely, her eyes dark pools of fear.

"We'll be back," Peter said, nodding to his mother. "Just as soon as we straighten this out." Gripping Beatrice's hand, he led her to the patrol car.

What could it mean? It seemed cruel to haul the vulnerable young woman away like a criminal. Anne cringed, aware that birds were singing with a jubilance more appropriate for a garden party. Beatrice had loved Alexei. Surely, she wouldn't want to hurt him. Vera, with her temperamental outbursts, seemed more likely to be involved.

An interpreter would put Beatrice on a more equal footing. But was Peter getting involved in something that would come back to bite him? The sun's warmth had evaporated, leaving her chilled as she retreated inside Grace Arbor.

Chapter 11

$\int$hane left the truck on the side of the road and strolled past the house where Beatrice lived. She'd be at work now, but he knew he would find Vera out back in the hen house, fussing over her biddies. *Clucking just like one of them*, he thought grimly. He parted the scraggly shrubs, revealing the lean-to coop that housed the old woman's pride and joy.

Beyond the low structure with its flat roof lay a broader hedge of lilac bushes that neatly separated the coop from the northern-most border of the Grainger estate. He paused, feeling the tension in his neck. He narrowed his eyes and took in the acreage that lay uncluttered next to the private wood where Alexei had been found.

The house beyond stood like a magnificent specter, alluring in the shadow of great trees surrounding it like watchful border guards. A rectangular sign advertised the estate in large, loopy calligraphy. It had been freshly repainted in dark green and garnished with curling vines. *Grace Arbor.*

He felt an unreasonable resentment as he studied the smooth lines of the house, its gabled roof, and dark shutters that guarded its secrets. He grimaced as he watched. He knew every inch of the place, had searched it thoroughly when Uncle Lance had sent him out to do the preliminary survey for the pending contract. He'd explored every corner with the most sophisticated equipment he could rent, sure the stash would be there. But his search had yielded only a new batch of blisters and an ache along his spine.

It wouldn't be easy to look anymore now that someone has bought the house. Lair had told him that it had been rented a few dozen times and left empty until a year ago when the city couple had begun to make noises about purchasing it. Shane pictured Anne Westin, a middle-aged lady with grand airs and fancy shoes like she had worn at the funeral.

Most women without a man around would have gone flying back to wherever they came from if a body had been found on their land. But she hadn't given any hint of backing away. She was even trying to make friends with her neighbors. He kicked a stone at his feet and watched it tumble along the line of shrubbery. Maybe he'd have to do something about that.

It had seemed so easy in the beginning. He had an advantage over the simple residents of the dead-end town. They were mostly country hicks anyway, who wouldn't know a gold mine from a field of alfalfa. At first, he thought he might die of boredom in the quiet town that rolled its sidewalks up at nine. He'd only stayed on the chance that the rumors about Alexei Popov were true. Opportunity was knocking, and he had a chance to hit it big.

He let the branch fall back in place, obscuring the elegant home from his view. Grace Arbor was a stupid name, he thought. It was the British who named everything, wasn't it? He turned his attention back to the house where Beatrice's bedroom window shade had been pulled down against the afternoon heat.

He was restless, weary of waiting. He thought his old charm was working, that she would confide in him. But despite his efforts to earn her affection, she seemed wary. As if she could afford to play hard to get! He ran a hand through his hair. He needed another talk with Vera, much as he disliked the idea.

Someone had to keep an eye on Beatrice and that nosy neighbor who had taken too much interest in the affairs of her new community.

He watched Vera move through a row of chickens, thick arms surprisingly agile as she relieved the hens of their smooth brown eggs. They clucked vague warnings and preened their feathers while she hushed them in low, guttural murmurs. He frowned and focused on the woman in the colorless sweater hanging loosely over her bulky dress. She wore heavy stockings and high-top shoes that looked like they'd sloshed through the hen house too many times. The hem of her dress was torn on one side and hung beneath her left knee when she bent to fill the noisy birds' water troughs. Plucking an egg from beneath a squawking hen, she placed it into a wire basket.

Shane grimaced with distaste when the hen flapped furiously, scattering feathery debris into the dusty air. When Vera turned to shoo it away with an angry sweep of her arm, she saw him. "What you want?" she asked, her lower lip protruding like a sulking child's.

He crossed his arms over his flat stomach and leaned against a rough-hewn post. "Is that any way to greet a friend?" He regarded her coolly. *What am I doing talking to a foreign farm woman in a smelly hen house?*

"I got work to do," she sputtered, transferring eggs from the basket into worn crates stacked in the corner. When she bent over, the red scarf on her head flipped up, revealing the black bundle of hair at the nape of her neck. Her skin was surprisingly unwrinkled for a woman so old.

She must be 70 at least. He watched her with an amused smile and then assumed a relaxed air. "Ah!" he said, "but maybe we won't have to work so hard for long, dear lady." He slung his jacket over his left shoulder and took three precise steps forward, then paced back and forth as though puzzling out some knotty problem.

Vera eyed him sullenly, one hand on a wooden beam above her head. With the other, she covered a brooch shaped like a cluster of green grapes, its brilliance clashing with the shapeless gray sweater. He wanted a closer look, but Vera always covered it when she noticed him staring. He was pretty sure it was part of a fortune in jewels. She was a fool to wear it. One of these days, someone would hit her over the head for it. But he supposed she was too dumb to be afraid.

He forced his eyes away from her heavy breast with the sparkling jewel and gave her a coy half-smile. "You—uh gotten little Bea to talk to you yet?"

"You forget. She ain't much for words," Vera said with tired irony.

"Miz Popov, you amaze me," he said in mock dismay. "Don't you know I'm trying to help you? After caring for little Bea all those years, you should have something for your trouble." He regarded her through narrowed eyes. "I can make it happen."

He had met the Popovs when he came to work for Uncle Lance, which hadn't been his idea. People were always making decisions for him, telling him what he should or shouldn't do. And what had it gotten him? Still, he needed a place to settle for a while, to think about what to do next. He decided to put up with this one-horse town for a little while on his way to something better. He was smart enough to make it big. After all, everyone said he was clever. If he could just get these annoying towns people to cooperate!

Vera Popov's heavily accented voice interrupted his thoughts. "I know what you try to do. I know." She shook a finger in his face. "You think you have Alexei fooled. But he die on you!" She laughed then without humor and pushed past him with her basket of eggs, her lips fixed in a childish pout. "There ain't no treasure."

"He buried it. You know he buried it!" Shane whispered fiercely, taking a step toward her. "Maybe you found out where and dug it up yourself." He grabbed her arm as she moved to swing away from him. It galled him to think that after all he'd put up with, the whole thing might be a hoax. But no. Hadn't that old fool been digging up the ground all over this place? It had to be here. "Maybe you're holding on to more than that pin," he said with forced control and grabbed the corner of her sweater, pulling it open to reveal the emerald brooch.

Vera yanked it away from him. "You crazy!" she hissed. She turned her back on him, but her fingers trembled on the egg crate.

Shane thrust his hands into his pockets. There had to be a treasure. Alexei couldn't have been fooling him all this time. He couldn't have started all those town rumors himself.

Suddenly, the sound of an engine ended their stand-off. Shane turned to see a car rolling up to the curb in front of the house. It was the car he'd seen that morning at the Grainger mansion. He chewed the inside of his cheek and squinted. Beatrice was inside, small and pretty, in the passenger seat. Like a picture posed in a frame, her hair waving back from her white face. What was she doing in that stranger's car?

A man in a brown leather jacket got out and came around like a chauffeur to open Bea's door. He was tall and gangly with light brown hair and glasses. *One of those Ivy League college types,* Shane thought. He thrust the hair off his forehead and watched them approach.

As they neared, Shane saw that Bea's eyes were red. She was dabbing at her nose with a tissue. Had the locket been found? He'd planted it in the woods to keep the authorities from sniffing around him. It had been so easy to steal it. Like taking candy from a baby. He went toward them leisurely as though he'd waited all day just for them to come calling. He couldn't help but see the look Bea gave the guy beside her, and he felt a pang of unreasonable jealousy.

"Bea—we've all been worried about you. I was just asking your aunt about you. You okay?"

Beatrice looked from him to Vera and back again as though bewildered. Her eyes glistened, but she said nothing and looked up at the tall man by her side as though the answer were written on his face.

She's fine," the stranger said. Ignoring him, he turned to Beatrice, saying something in sign language. Vera glared at them when he laid a hand on her shoulder, and Shane made fists at his sides.

He clenched his jaw. *What was this stranger doing with her?* Shane hated the superior look on his face, the strong jaw and prominent nose, the brown eyes set in deep behind dark-rimmed glasses. Shane cleared his throat noisily. "I'm a friend of Bea's. Shane Eldridge. You—uh—from around here?" He waited, looking the intruder over and waiting for him to introduce himself.

"Peter Westin," he said without taking his eyes from Bea's face. He handed her a white card as she stepped back, clutching a small blue handbag. His voice was low and deep as though he didn't want anyone to hear, and he worked long fingers in the air the way Bea did.

So, he knew sign language. Big deal!

Peter Westin. He had to be related to the lady who bought the Grainger place. Shane edged toward Beatrice. He put a protective arm around her shoulder, eager to draw her attention away from the Ivy leaguer. "I'm here for you," he said with careful precision, commanding her eyes.

She eased out of his grasp and tugged her jacket around her shoulders. "Thank you," she said softly, but the words were for Peter Westin, and she had a dreamy look that Shane hadn't seen before. She walked away toward the house, her tennis shoes making soft swishes in the grass, Vera following without a word. The two men were left facing each other.

"I didn't get your name," Peter said levelly, his eyes cold and calculating.

Shane drew himself up to his full height, which wasn't enough to meet his opponent's gaze squarely. "Shane Eldridge," he repeated evenly. "Bea and I are old friends. Fact is, I'm a friend of the family. I was just telling Mrs. Popov how sorry I was to hear about the old man dying and everything."

Westin's penetrating stare unnerved Shane. He was one of those guys the world had smiled on—silver spoon and old money. He'd probably never had to do a day's work in his life. Shane stiffened, but he forced his most winsome smile. It wasn't good to antagonize the neighbors and make them suspicious. He shrugged his shoulders and looked off toward the house. "Bea needs someone to look after her." He cast a nonchalant glance at Westin. "You seem pretty good at sign language."

Peter Westin made no move to shake hands. His mouth remained fixed in a grim expression.

Shane hurried on. "The poor girl was fond of the old guy. Rotten luck him dying and all. Seems she got a bad deal all around, being deaf and … " Something in Westin's steely glance stopped him short.

Peter turned away, walked to his car, and folded himself inside without looking back. Shane followed and leaned in the open window just as the engine roared to life. *Where does this guy get off acting so high and mighty? Who does he think he is?* "Little Bea needs all the help she can get," he said as genially as he could muster.

The car lurched. Shane had to step back fast to avoid the spray of gravel that spattered his new jeans. He cursed and clenched his teeth as the car sped away. What he wouldn't give to put his fist into the clean-cut face of Mr. Peter Westin. But he had kept his cool. He congratulated himself as he brushed dust from his pants. He had to keep a low profile, at least for now, until he could get his hands on the treasure.

He dug his fists into his pockets. Things were not going well; he had to think. He had to find out where the stuff was before things spiraled out of control. He had to get Bea to tell him. But he couldn't talk to her now, and Vera was in no mood to consider a truce and help him, even though he'd promised she'd not go empty-handed. Could he count on her greed?

He got into his truck, or rather Uncle Lance's truck, and gripped the steering wheel hard. This was not the way he'd planned it. Uncle Lance was sick of him; likely he couldn't wait to get rid of his pain-in-the-neck nephew. He'd made that clear only that morning. He'd only taken him in because of his promise to his mother. He pictured her white-faced and still, and his eyes began to sting as he revved the motor angrily. What to do now? Old Alexei hadn't turned up the treasure, and now someone else was vying for little Bea's trust.

He spat through the open window. There was a gold mine here. He was sure of it. He could almost smell it. Something in his gut reacted. "Steady, man," he told himself, gripping the wheel. He squared his shoulders and looked at himself in the rearview mirror. "It'll just take some brains and patience, Shane, my man." And he roared away from the Popov property, drumming his fingers to the rap beat coming from the radio. Gradually, he began to feel calmer.

Chapter 12

Beatrice's heart thumped wildly in her chest. She tried to scream, but no sound came. A great, burning star was moving toward her, its sharp points menacing and hot. Any second, brilliant tentacles would pierce her. The star would grasp her, crushing, swallowing her.

She woke suddenly, panting as harmless sun rays danced across her bed. She fell back against the pillow until the dream gradually wore away. Then she remembered. Chief Mackowitz with the locket in his big hand—just below the gleaming star on the blue field of his shirt. It had mesmerized her, making it hard to answer his questions about Uncle Alexei.

The authorities thought he might not have had a heart attack but that someone had been with him that night. They had found evidence—her locket. How could it happen? And how could they possibly think she could have been there and not helped him?

She had missed him when she was away at the institute for the deaf—the tenderness of his rough hands, his wild stories. When she returned, she had been shocked by the absent look in his eyes, the vague, half-spoken phrases that made little sense. She wanted to take care of him, to prepare his favorite raspberry tea, and sit with him under the trees.

But he was gone. She would never know his gentle touch again, never see those eyes that burned with some age-old secret.

A sob caught in her throat. At least he was free from the curious gazes of people, free from Vera's nagging. Free from whatever it was that drove him to dig up the ground. Was he truly at rest now?

What happened when the door closed on life? Did another door open, or were you trapped in some alien atmosphere that swallowed you up—like in her dream? She shivered despite the comforter drawn up to her chin.

A teacher at the institute said that God created people like Himself to love and to be loved. Beatrice sighed. It sounded like such a lovely story. If only she could believe it. And maybe it was true—for some people, but not for her. She'd always known she was different. She had prayed to Him when she was a small child, begging God to make her hear.

She had read Mark Twain's story about a boy with a clubfoot who believed God could heal him—make him normal. It would happen if he prayed hard enough or had enough faith. Hoping to impress God with his earnestness, he pushed away the comforting little rug on his bedroom floor and knelt on the hard boards to pray. He took off his shirt and said his prayers naked to show his humility. When he woke up, he touched his foot, believing that God had answered, but he found it just as before—deformed and ugly. A lump formed in her throat. Perhaps she, too, had not been found worthy of God's attention. Or maybe He, too, was deaf.

She'd learned a lot since her childhood days—how to eat without causing people to stare, how to avoid the noises the human body made. She'd learned how to water plants without overflowing the pot. Other things, too, that hearing people never had to think about. And she'd learned that nothing was going to change her deafness.

At least she had a job now. She felt a rising in her heart. Maybe one day, she'd have a car and roam the beautiful hills.

No more pedaling her bicycle into town and arriving at work sweaty and exhausted. She drew in her breath. Then, too, there was Shane. Was that admiration she saw in his eyes? Did he really care about her? A girl could live with a lot of things if someone loved her.

She remembered how Shane had comforted her when he took her to buy ice cream and how his hands had moved against her back, soothing and warming. She had felt the soft vibrations in his throat when he spoke. "My little Bea, you should talk more," he had said when she finally found the courage to speak without using her hands.

He had told her he was sorry about Alexei, but when his hand traveled up from her waist, she had breathlessly squirmed out of his arms, afraid and delighted all at once. She liked being cared for by a handsome boy, but sometimes, she was afraid when he was close to her.

She crawled out from under the warm blanket, wondering about him, about Alexei, and what they talked about. Why did Shane come around? Even Vera tolerated him. She usually had time for no one but her hens and the lazy hound that traipsed behind her.

Beatrice slipped into jeans and her favorite blue sweatshirt, the one she had worn the day she and Peter Westin had found the deer in the brush. She paused before her mirror. Peter had been kind—treated her like someone important. She liked it. She liked it a lot.

She had never had a boyfriend until Shane came along. Could the sophisticated, well-educated Peter Westin like her, too? At least he had taken time to help her. She had been so glad for his comforting presence when the policeman had come looking for her.

"Call me if you need me. Anytime," he had said before leaving her door.

She turned away from the confusing rush of feeling and left her room. It was Sunday, the day some people went to church, a day to reflect on the God who supposedly watched over the universe He had created. If He was watching, He seemed to have no time for her. She walked into the kitchen feeling guilty about her irreverent thoughts. Would God be angry?

Aunt Vera wasn't up yet, and the house seemed deserted. She liked the early morning when the light crept in through the shades and the air smelled lemony. The faded linoleum was cold beneath her bare feet as she passed the old stove with its crusted burners, the scarred table, and the chairs with yellow vinyl seats. One of those chairs would be empty today and for all the days to come.

She swallowed and turned away to the old pine sideboard. The dish Mrs. Westin had brought lay empty and unwashed. She should take it back to the lady. Vera wouldn't. Beatrice sighed. She'd been prepared to dislike Mrs. Westin, too, but the new owner of the grand house had been kind to her. And her son, too, had been kind. She formed his name on her lips. Peter…

Chiding herself, Beatrice opened the refrigerator door and closed it again. She ran her fingers over the checkered towel that hung near the stove, wanting to touch everything, every place that her uncle had touched. She even peered into the worn raffia wastebasket under the sink.

Suddenly, she stopped, hand poised over the basket. Scraps of paper torn into small bits lay in the bottom of the raffia container. She picked up the closest piece. The letters "Bea" appeared. She dropped to her knees and began sifting through the scraps. The same handwriting appeared on all of them. She began to fit them together on the kitchen floor. Suppose Vera came in? She stuffed all the pieces into her jeans and returned to the privacy of her room.

She waited, tested the floor's vibrations with her bare feet, and then emptied the scraps onto her bed, turning each one over carefully. The writing was wavy and unsteady. Who had written words that included her name? And why would Vera tear up the message? Was it a letter meant for her? Or was it simply *about* her? Anger and frustration churned inside her as she tried to decipher the fragments. But the more she worked to assemble the tiny pieces, the more frustrated she became.

Vibrations on the floor warned her that Aunt Vera was passing her room on her way to prepare breakfast. Beatrice gathered the scraps, stuffed them into a shoe box, and carried them to the kitchen.

Vera poured water into an ancient coffee maker that leaked if the plastic cup wasn't set in just right. She was dressed in her checkered house dress, her hair rolled against the back of her neck. If she saw Beatrice, she made no indication. Beatrice waited until Vera began to break eggs into a chipped ceramic bowl. Then she dropped the shoebox onto the table with a loud crack.

Vera narrowed her eyes at the sound. "What's that?"

Beatrice turned the box over and poured its contents onto the table. When the last scrap had fallen, she said, "These were in the waste basket."

"You go through trash?" Vera asked dully and turned her back. Any further comments were offered to the four walls or the ceiling.

Beatrice drew in her breath angrily. She walked around to face her aunt. "I saw my name," she said with forced calm. "Was this a letter for me?" She spoke without signing, clenching her hands at her sides.

"You got fancy ways since you go away," Vera said, frowning.

"I just want to know if this was a letter for me. I want to know why you didn't give it to me." Her heart raced. "Please!" She would not let her aunt see her cry.

Vera returned to the eggs, and Beatrice had to read her lips in profile. "It was nothing. Nothing. Go now. Make toast."

Beatrice waited, watching Aunt Vera's sausage-like fingers on the spatula, then whirled away and left the house, carrying the shoebox in her arms, stiff with anger and frustration. The wind tore at the cover, lifted the scraps, and sent them flying. She covered the box with her jacket and stumbled across the yard and through the hedge that led to the Grainger house. The house that now bore the name "Grace Arbor." Mrs. Westin had said she could come as often as she wanted to tend the fawn. She would hide herself inside the warm shed.

The grass was wet beneath her feet, and the fragrance of honeysuckle was sweet on the brisk air. Somewhere, a morning dove crooned as she stepped inside. She dropped the box in the waste barrel near the door. She had lost most of the pieces anyway. She would never know what was written on them.

Brushing away tears, she dropped to her knees by the little animal's stall. She rubbed its head, inhaling its earthy sweetness. It had come to trust her and nuzzled her hand with its cold nose. It felt good to be loved, if only by a fawn. She stroked the furry neck, determined to banish thoughts of a ruined letter—if indeed it was a letter. She wouldn't think about what might have been said about her. Or to her?

She jumped up in sudden alarm as she became aware of someone's presence. Peter stood in the doorway with light brown hair tousled from the wind or sleep.

"Are you all right?" he asked, long fingers forming the question.

She nodded and sniffed back her tears, continuing to stroke the tawny neck. "He's not so afraid now. I think his leg is better."

Peter knelt to examine the animal's leg with its splint and bandage. "You're right," he said, looking at her intently. "Before long, he'll be running all over the place. You're a good nurse."

Beatrice smiled as the fawn nuzzled her jacket pocket. She pulled out the baby bottle with its oversized nipple as Peter dropped beside her on the hay-strewn floor. The little deer tugged on the bottle, huge eyes eager. Beside her, Peter watched, lips curved in a smile. Beatrice felt a strange happiness. If only this sense of warmth and well-being could go on forever. But nothing was forever, was it?

"I'm sorry about last night," Peter said. "You were pretty brave through it all."

She searched his eyes. Did he really think she was brave? She hadn't felt brave when the detective had come for her and questioned her with dark suspicion in his eyes. She had struggled not to cry or run but to concentrate on Peter's presence beside her. "Thank you for helping me."

"Beatrice is a strong name," he said, watching her feed the little deer. "A bit old fashioned and long, but a good name."

"I have a name sign. It isn't very long,"

He looked at her curiously. "How do you make it?"

She curved her fingers and wove them nimbly. "It means 'one who stands tall.'"

His eyes lit up. "Yes, it suits you," he said, smiling, and copied the sign, his fingers so close to hers that they nearly touched. "Tess," he said. "I'll call you Tess for short. It's a strong name—and not so formal."

"Tess," she repeated carefully.

"Like *Tess of the d'Ubervilles*. It's from a novel by Thomas Hardy. The heroine's name means one who stands tall. She was good and very brave."

Good? Brave? She was neither of those things. But could she one day be good enough for him? She looked away from his earnest brown gaze. For now, it was enough that he was here beside her.

"I have to leave tonight, Tess," he said suddenly. "I have to go back to work." He paused as though he wasn't sure how to continue. "But I promised Mom I'd go with her to church this morning." He smiled. "Afterward, we could go for a drive or something. That is, if you want to."

Did he really want to be with her? Her breath caught. "I'd like that," she said, surprising herself.

"Would you like to go with us—to church?" he asked, stroking the fawn's nose.

She shook her head, thinking about the charges she had leveled at God. "I—I don't go to church."

"My mother—church is important to her." He looked away as though something troubled him, and he didn't speak for a long moment. Then, "All right. No church. I'll pick you up about three then. That okay, Tess?"

When his lips formed the name, her heart beat hard and fast. Did it make a sound? Could Peter hear it? "Three," she said, overwhelmed with feeling, and made the signs to indicate that she would be ready. Then she ran from the shed without looking back.

Chapter 13

*P*eter led his mother along the tree-lined path from the parking lot to the polished log church with its low windows and cross at its apex. He took her arm, not because she needed steadying but because he simply wanted to protect her. Dad had always been there to shield her. Now, she was alone in a strange house, living on land that had already claimed one life. For reasons he couldn't quite fathom, she was determined to stay despite his attempts to dissuade her.

"Have you ever seen so many trees?" she exclaimed as they walked under an arch of slender white birches. Leaves fluttered like oval stars on the spare branches, and sunlight danced through them, patterning the earth like a grand lady's lace shawl.

Peter smiled as he ducked to clear the foliage. "I read somewhere that forest comprises some fourteen million acres of Wisconsin land. That's about 42 percent of the total state. Amazing, isn't it?"

"Leave it to you to come up with statistics like that," she said, glancing up at him fondly. "I guess 'Grace Arbor' is a fitting name for my place then."

He inclined his head toward his mother. She moved gracefully in her long blue skirt and white ruffled blouse. Her hair framed a radiant, expectant face. A face, Peter thought, that said she welcomed you—whoever you were—and cared about you.

He had always thought of his mother as beautiful, but not in the womanly way he saw her now. No wonder dad had loved her so much all their years together. His parents' strong love for each other had been a stabilizing force in his life. His North Star, he suddenly realized.

But she had been left alone in a dark and often frightening universe. It seemed to Peter the worst injury, and he felt the muscles in his neck tighten. He never pretended to know the ways of God, if indeed He existed. He drew in his breath. It would pain his mother if she knew what he was thinking.

"I'm glad you're here, Peter," Anne said softly. "People here welcomed your father and me so warmly when we visited. I don't expect they've changed much."

Peter caught the tremor in her voice and once again reeled at the unfairness dealt her in the prime of her life.

By the time they slid into a pew, parishioners had taken their places, including the choir in crimson robes accented by white collars. The organist played "Ode to Joy," long fingers dancing over the keys. Peter studied the hands, ignoring small movements around him in the sanctuary and that his mother was praying. He could see her bowed head from the corner of his eye while music from the organ spilled around them. Something stirred in Peter—a yearning he couldn't identify.

A silver-haired man in a gray suit appeared across the aisle, striking blue eyes trained in their direction. He reached out a hand to Peter's mother and wished her a good morning.

"Hello," she whispered back and returned her gaze forward. But a light blush on her cheek remained. Peter nudged her and raised an eyebrow in silent inquiry.

"Lance Crane," she said into his ear. "The realtor I told you about. Your father and I met him last summer." But there was no time to discuss this new bit of information. The service had begun.

Around him, voices lifted the strains of the first hymn. Modern worship techniques hadn't yet invaded this quiet parish, for no overhead screens projected text over pastoral backgrounds. The hymns, for the most part, were familiar. He'd sung them often enough growing up. But it had been a long time ago. He was surprised now to enjoy their cadences, which mitigated his discomfort.

The music and sermon washed over him like waves on a barren shore. He could hear everything and nothing in a sort of blissful reverie. It might have gone on this way except for the final hymn, which had been his father's favorite and suddenly drew him up short.

This is my Father's world.
O let me ne'er forget
That though the wrong
Seems oft so strong,
God is the ruler yet.

As the benediction ended and congregants moved to the narthex, the words of the last stanza stung him. *God is the ruler yet.* Was He indeed the ruler of a world that had in so many ways violated His precepts, a world that had been itself violated? With other scientists involved in his industry, Peter struggled to preserve the Earth, which seemed doomed to ultimate destruction. If God were indeed its Ruler, why didn't He do something?

Would earth and Heaven indeed be one, ending the cosmic question with its endless debates? Did it all hinge on His incursion into the world in the person of His Son? Was He the answer to the world's dilemma, as his parents believed? Someone had written that He had taken his own medicine and become a man. He had thought it worthwhile to be born into poverty and to experience humiliation and death to redeem the world.

In a flash of insight, Peter realized that he, too, had been working to reclaim the world. But was it a world only God could save? The thought disturbed him enough to send him hurrying down the stairs at the final amen.

He waited by the car, glad that his mother's attention was diverted by her friend with the silver hair. They stood talking, their faces earnest, as people walked by. The moments stretched. And yet, it gave him time to put this strange rise of feeling into perspective, the unusual stirring in his soul. It had been a long time since he had felt so torn, as though he were suspended halfway between prayer and a curse.

Later, he and his mother were finishing dinner at a restaurant near the church. They lingered over coffee, Peter trying to keep up a lively conversation but finding himself absorbed in a raging inner conflict. It was bizarre, well beyond his comfort zone, and he kicked himself mentally. He marshaled his thoughts, focusing on his mother.

"Mom, it's all so different here, so remote. Are you going to be all right?"

She smiled a slow, thoughtful smile. "I'm going to be fine, Peter. It has been a rocky start, and I'll admit I've had some anxious moments." She patted his hands folded on the white tablecloth, and a frown appeared on her forehead. She started to say something but stopped.

He waited, knowing she was editing her thoughts.

She gave his hands another pat and leaned back in her chair. "Really, you mustn't worry about me, Peter. I'm content here."

"And you're not lonely? I mean, you don't have any friends yet." *Except for Lance Crane, perhaps?* He recalled their heads bent in conversation. Did they share more than real estate?

"There will be time for making friends," she said quickly. "I've been getting out. I've had dinner on the town and even attended a civic gathering." She laughed gently. "Do you think Alexei would have liked his funeral described as a civic gathering?"

"What about Tess?" Peter asked.

"Tess?" His mother's hazel eyes widened.Peter shrugged. "Beatrice. It's a nice enough name, but it's so archaic. 'Tess' fits her better. It's not exactly a nickname. It's her name sign, or what her name stands for."

She smiled, looking at him intently. "I like it."

Peter felt a strange restlessness in his stomach as he thought of Tess. He recalled her white hands gently stroking the fawn, the violet eyes filled with concern. Who would befriend and support Tess now? The man with the noxious swagger and pseudo-romantic name? Peter disliked him immediately, especially when he referred to Tess as "poor little Bea," as though she was somehow inferior. If he felt himself above her, why was he playing up to her? "What do you think will happen to her now that Alexei is gone."

"She'll miss her uncle," his mother said quietly. "Now there's just Alexei's sister, who seems rather cold and unfeeling, but appearances can be deceiving, I suppose."

Peter studied a coffee stain on the tablecloth, recalling the woman with the permanent frown. "She's not exactly the nurturing type, is she?"

Anne curled her fingers around her napkin. "I wish I knew what I've done to offend her. I want to be a good neighbor, but there's something about me she dislikes and distrusts." She looked across the table at her son with an arched eyebrow. "But Beatrice—or Tess—seems to have taken to you rather quickly."

Peter raised his cup to his lips but stopped short of drinking. He'd been dissatisfied with the girls he'd dated, most recently with the beautiful, cultured Jennifer Stratton. The contrast between the sophisticated Jen and the unaffected niece of Alexei Popov intrigued him. Tess had an innocence he found oddly charming. She seemed a part of all nature—untamed, mysterious, and free.

"How do you think her locket got in the woods, Mom?" he asked quietly.

Anne shook her head. "I don't know. I keep wondering. Why didn't they find it if it had been there in the original search? Beatrice might have lost it at the spot after her uncle died." She pursed her lips. "But it could have been planted there by someone."

He paused, remembering that the necklace wasn't simple costume jewelry, not the kind a girl—even an unsophisticated one—would be careless about. But how Tess came to own so expensive a piece of jewelry was another puzzle. "You don't believe that nonsense about buried treasure, do you, Mom?"

She played with the folds of her napkin. "Margaret Morris told me about a local legend that has circulated for some time. The story goes that Tess's grandmother had some connection to a noble Russian family and fled the country as a young woman with Alexei, a trusted servant. She had a daughter who died after giving birth. So the child—Tess—was raised by her grandmother who, oddly enough, bought Grace Arbor—or the Grainger house as it was known then—some 20 years ago or so."

Peter frowned. Rumors abounded in small denizens like the town his mother had chosen to make her home. "I heard Alexei himself started those rumors." It was too strange to be true. He wondered what Tess knew of the rumors and what she thought of them. "Pretty wild, I'd say."

Anne made a little tent with her fingers. "Supposedly, after the Grandmother died, Alexei and his sister took her in. She was only a toddler—two or three years old. Have you talked to her about any of this, Peter?"

"No, but maybe I will. We're going for a drive this afternoon." He picked up the check and pushed back his chair without waiting for his mother to react to this bit of news. He could feel his ears grow warm and sense her penetrating gaze on him.

They left the restaurant, and Peter's mind filled with thoughts of Tess. How different her life had been from his. He'd been fortunate enough to have two parents who nurtured and loved him. Tess had lost her family, and now the one person in the world whom she had loved was dead.

"Hello again!"

Peter turned to see Lance Crane climb out of a late model jeep. A younger man in a sleeveless tee shirt and spiked black hair came around from the passenger side, long legs pumping on the concrete. Peter instantly recognized Shane Eldridge. Ironically, the two had chosen the same restaurant, arriving just as he and his mother were leaving.

"We've just finished," his mother said brightly. "The roast beef was delicious." She paused and turned toward the young man, her face a study in confusion.

Crane cleared his throat and ran a hand through his shock of silver hair. "My nephew, Shane Eldridge," he said.

She shook the young man's hand and turned to Peter as though to introduce him.

Shane's hand was clammy and hot. Peter released it quickly, stifling an urge to wipe his hand on his pants. "We've met," Peter said.

When the two had gone, Peter helped his mother into the car. "That Eldridge character is your friend's nephew?" He worked to keep the disapproval from his voice.

Her brow furrowed. "I didn't know," she said softly. "I saw him at Alexei's funeral with Beatrice but didn't know who he was." She offered no more, and they drove back to Grace Arbor in silence.

What did his mother really know about her friend Lance Crane? *One shouldn't judge a book by its cover, of course—or a man by his companions*, Peter thought as he pulled away from the restaurant, but he couldn't help the rise of anxiety that came over him.

It occurred to Peter that he might pray for his mother's safety, and he was startled by the notion. He hadn't prayed in years, so where had this strange urge come from? Maybe everyone prayed to some god in times of stress or worry. And he was worried. His mother was alone in a strange town with even stranger neighbors. He wondered if God would be inclined to send a guardian angel or two.

Chapter 14

Tess let her hair drift off her brush as sunlight streamed in the window of her upstairs room. The red-gold strands sparkled with electricity, and she wondered what it would be like to be powerful and beautiful like lightning across a summer sky.

Uncle Alexei used to cover his ears during a storm and search the sky with a worried frown. "Thunder," it was called, but Tess couldn't imagine a sound that scared children and sent dogs scurrying under the bed. Though she had always found lightning and rain beautiful to watch, the wildness in Alexei's eyes until the storm eased had made her afraid.

She studied her face in the mirror and pressed both hands to her neck, touching the little indentation where the gold locket had nestled. Anxiety gripped her as she remembered Chief Mackowitz and his frightening questions.

How had her locket gotten into the woods? She hadn't been near the cordoned-off spot since that terrible day. When she wasn't wearing the locket, she always placed it carefully in the faded blue box on her dresser. She stared at her image in the mirror. The violet gaze that looked back at her belonged to a fearful child, not the strong woman she longed to be, one who would stand tall as her name sign indicated. *Tess.* She repeated the name, imitating the shape Peter gave to the name.

He said she was strong, like the character in Thomas Hardy's novel. But she wasn't strong like the innocent heroine who was seduced by the family's dissolute heir and secretly bore a child who died. Later, she meets an idealistic man who rejects Tess when he learns of her sexual past. She dropped the brush on her dresser. Peter was waiting. She smoothed her cotton sundress and climbed down the narrow, uncarpeted steps, her heart racing with every step.

He was leaning against the car door, a look of calm pleasure on his face. The sun burnished his dark hair and bleached his shirt to a brilliant white. She smiled as she went to meet him. All he needed was a white horse and perhaps a shield and spear like Sir Galahad. *You are a child!* she told herself.

"Hello. It's a beautiful day," she said lamely, wishing she could be witty, charming, or mysterious. Still captivated by the image of a storybook knight, she could think of nothing clever to say. She got inside the car and tucked in the folds of her skirt.

As they drove past meadows of Queen Anne's lace, cornflower, and sumac, Tess began to relax. She liked the easy way Peter steered the car, rounding the curves and avoiding ruts in the old post road. She watched his hands resting lightly on the steering wheel, liking the smooth arcs of his fingernails and how thin dark hairs clung to his knuckles.

"My mother really likes it here in the north country," he said, turning to her. "She likes her house."

He remembered to look at her when he spoke so that she could easily read the words on his lips. She liked that about him. Many people didn't do that, thus excluding her from their conversation. "It's a good house," she said, savoring the wind that ruffled her hair and the fragrance of Norwegian Pine wafting through the open windows. As a child, she had always wanted to be somewhere else, even to be someone else, but no foolish choices were available, not to someone like her. She had learned to be content.

They reached the north end of the waterfall, near the place where they had rescued the fawn. Peter parked the car, and they stood awhile to watch the water rush over the rocks. Tess inhaled the fragrance of clover and wild foxglove and felt the sun's kindly burn on her shoulders. Had it been only days since she had first met Peter here? Why did it seem that she had always known him, known that they might once have been attached to some great umbilical cord of the earth?

"I brought Cokes and ice," he said. "I thought we could cross over to the other side and watch the falls from there."

She nodded, and they climbed to a flat ledge on the rocky expanse. Peter helped her onto a wide outcropping, and they sat to view the panorama. Slender poplars on both sides of their "window seat" offered sun-dappled shade. Light mists sprayed their faces as water rushed down into a pool of frothy cream.

"Uncle Alexei said the water makes a beautiful sound," she said wistfully, drawing her knees up and clasping her arms around them.

"I wish you could hear it," Peter said, his brown eyes gentle.

"But I can feel it," she said quickly, not wanting him to feel sorry for her. "The vibrations are strong and powerful, and everything seems to stop when the water falls away."

"Amazing," he said, shaking his head and smiling. "That's exactly the way it is."

His brown hair curled around prominent ears that kids might have made fun of when he was a boy. But Tess thought they gave the man character and depth. She would like to trace her fingers around their smooth contours. Warmth crept up her neck, and she looked away as though her thoughts might be revealed.

Peter poured soda into a plastic tumbler and handed it to her. "Tell me about your uncle," he said when she'd taken a drink and set it down again.

She studied him. Was it idle curiosity? Or something more? Shane was also interested in Uncle Alexei. He called him a friend and asked her about the foolish town gossip of a treasure he supposedly had. Would Peter have been Alexei's friend too?

Things just weren't always what they seemed; people weren't either. A memory from her childhood returned. Mallory Wilson had pretended to like her. She had even bought her a box of Swiss chocolates as a token of friendship. But one day, Mallory and her friends chased her over the meadow, sticking their fingers in their ears and fluttering them to mimic sign language.

"Do you mind talking about him?" Peter looked earnest as though she might have been offended by his question. "About your uncle, I mean. I don't want to pry or stir up sad memories."

"No, it's all right," she signed. She twined her fingers absently where they rested in her lap. "Uncle Alexei used to take me to places he loved, like Cotton Woods and Old Hollow River, and Tanner's Falls. Sometimes, we'd fish or look for swallows' nests or Indian Paintbrush. When I was little, I made necklaces from them, but they were very prickly." She stumbled on this last word and wished she had not tried it. "Rs" were the hardest.

If she garbled her speech, Peter seemed not to notice. He listened as she told him how her uncle had placed a garland of flowers on her head and crowned her queen of the meadow. "I can see his face so clearly—his dancing eyes and crooked smile." She recalled his rough hands on her cheeks, and a lump formed in her throat. She couldn't go on.

Fresh grief welled up from some hidden place, and Tess ground her fingernails into her palms, swallowing desperately. She didn't want to cry—for Peter to think she was a child. She dropped her head down onto her arms to hide the tears, but her body made little jerks she knew would give her away.

Peter's arms came around her. He held her gently, and she felt the quick beating of his heart until he moved back to look into her eyes. "Tess. I'm so sorry. We don't have to talk about it if you don't want to."

She let him draw her toward him again and, this time, clung to him, feeling the vibrations his voice made. If they stopped, she too might cease to be.

After a moment, he moved back and looked into her eyes. "I think your uncle would be very proud of you." He stroked her cheek, his hands gentle. Then he added, "He's gone, but you'll be together again someday."

She stared. If only she could believe she would see Uncle Alexei again in some bright, beautiful place. She waited, watching his lips.

"My parents always said that death isn't the end, that souls are eternal and..." The flow of words stopped.

She pressed a fingertip lightly against his chest. "Is it true? Is it really true?"

The rhythm of his heart seemed to skip a beat, then resume. He was looking beyond her at something only he could see. His lips remained closed.

"Is it, Peter?" she urged.

He reached a hand into the thermal container. "Our drinks are warm. We need more ice."

She felt his shift in mood. The moment passed—the strange, shining moment that had made her heart leap. Was he treating her like a child who couldn't take the hard truth? *Of course, he was. He was placating her.* She would never see Uncle Alexei again. There was only now—this present moment to live and perhaps, if you were lucky, to love.

Tess sipped her drink without speaking or looking at Peter. She watched the changing scene, the water's ebb and flow. What would it be like to stop time, she wondered, to stay here forever without thought of tomorrow or regret for the past? To blot out death and what might come after it.

But the moment ended. *Peter will go back to the city and his job. He will come again to visit his mother, perhaps even wave if he sees me. But only a child would believe that Peter is really interested in a girl like me.* She leaned back against the rock, feeling the elation of the past few moments slip away.

Presently, he spoke again. "My mother tells me there's some gossip about your uncle and a treasure buried somewhere in town."

"A lot of nonsense." She shrugged and felt the cold hardness of the rock. "Uncle Alexei started the whole silly thing." She paused, remembering the embarrassment of people laughing behind their hands. "It wasn't his fault," she said. "The stories in his mind comforted him."

Peter sat still on the stone, watching her.

"He loved to make up stories," she added, pushing into the memory. "He said people from his country were great storytellers. Tolstoy and Dos..." She stopped, afraid to try the difficult name.

"Yes," Peter said with a quick smile. "Some of the world's greatest novelists were Russian."

The spray from the waterfall cooled her cheek, and she closed her eyes as Uncle Alexei's face lingered in her mind. He had told her many stories. Why had he never told her about her mother? Why did he look so sad when she asked about her or her grandmother?

"Past is gone. Better to forget, *lapushka*," he would say and turn away. She frowned at Peter, feeling a rush of anger. "*Lapushka* means little cat—kitten," she said more softly. "People called him crazy, but he wasn't."

Peter threw a pebble into the stream below. After a long moment, he said, "People say he dug up the ground everywhere, looking for treasure."

"Silly gossip for old women," she said, rolling her eyes and signing emphatically.

"Like Miss Morris?" Peter queried, watching her curiously.

She searched his face, thinking of the kindly Miss Morris who had always spoken to her respectfully, as though her opinion mattered—unlike Aunt Vera, who didn't like her. But who did Aunt Vera like? Tess frowned, not wanting to characterize Miss Morris as a silly gossip. "She was my uncle's friend. She was good to him." She watched the ripples widen as Peter dropped stones into the water below. "Uncle Alexei didn't have many friends."

A toad had hopped onto the ledge just below them, and she followed its erratic progress before continuing. "He was happy with her because she was his friend."

"Tell me about her," he urged.

She took a deep breath and let it out slowly. "Aunt Vera doesn't like her." She paused. "Aunt Vera says I shouldn't talk to her."

"Everyone needs someone to talk to. I'm glad your uncle had a friend." Peter's gaze was gentle.

Tess swallowed against the lump in her throat. Someone to listen, to care what you thought, what you felt. Was Peter that kind of person?

Why was she kidding herself? In a little while, he would be gone. There would be no more walks in the gathering dusk or conversations in the cozy shed with the fawn nuzzling their pockets and drinking milk from their hands. Peter would return to the city and his sophisticated friends, and she would be forgotten.

He would go back to the beautiful lady with the pink fingernails. To someone who didn't speak funny. *She'll be waiting for him, beckoning him with those curvy hips and sultry eyes.*

She reached for her sandals. It was time she stopped being foolish and pretending she could hold the interest of someone like Peter. Let him go back to his girlfriend. She didn't need him to feel sorry for her!

Peter had gotten up when she did. His gaze had gone from gentle to doubt or puzzlement. She looked away as they packed things away in the cooler.

When it was done, she picked up the blanket they had been sitting on and shook it with quick, hard snaps. He shouldn't have made her care for him. Not when all he was doing was being kind to a disabled girl who had lost the only person in the world who loved her. It would have been kinder to leave her alone in her silence—alone in the only world she understood.

Peter stood quietly on the rock ledge, facing her. The sad puzzlement lingered in his eyes, but quietly, he spoke. "Today was great. I'm glad we came."

She wanted desperately to run. But she straightened her back and gave her hair a nonchalant toss. "Me too." She turned away to climb down the rocky ledge to the place where the car was parked beneath a spreading sycamore tree. She would lead the way; she didn't need him to hold her hand. She hurried to the car, not waiting for him. She knew it was a childish way to behave, but she couldn't help it.

As they drove back, Peter glanced at her occasionally, and Tess could see the confusion in his handsome features. How could she possibly explain what she was feeling? She didn't understand it herself. If she could just run to her room and shut the door.

When Peter stopped the motor, she forced herself not to grab the handle and jump out. She told herself to remain calm as he took the keys from the ignition and laid them slowly on the dashboard. He turned to her and gently lifted her chin. "I'm sorry if I upset you, Tess. I didn't mean to."

Ashamed, she looked away, his touch burning her face. She couldn't speak. She had longed to stop time when they were sitting on the sunny rock, the mist from the waterfall cooling their faces. She had felt protected and cherished. But a girl was a fool to trust such feelings.

"I have to leave tomorrow morning," Peter said gently, "but I'll be back." He paused, holding her with his eyes. "If you need to talk to someone while I'm away, talk to my mom. She wants to be your friend."

She couldn't speak. Everything inside would melt, break away, and disappear like an iceberg into the ocean. She flung the car door open and ran into the house.

Chapter 15

Anne looked at the clock on her desk and realized she had worked through supper. It was nearly eight o'clock. She exited the computer program and stretched the stiffness from her bones.

Switching off the light in her study, she ventured into the kitchen, where the shades had not yet been drawn against the ebbing light. It had been a surprisingly quiet week. In the last few days, even Mackowitz had stayed away, though the garish tape still marred the pristine beauty of the estate on which summer lay deepening like ripe fruit.

Seven days had passed since Peter's visit, but he had called almost every night and seldom failed to ask about Beatrice. "Tess," as he called her. *Whatever name she goes by, she's an enigma,* she thought. The girl who had been cold, even hostile, now occasionally looked at Grace Arbor curiously when she came to care for the fawn. There had been no more childish poison pen letters.

No doubt Peter was responsible for the change in her. Always sympathetic to the marginalized, he would naturally be attracted to the girl's vulnerability. Nor would her willowy figure and creamy skin be lost on him. And it seemed that Tess had been good for Peter, too. He seemed less consumed with his job and more faithful in his calls to Grace Arbor. But she couldn't help feeling that the girl was only part of what was happening with Peter.

She recalled how he had appeared moved by the church service and hurried away when it ended. Was Peter beginning to give his childhood faith a second look? Was he rethinking his old arguments about the blindness of belief? She sighed. Faith might seem blind, but it had eyes that could pierce the darkness. She longed for Peter to see the light.

She whispered a familiar prayer for Peter and Dawn. Her grown children had their own lives but were never far from her thoughts and yearnings. She grabbed her denim jacket. It would be dark soon, but she needed a walk.

Following the driveway to the road, she strolled along the border of sumac and wild blackberry, inhaling the brisk air. The moon was a pale crescent tucked in the cradle of sky. Lightning bugs flashed, and crickets rasped their inscrutable melodies. She liked the swishing sounds of the wild grasses and tree branches and felt pity for the young woman who could not hear them. How did Tess endure the isolation such silence must bring? Someday, science might make a discovery that could allow deaf people to hear. Peter said electrodes might one day be implanted directly into the ear to stimulate the cochlear nerve.

When she reached the end of the fence dividing her estate from her neighbors' property, she turned back to look at Grace Arbor, couched in burgeoning shadow. Dark shrubs surrounded the shed with the recovering deer, and beyond it lay the forest where Alexei had been found. She shivered and pulled her jacket closer.

Suddenly, she was startled by a light flickering among the trees. It was too bright to be lightning bugs, and she hadn't heard any cars passing along the road. What was it? She felt the rapid rise of her pulse. Something was moving in the thick foliage. Unsteady strokes of light accompanied it as though someone ran with a flashlight.

She raced to her back-porch steps. *Go inside, lock the door,* she told herself. *Call Mackowitz.* It was probably someone on his force. Someone was always turning up at odd hours, finding another reason to check the site. But why would they explore this late in the day? It had to be nearly nine o'clock.

She hesitated between the porch and the driveway, fear giving way to frustration. It was enough that she had to put up with investigators and technicians showing up, but they had no right to invade her privacy so late without warning. She zipped up her jacket and stalked toward the woods.

Suddenly, the flashing stopped, leaving everything engulfed in shadowy twilight. She stopped to listen for a sound that might identify the invader. She crept on her rubber-soled shoes along the edge of the woods but could hear nothing. And the light had vanished, turning the darkness malevolent and threatening.

She inched forward, the damp ground seeping into her shoes, and realized her folly. What if it wasn't a policeman out there or a foolish girl testing her neighbor's resolve to remain at Grace Arbor?

"Hello!" she called, startled by the sound of her own voice. "Who's there?"

Almost immediately, she heard crackling branches and the sound of retreating footsteps that were too near for comfort. "Who are you?" she shouted, moving deeper into the woods. "What are you doing here?"

Someone was running several yards ahead, visible in the shifting moonlight through the foliage. Recklessly, she followed until a clearing in the woods led to an access road and then a highway.

Headlamps glowed from what must be a car parked on the edge of the road. But the light effectively blinded her. The stranger in the woods was running toward it. When he was almost upon it, he was caught in the glare of headlights. Anne could make out a blue jacket with an emblem emblazoned on it. The intruder raised an arm to shield himself from view and leaped into the waiting car.

She stood trembling as it roared away. What had the trespasser been looking for? If she hadn't frightened him off, would he have entered her home? Was he planning to rob her? Or harm her?

Her mind whirled. She had left her house unlocked to take her walk. Thankfully, she hadn't gone far. Who would have thought she'd have to bar her doors in a lazy little town that rolled up its streets before dark? Thoughts, rational and ridiculous, swirled in her brain until she became aware that the dampness was seeping into her clothes. Shivering, she ran back to the house and drew the double bolt.

Should she call Peter? But what would she tell him? She didn't even know if she'd been in any real danger. Whoever the intruder was, he had run away like a scared rabbit. Besides, what would Peter do so far away?

But to do nothing was hardly an option. Trespassing was not only disturbing and disgusting; it was illegal, and anyone would be a fool to tolerate it, however innocent it might have been. She dialed the police department, and after the third ring, Mackowitz himself responded with infuriating calmness.

"No, Ms. Westin. I didn't authorize any investigations on your property tonight."

"But someone was in my woods," she stated flatly.

"Any idea who, ma'am?" he asked.

Should she incriminate someone based on wild possibilities? A woman dressed like a man. Tess in a man's jacket? But the intruder had been taller. Could it have been Vera? But she was heavier and couldn't have run that fast. She searched her mind for possibilities. How many people did she even know in town?

"I couldn't see who it was," she said weakly. "It was just a few minutes ago—about 9 o'clock. It was too dark." What could she say? She'd seen only a shadowy figure in a blue jacket. The image clung, playing itself repeatedly as though trying to tell her something. Had she seen a jacket like that before? She searched her mind for possible suspects, but it could be anyone. Someone she didn't even know. Maybe someone who believed the gossip about treasure buried somewhere in the vicinity. It was absurd—so like something in a fairy tale. Surely, no one gave any credence to it. The one man who did was dead.

A memory came like a thunderbolt, and she let out a gasp. She had seen a sports jacket like that! The bold color in the headlights matched the wearer's eyes—blue, deeply blue, like a sea at dusk. Had the letters on the jacket been "Cubs?" Another image returned with a jolt—a pickup truck idling near her home last week.

Both came with a name attached: Lance Crane, a diehard Chicago Cubs fan.

It was unthinkable. And yet, she wouldn't be the first woman to be fooled by a handsome, attentive man. Hadn't he seemed more than willing to call off the sale of Grace Arbor when the trouble began? Maybe he wanted her gone and was taking more desperate measures to hold Grace Arbor. After all, why hadn't it sold in 20 years? There had been one or two short-term rentals but no sale. True, the property was remote and expensive, but—

"Ms. Westin?" Mackowitz prodded.

She drew in her breath and forced herself to be calm. "Yes, please do send someone by. Whoever it was might still be around." She hung up with trembling fingers and stared at the silent telephone.

Richard had liked Lance. He had trusted him. She had been drawn in, too, warmed by his sensitive and supportive ways. She replayed the evening he'd taken her to dinner. The pall of loneliness had dissipated while they talked in the flickering candlelight.

But the rude young man in the restaurant was his nephew! Why hadn't he told her? Why hadn't he introduced him when he stopped at their table with Joe Lair? What did she really know about Lance Crane? And could there be more than one Cubs jacket in this community?

With her hand still poised on the phone, she saw something moving beyond her kitchen window and froze. Anyone coming near would be visible in the porch lights. She ran to the window, her heart in her throat.

The figure moving slowly toward the shed had long red hair and carried a pail and blanket. Tess, her white blouse like neon in the darkness. Had she been running away from the woods only a few moments ago wearing a jacket? A blue jacket with a Cubs logo?

She watched Tess continue toward the shed, saw her lift the wooden bar, and go inside. Anne stepped onto the porch, her breath coming in gasps. Where was that police cruiser?

Seconds later, Tess came running out of the shed, her face a white mask. She looked one way, then another, hands flailing. She dropped the bucket, its contents spilling onto the grass.

Anne raced across the lawn. "What is it? What's happened?"

Tess made agitated gestures that Anne was powerless to interpret. "Where is he?" Tess gasped, turned from Anne to the open shed door from which she had just emerged, and ran toward it.

Anne hurried after her to the place where the fawn with the bandaged leg usually lay. It was empty! She thrust aside boxes and barrels and turned over bales of hay.

"He can't be gone," Tess wailed, signing with anguished strokes. "He wasn't well yet. He's only a baby!"

"I don't understand. The fawn couldn't have gotten out alone, and no one has been here to ... " Anne stopped, searching the girl's face. Was her dismay genuine? Could this be an act, a way to stir up more trouble? First spying on her, then leaving a threatening letter, now blaming Anne for losing her pet.

Tess backed up with jagged steps, her violet eyes wide as she glared at Anne. "What have you done with him?" She stumbled over the words as she signed.

"I haven't done anything with him," Anne said quietly, hoping to diffuse the girl's anger. Did she believe she would deliberately turn the fawn loose? It was ridiculous. "He can't have gone far. We'll look for him. We'll find him."

But the girl nearly tripped over the discarded pail as she fled and disappeared through the thick bushes.

"Wait!" Anne called, but her words fell on the empty air.

What had happened? The fawn couldn't have escaped on its own. Someone had to let the animal loose, but who would do that? Anne watched the trembling branches of the hedge that Tess had passed through. It wouldn't do any good to go after her. She had no explanation to offer. She had failed to keep the animal safe; Tess blamed her.

The sheriff's car pulled up the driveway and stopped.

"You all right?" Mackowitz asked through an open window.

"No," she said sternly. "Everything certainly isn't all right. Someone was trespassing and took off when I tried to follow."

Mackowitz rubbed a hand through his spiky crew cut. "Been checking things out, ma'am, but there's no sign of anyone around." He pursed his lips and looked at her with confusion and amusement as though he suspected she might be overreacting. As though she were some highly-strung city woman who ran to the police every time someone looked at her cross-eyed?

"Someone was there!" She said firmly and pointed to the woods. "Whoever it was ran off when I called. And there's something else."

"What's that, ma'am?" A pencil behind the Sheriff's ear hovered precariously on its perch.

"The injured fawn we've been keeping in the shed is gone. Someone broke in and let it out. Tess came a few minutes ago to feed him, but he's gone!"

His eyes rolled up in confusion.

"Beatrice," Anne amended. "Alexei Popov's niece. We call her 'Tess.' She was here."

"That's what's missing? A deer?" He moved to the door and examined the lock and wood casing with thick fingers.

"What's missing isn't the issue here," Anne said, working to cool her rising temper. "Someone was sneaking around and would not identify themselves when I confronted them."

"Them," he said dully. "There was more than one?"

She let out a sigh. "I say 'them' because I couldn't tell whether it was a man or a woman who ran out of the woods. I think it was a man. I don't know for sure. Look, I know what I saw, and you must take this seriously in light of what's happened."

"Of course. Of course." Mackowitz licked his chapped lips and wiped them with a handkerchief.

"I'd appreciate it if you'd look around for the fawn. It has an injured leg. Tess—that is—Beatrice has been taking care of it in my shed since she and my son rescued it. She's terribly upset about it."

"We'll do what we can." Mackowitz raked his fingers over his crew cut and gave a dubious shake of his head. "Deer aren't easy to trace. Even the young ones can move pretty fast. He's probably long gone."

"With a badly injured leg?" She wrapped her hands over her elbows and exhaled in an exasperated stream.

He raised shaggy eyebrows. "Are you all right?"

No, she wasn't all right, and things were getting crazier all the time. It was on the tip of her tongue to mention the blue jacket—but suppose it wasn't what she thought? "I appreciate your coming," she said wearily.

As Mackowitz backed down the driveway with a wave and a promise to be in touch, she longed for peace and the comfort of home. But these comforts would not be hers. Not tonight.

Chapter 16

Anne woke, still puzzled over the strange events that had occurred. It was time—indeed, long past time—that she learned about previous occupants of Grace Arbor, especially about the Russian woman who had owned it long ago. It hadn't occurred to her or Richard to delve into its history before. A house was a house; previous tenants did not define or diminish it. Did they?

But someone had been trespassing on her property—running through the woods with a flashlight, sending a crude message. And someone had released a wounded animal from her shed. More importantly, what had happened to Alexei, and who had been in the woods with him when he died?

None of it made sense. Everything revolved around Vera and Tess reacting to the presence of a stranger moving in next door. Some small-town citizens could be very provincial in their attitudes. But what if it was something more?

As for Alexei—poor, demented man digging in the woods. Like a war veteran with post-traumatic stress syndrome, perhaps tormented by some leftover nightmare from his past. He was harmless, everyone said, and laughed at his tales of buried treasure, at the odd gleam in his eyes, and wagged their heads pityingly as he toted a shovel over his back. Peter said that Tess believed the tales were harmless nonsense. Lance had agreed.

But Vera had lost a brother and Tess, an uncle she had loved.

Maybe Alexei knew something others didn't know. For years, the Russian government had tried to suppress what really happened to the last ruling Tsar. The curiosity even led to the exhumation in 1991 of Nicholas II, his wife, and three of their five children as well as four servants. The discovery of two missing children spawned speculative tales such as Twentieth Century Fox's *Anastasia*.

After Margaret had talked to Margaret about Russian history, she looked up information on the Romanov Dynasty. The account was chilling. The family, aware of the unrest and the loss of trust in the government, must have suffered greatly, even before they were captured, pulled off a train headed for Moscow "for their protection," and taken to a "safe house" in Ekaterinburg. The "Impatiev House," fenced in on all sides, had been taken from a wealthy Jewish burgess. The conditions were brutal; the captives endured hunger and isolation, humiliation, and cruel punishments.

But nothing could have prepared them for the slaughter that occurred in the cellar of that house. Their protectors became their assassins. Nicholas II was the first to fall. The daughters did not die from the first shots, which rebounded off jewels sewn into their corsets. Even bayonets could not penetrate, and the assassins eventually shot them in the head at close range.

Anne shivered. After long years of silence and speculation, the Romanovs had been canonized by the Russian Orthodox church and acclaimed for their "humbleness, patience and meekness."

Purported missing jewels had never been found. Could Alexei Popov really imagine himself in that saga? It boggled the mind.

And did it have anything to do with his death in the woods? A disturbing image of a shiny blue jacket pressed into her consciousness. If Lance had been in the woods last night, what was he doing? Had he unlocked the shed and released the fawn? Why? It just didn't gel with what she knew of him. Her heart rejected it. But thinking with the heart and turning off the mind was a dangerous practice.

It was hard to forget the previous summer—Lance fishing off the dock with Richard or skimming the LaCroix River in his maroon runabout with "Rosie-O" in white and gold calligraphy on the starboard side. He'd named it for his wife, and when she became ill, he had taken early retirement and moved from Chicago to build a log home in Wisconsin's north country. Here they had spent her final days. Now Lance was alone.

She had warmed to his friendship, feeling a special connection. At first, she thought it was simply because Lance had been Richard's friend. But it had become more than that. Had it all been an act? Was there some other motive for his kindness and attentiveness? She recalled the tender way he looked at her and his whispered comment: *He was a lucky man, your Richard.*

Anne spent the morning at the microfiche machine reading until her head ached from line after line of tiny print. The library was small and stuffy, and she was too warm in capris and a light cotton blouse. She had found only a brief obituary:

Svetlana Grainger, a recent resident, died after a brief illness. She is survived by a granddaughter, who is six months old and has been placed in temporary care.

A photograph of poor quality accompanied the 1972 notice, showing a woman with graying auburn hair and finely molded features who bore a vague resemblance to Tess. How much did the girl know of her past? Was she aware that her grandmother had lived at Grace Arbor? Was that why she stood at the border of lilac bushes gazing with such longing? Why hadn't the house been reserved for her instead of going to a real estate buyer? And why hadn't Lance shared its background if he knew about it?

She'd think better with coffee and something to eat since she'd had neither that morning. She left the library, rounded the corner, and nearly collided with Lance Crane.

He reached out to steady her, surprise etched in his face. "Are you all right?" He bent to retrieve her purse.

"It's my fault," she said breathlessly, pushing back the hair that had fallen over her forehead. "I wasn't watching where I was going." She probably looked a sight. But why should it matter? Frustrated at her embarrassment, she allowed herself to look at him closely. Was there something in those vivid eyes to give him away?

"No, it's my fault!" he countered. "I'm so sorry!"

He looked fresh and disturbingly handsome in khaki slacks and a polo shirt the same color as his eyes—blue and unruffled as a calm sea. Nothing in his manner hinted that he might have been hiding in Grace Arbor's woods with a flashlight the night before. He looked the soul of innocent gentility.

"Please," he said, his hand on her arm, "let me make amends. Lundstrom's Bakery is just down the street. I was headed there. Can I buy you a cup of coffee?"

The better part of wisdom urged her to decline, but maybe he would give himself away, or she would be able to see something suspicious in him. "All right. Yes."

The bakery was small, with a wide counter area and a few tables for eat-in guests. Anne followed Lance to a table set with wrapped plastic cutlery and a vase holding a single carnation. After settling her in a chair, he sat across from her. The waitress brought coffee and menus.

"I'll have a cherry Danish," Lance said, raising his eyebrows in Anne's direction.

"Sounds good. I'll have the same." She added cream to her coffee and stirred slowly, aware of Lance watching her. Was he worried or curious? Apologetic? Guilty?

"So, where were you off to in such a hurry?" he asked with a smile.

"I was coming from the library," she said, stirring her coffee. "I was looking for some information on the former owner of my property." Would he be concerned about this? But he seemed to be waiting for her to say more. The waitress set two plates before them and rushed off to help other customers.

Anne took a sip of coffee. "Didn't find much," she went on casually. "Twenty years ago, a Russian woman died there, left a granddaughter—Beatrice, who the Popovs raised. What I don't understand is how the house became salable property."

"I asked the same thing when I came here," Lance said. "The woman bought the house outright—had to be a good 20 years ago or more. But she defaulted on her payments, and the house was sold to recoup the back taxes. The agent who handled it has moved on." He paused, narrowing his eyes in thought. "I inherited the listing when I moved here from Chicago."

"Yes, I noticed the date on the obituary."

Lance finished the last bite of Danish and wiped his mouth on his napkin. "Why all this interest in old history, Anne?"

"Well, after all that's been going on ... " She thought of the letter that Beatrice might have written and what had just happened the night before. She searched his face for some sign that he was hiding something.

"Mackowitz still looking under rocks out there?"

She nodded.

He gave her an incredulous look. "Our police department has too much time on their hands. They already determined it was a heart attack and released the body for burial."

"There are footprints, which could be anybody's," Anne offered reflectively. "I don't imagine Alexei was the only one to cut through those woods. But the blood on the tree was Alexei's." She contemplated her analysis. "It could easily have gotten there when he fell. But then there's the locket suddenly turning up at the scene. Peter says they questioned Tess about it—scared her half to death."

"Tess?" Lance narrowed his eyes.

"Beatrice. Peter calls her 'Tess.'"

"'Beatrice' *is* quite a mouthful for a young woman," he said thoughtfully, taking a long gulp from his coffee mug. "And you think all that's happened is connected to a woman who died 20 years ago?"

She shrugged. "I don't know." She paused, then before she could consider the wisdom of her words, asked, "Lance, you seen any Cubs games recently?" It was hardly a reasonable segue.

He said nothing for a few seconds, his face a study in confusion or expert acting. "Only on television; I haven't been back to the park since moving up here." He paused, grimacing, "I still hang onto my old jacket, even though they haven't exactly been making headlines."

She smiled to cover her anxious thoughts. Had he been making his own headlines last night at Grace Arbor dressed in the jacket she'd seen hanging in his office? A tense silence passed between them. She could hardly come right out and accuse him, could she? But how many Cubs jackets could there be in the small community, made up mainly of Minnesota Twins fans? She nibbled at her Danish and sipped her coffee uncomfortably.

"Anne, are you all right? Has something happened?"

She searched her mind for a way to respond. *You should know! Sneaking around my property in the dark!* Instead, she offered, "It's just a letter I got..."

"Letter?"

"Message really," she said hesitantly. "It was a few days after Alexei died." She floundered, thinking how ridiculous it sounded—how melodramatic. "I found it under my front door—a crayoned message telling me to go home."

Lance said nothing for a few seconds, his frown deepening. "What does Mackowitz say?"

"I—I didn't tell him about it. It was probably Tess's doing. She's been pretty upset that I'm living here. Vera, too, for that matter. But Peter's been trying to help her sort things out. We were making progress in the neighborly relations department, but after last night—"

He leaned in, eyes wide. "What about last night?"

Oh, so innocent! She worked to keep her response level. "Someone broke into my shed and the fawn got out."

"You had a wild deer in your shed?"

"A fawn. Tess and Peter rescued it by Tanner Falls, and I've been keeping it in my shed. I gave her a key to the padlock, and she has been coming back and forth to feed it. Anyway, the poor thing's gone, and Tess blames me."

"Maybe she forgot to lock up," he suggested, brows drawn together.

"I don't think so," she said quietly, looking down. "Besides, I saw someone in the woods last night. He—uh—had a flashlight. I chased him, but he ran off." She glanced up, but his features remained inscrutable. "I phoned Mackowitz. He came out right away, but he didn't find anything."

Lance paled beneath his tan and dropped his cup onto the table. "This is my fault! I should never have sold that house to you. It's those ridiculous rumors of treasure. It gets people stirred up—especially kids." He ran a hand through his thick gray hair. "They usually wait until Halloween to haunt the place. Now that they've found Old Alexei dead, they're going at it again. And here you are in the middle of it."

Was this another ploy to get back the property? She cut him off. "I've no intention of giving up Grace Arbor—no matter who tries to run me off." She could hear the coldness in her voice. And she was tense from withholding all that she was thinking.

She felt tight enough to explode! She stood and let her napkin fall to the floor. "I have to go."

"Anne, please, wait..."

She turned away and strode to the door. She didn't even offer to pay for her coffee, something she would never have done in saner moments.

She drove back toward Grace Arbor but slowed when she neared her neighbor's old house at the top of the rise. She hadn't seen Margaret Morris since the day of Alexei's funeral and wondered if she was all right. Suddenly, she felt the need for friendly company. Besides, she wasn't ready to step inside the quiet interior of Grace Arbor.

She climbed the porch steps where a scarred bench with handmade cushions languished, their colors diffused in dappled sunlight. On one end, a faded straw hat lay discarded like lost love. Anne recalled the elderly woman's memories of Alexei and how she had spoken of him with such tenderness and sorrow. How close had the two of them been?

After a few moments, a shaky voice answered her knock, inviting her to enter. The house smelled of dampness and inactivity, and she shivered as she entered the dark living room. The room was a page from a history book with its russet, gold, and green colors and the ancient chairs blooming with crocheted doilies. Floor lamps with yellowing shades brooded over the furniture, and photographs browned in their frames on dusty tables.

Anne walked toward the back of the house, and when she passed an open door, she caught sight of Margaret. She was in bed, a flowered quilt drawn up to her chin. Straggly hair splayed on the pillow, and her face was white as marble. The afternoon's amber light thinned to narrow ribbons through the window near her bed.

Margaret inclined her head slowly toward Anne, her eyes growing wide. "Forgive an old lady for not getting up," she said. "I'm not feeling so well today."

Anne knelt beside the bed and took her hand.

"But I'm so glad you've come," Margaret said. "I prayed you would." She pushed herself up on the pillow. "Don't look so grave. It's just my rheumatism acting up."

"I wish you had called me," Anne said. "I would have come if I had known you were ill. What can I do?"

"Don't worry. My doctor prescribed something." She nodded toward a bottle of pills on the bedside table and returned her serious gaze to Anne. "Please," she said, coughing, "that's not why I hoped you would come. I need to know about Beatrice. Is she … ?"

"She's all right," Anne said quickly. She wasn't really, but what could she say without upsetting Margaret?

"I must see her—and very soon!" Margaret took a rheumy breath, her eyes registering anxiety. After a moment, she began to cough again.

Anne's pulse quickened. "Can I get you some water?"

She shook her head and drew a hand across her mouth as though willing the spasms to cease. "No. Listen, Anne, please." She resettled herself against the pillows. "I wrote several letters asking Beatrice to come." She coughed again but refused the water Anne offered. "I told her it was very important, but she hasn't come."

Anne waited, surprised and confused. Why would Tess ignore a letter from someone who had been her teacher and friend?

"Please, you must tell her to come," she pleaded. "It is urgent." Margaret reached under the quilt and pulled out an envelope. She pressed into Anne's hand. "Give this to her, and please … tell her she must come to see me soon."

"Of course—"

Then she lay back on the pillow and closed her eyes. "Go now, Anne, and thank you."

What could be so important? Did she expect to die? Anne left the elderly teacher's house, clutching the cryptic letter.

Chapter 17

Tess rode her bicycle home, gripped by a strange sense of something about to happen. She couldn't tell if it was a good something or a bad something, and she lifted her face to the cooling wind as though it could reveal the secret. Just the day before, she had opened Peter's surprising letter with trembling fingers. *He was thinking of me!* She read it over and over before tucking it safely under her pillow to read again, but already she knew the spare lines by heart:

Dear Tess,
Thank you for the time we spent together.
I'm sure the little deer is healing well with your expert nursing. I hope you are okay. I look forward to seeing you again soon.
                                                                              Peter

She rehearsed the message again in her mind, recalling the tenderness of his touch when they picnicked by the waterfall. That he might really care for her filled her with joy and a singular dread. What if it was a cruel hoax? Still, maybe there was a God in heaven who sometimes let good things happen—even to her.

She had liked Peter from the first moment they had met. He had been so gentle with the injured fawn and with her. She bit her lower lip, gripped by the image of the vacant shed and the door gaping on its hinges. What would he think when he learned she had lost the little deer they had rescued together? Short of a miracle, it had probably been devoured by some wild animal or hit by a car.

She had instantly blamed Mrs. Westin and ran like a bad-tempered child. *Why didn't I wait for her to offer some explanation?* It was immature and silly, but she had felt too hurt and betrayed to think the situation through. Maybe it wasn't Mrs. Westin's fault. But how could the animal have escaped on its own from the shed?

Was Peter's mother an enemy? Maybe Peter, too, was not what he pretended to be. Since Uncle Alexei died, everyone suddenly wanted to talk to her—Shane Eldridge and other neighbors who usually ignored her. Even people at work were asking about a rumored treasure.

It was ridiculous. Ridiculous, yet where *did* the money come from to send her to school? If only she could trust someone to tell her the truth about it all.

"I saved it, honey," Uncle Alexei said when she had asked. "I save long time. I keep the money for you, my *lapushka*."

Vera objected when Alexei talked about a place where deaf people learned to read. "She don't need no schooling." Tess had turned away, not wanting to know what else her aunt said. Uncle Alexei had believed in her and wanted her to learn. She would always love him for that.

She had worked hard at school, anxious to make Uncle Alexei proud, but when she returned, she had found him odd and childlike—not his old self. In the days following her return, she had to gently remove the shovel from his hand and lead him home like a child. One thing was sure. He was gone now, and life would never be the same.

The long stretch of pedaling uphill had winded her, and she stopped at the bridge to rest. She was in no hurry to get home. Aunt Vera had been particularly moody that morning as she spooned thick oatmeal into bowls. "You were out late last night—over there." She thrust her head in the direction of the neighboring estate.

"I had to find something I lost," she said and sprinkled sugar over the contents of the bowl. Knowing her aunt would be angry, she didn't want to talk about the fawn in Mrs. Westin's shed. Vera didn't want to be "beholden" to anyone, especially the rich city neighbor, who "don't belong here!"

Tess recalled Vera's frown and the strands of uncombed hair brushed back furtively from narrowed eyes. "You were there again, weren't you?" What Aunt Vera didn't understand often made her angry. When she asked Uncle Alexei why Vera was the way she was, he always told her to be kind. "My sister has had hard life, *Lapushka*. Hard life."

Vera had demanded to know what Tess was doing at the neighboring estate. "Oh, just looking for something I lost on my way home," she had said, signing the words and concentrating on her oatmeal. It bothered her to lie to Aunt Vera. Even as a child, she'd been able to outwit her aunt and get what she wanted. Still, in some ways, Vera Popov could be crafty too. She stood at the table's edge, peering at Tess. "You no find, do you?"

Did her aunt know about the fawn? "No. No, I didn't."

"Ain't nothing there. I told you not to listen to those tales."

Vera hadn't been talking about a little lost deer, Tess realized. She meant the treasure Alexei had been looking for—the silly story people talked about behind their hands.

"No. It wasn't that. I was looking for—" Tess would have explained about the fawn, but Vera whirled around and strode to the door.

Now, as she remounted her bicycle, Tess puzzled over Aunt Vera. She had grown increasingly agitated since the funeral, spending most of her time with the hens. Sometimes, she washed the eggs two or three times before filling the crates. Tess would have to make supper for them both when she got home. They ate quickly and silently, and Vera would go back out to her chickens. No, Tess was in no hurry to get home.

She swerved around a rock in the road. What was to become of them now that Alexei was gone? How much longer could she go on living where she was not wanted? Had Vera ever liked her? A deep loneliness welled up, and tears stung her eyes. Suddenly, a truck pulled alongside her, and Shane Eldridge leaned out a window and grabbed her handlebars.

"Whoa, there!"

She hopped off the bike, aware of her windblown hair and faded lipstick, and hated that he was always turning up unannounced.

"Bea!" His spicy after-shave drifted toward her. "Let's go for a ride. Dump your bike in the back of the truck, and we'll get a Dairy Queen. What do you say?"

"I should get home," she stammered.

"Come on. Just a little ride. I promise I'll take you right home after that." He was like a puppy begging for a bone. She laughed at him as he hoisted the bike into the truck's bed and returned to the wheel. She climbed in the front seat, and Shane peeled away, one arm flung over the back of the seat.

He closed one heavy-lidded eye in a slow wink. She couldn't help but be flattered by his attention. He was so tall and good-looking.

"What's your pleasure, my fair lady?" Shane asked when they pulled up to the drive-in window.

"A chocolate cone," she said decisively. It was supper time, and her appetite would be spoiled, but like as not, Aunt Vera wouldn't have supper ready anyway.

"Chocolate it is." Before handing her the cone, Shane swiped it with a wide lap of his tongue. "Just testing it," he said with a crooked smile. Then he pulled away from the window so fast she had to brace herself against the dashboard to keep from dropping the cone. Laughing, he rolled the window down as they sped toward the community park.

He had switched on the radio, and the vibrations from the music thumped under her feet. "Too loud," she said.

He gaped at her in surprise.

"Your truck's shaking," she explained. "I can tell by the vibrations. Everybody in town will hear."

"Oh, I thought maybe you'd been healed or something!" He assumed the grand air of a show preacher and cocked his head from side to side. "I thought maybe the big Man upstairs sent a lightning bolt. Heal! I say, heal!" he bellowed in mock delight.

Tess swallowed a lump of ice cream so large it hurt her head. "That's not funny." She didn't like it when Shane made fun of people or God.

He raised a dark eyebrow. "Okay. Just making a joke." He rolled the truck to a stop along the lakeside and turned to her. "I have to say you hear pretty good for a deaf girl."

"I have to get home, Shane," she said wearily. She needed time to think and apologize to Anne Westin for how she behaved when the fawn disappeared. It was time she acted like an adult and faced things instead of running away. She also needed to know what Aunt Vera had been talking about that morning.

"Don't you have time for me anymore?" Shane asked with an injured look.

He was too cocky to take seriously, and she laughed at him. "I have things to do," she said, finishing the last of the cone. "Thanks for the ice cream."

"Sure," he responded, starting the motor with a shrug. The playful look was gone, and she imagined seeing his pale eyes grow icy behind his dark lashes.

They rode without conversation, Tess feeling the coolness of his mood and seeing his jaw twitch. His knuckles were white on the steering wheel. He had turned up the volume on the radio again, and the vibrations shook the car. When they were about a half mile from her house, he pulled over to the side of the road. Shifting into Park, he looked at her with piercing eyes.

"I told you, I have to get home," she said warily.

"I know, I know. I just want to talk a little." He turned and stretched his arm over the steering wheel to look directly into her face. He smiled, but his pale eyes were cold when he pulled her suddenly toward him.

She stiffened. She had never really been afraid of him before, but he was different now. So fierce and intense. She felt herself tremble.

"You know, my little Bea, you're beautiful. I've always thought so, you know." He held her with a strong arm, his face so close she could see the furry hairs on his upper lip. "Yes, you're one beautiful woman." And then he put his mouth on hers.

"No, please." She pulled away, feeling his breath hot on her face and his hands digging into her shoulders. She struggled against him, feeling his rapid pulse mixed with her own frantic heartbeat. "I have to go home!"

"What's the matter!" he demanded angrily. "I just want a little kiss." He pulled her forward again. "Haven't I been good to you, my little Bea?"

She reached out and slapped his cheek. She had never slapped a man before, never hit anyone that she could remember. Her face burned with fear or shame or some emotion she could not have named as the vibrations from the truck's radio tore through her body.

Shane drew back. Hard little lines appeared around his mouth, and he rubbed the side of his face. "I bet you don't treat that Westin guy like that." He banged the steering wheel with the heel of his hand. "You think he's interested in you just because he helped you with that stupid deer?" He gave a short, mirthless laugh.

"Stop it! Stop it," she cried. She knew her words were slurred and jumbled. She must sound like an idiot. She signed the word "please," feeling small and helpless. "Please . . . "

"I bet you told *him* where your dumb uncle buried it!" He spat out the words. "That's what he's after, you know! Yes, of course you know," he finished with a little snort of triumph.

She bolted from the truck and ran to hoist her bike to the ground. He twisted around and leaned out the window, still shouting something. She jumped on her bike and took off. Glancing over her shoulder, she saw him laughing, his head thrown back.

She raced away with the scent of Shane's cologne clinging to her and feeling the pressure of his hands on her shoulders and neck. She steered toward home, taking the long way around. She wouldn't cut through Grace Arbor this time and risk meeting anyone.

But as she approached the expansive estate, she could see her neighbor at the top of the hill. Anne Westin was flagging her down, waving something in her hand and signaling her to stop.

Tess did not want to stop. But she was not a child; she was nearly 21 and should be able to take care of herself. She had to, didn't she? Who else would? Shane's taunts tumbled through her like a frame from a movie stopped in mid-roll. "You think he's interested in you because he helped you with that stupid deer?"

How did Shane know about the deer? She hadn't told anyone—not Aunt Vera or anyone at work. Only Peter and his mother knew about the fawn in her neighbor's shed.

I bet you told him where it is! Shane's accusation burned in her mind. He wanted something from her—something besides a kiss. Uncle Alexei's pretend treasure, she realized with astonishment. *He thinks I have it!* Was Peter after it, too?

"Wait!" Mrs. Westin called. "Please. It's important, Tess."

She stopped, suddenly too tired to go on. She dismounted, wiped the sweat from her face, and walked her bike slowly up the driveway. When she reached Mrs. Westin, she pushed back the kickstand and waited, wondering if her legs would hold her up. Peter's mother was probably angry, but it didn't matter. Tess was too tired, too weak, to care.

In a red silk blouse and white pants, Anne Westin seemed taller than Tess remembered. She smelled like gardenias, maybe lavender, or some fragrance she didn't recognize. Tess glanced up and saw that the eyes looking into hers held no anger.

"Are you all right?"

Tess nodded, not trusting herself to speak.

"You look exhausted," Anne said. "Sit down a while—please."

Tess shook her head. "I'm late," she stammered. "I have to get home." She forced herself to respond appropriately with words since Mrs. Westin didn't read sign language.

Mrs. Westin's eyes were soft and sad. "I'm so sorry about the fawn. I tried to find him." She shook her head, the soft amber curls glinting in the sun. "The police are looking, too."

"It's okay, Tess said wearily. Then she looked away, afraid to meet Peter's mother's gaze. "I'm sorry I ran off last night. I was afraid. I —"

"I'm so sorry, Tess. I don't know how he got away. I'm so sorry." She paused and stretched an envelope toward her. "But I'm glad you stopped because I have something for you."

Tess stared at the envelope with her name written in careful script. It was familiar, somehow. Where had she seen it before? Her breath caught in her throat.

"It's from Miss Morris. She said it is important that you have it. Tess." Mrs. Westin was looking at her steadily, appealing for understanding. "She's been trying to contact you, but you haven't responded to her letters." A hint of reproach touched the hazel eyes.

Letters? Tess knew nothing about any letters. She rarely received them except from her new friend from school and a cousin she hadn't seen since she was ten. And then there was Peter's letter safely tucked away under her pillow.

Peter. Her heart leaped at the thought of him. But Shane's taunt quickly flashed into her mind. Do you *think he's interested in you because he helped you with that stupid deer?* Tears stung her eyes, making it hard to see Mrs. Westin standing a few feet away with an envelope. She took it gingerly as though it might burn her fingers. Why was she being scolded for not answering letters she never received? "I don't know about any letters…"

Mrs. Westin was looking at her strangely. "Are you sure you're all right, Tess?"

"I have to go." Tess hopped onto her bicycle, clutching the strange letter. She knew she was being rude and childish once more, but she couldn't help it. Pressing hard on the pedal, she rode away as fast as she could, wanting to fly to her room and shut the door against the world—a world she didn't understand and feared she never would.

Chapter 18

Shane watched Bea wobble away on her bicycle, copper hair swishing with each rotation of the pedals. She was biking at a furious speed, turning at the fork to look over her shoulder. He wanted her to see that he was laughing, that he wasn't in the least affected by her refusal of his kiss, but the familiar sting of rejection burned inside him like a firebrand. He climbed back into his truck and slammed the heels of both hands hard on the steering wheel.

Now, he'd done it! He shouldn't have moved so fast, but he was tired of waiting for her to warm up to him. He'd been patient, careful not to push the subject of the buried treasure, but his sly probing and cajoling hadn't worked. She wouldn't talk to him about it, and she kept pretending it was a lot of nonsense in an old man's head.

And then there was Peter Westin playing up to her. He must have his sights set on the treasure, too. It had to be! What other interest could a sophisticated slick like him have in a deaf girl who'd probably never been kissed in her life?

Shane pressed harder on the accelerator. He had thought letting that deer go would clinch things in his favor. He'd been watching when they brought it into the shed, watching as he always watched. Little Bea would blame her high and mighty neighbor when she discovered it missing—precisely as he wanted her to do.

He'd felt only slightly guilty when the fawn looked at him with huge round eyes before bolting unsteadily away on three legs. He bore down on the pedal, heading automatically toward his uncle's house, his mind a maze of frustration.

He fumed as he drove. *Where could the old man have buried the stuff?* He'd searched every inch of the Grainger place—or "Grace Arbor," as it was called now. He had come at night, hiding his detector well under a tarp in his uncle's truck. If that woman hadn't moved in, he might have found what he was looking for. As for that nosy son of hers—

Shane cracked his knuckles. Things were getting out of hand. He had hoped the locket he'd snatched from Bea's room would avert suspicion and buy himself a little more time to get her to spill what she knew. He'd been careful not to get his fingerprints on the locket, then planted it carefully—not too obvious, but not too hard to find.

The police were sure to question her when they found it. He hadn't really thought they'd arrest her, but why weren't they digging around much anymore? There were no dogs or equipment or anything. That stymied him. He had to be careful. He couldn't let them connect him to the old man's death.

But he might have blown his chances with Bea. As he sped away, he turned up the volume on the radio to drown out the worry in his head. Somebody had to know something! Maybe the Westin woman had found Alexei's stash. She was smart. She would know how to handle things without a lot of noise. But so far, she hadn't done anything to make him think the treasure had been found.

Seeing her with Uncle Lance had made him nervous. That's all he needed, the two of them joining forces and nosing into his business. The smartest thing to do might be to give it all up and move on. Get out before they could connect him with anything.

But there was too much at stake. And it wasn't just the jewels Alexei had buried; it was Lair's next project. If the stuff was worth what they both thought it was—and if he kept out of the clutches of the law, they'd both be rich. He laughed despite his sour mood. It couldn't be hard to outwit the likes of these small-town policemen.

He pulled into the driveway and quickly decelerated when he saw his uncle on the deck turning burgers. Shane groaned. A confrontation now he didn't need! But he couldn't just take off either. That would be too obvious. He thrust his hands into his pockets and steeled himself for the inquisition that was sure to follow. He had again "borrowed" the truck and had still not carried out the assignment he'd been given.

Lance's silver hair gleamed in the sun, and Shane was struck by his uncle's unsettling likeness to his mother. Her face came to him now, her subtle smile. He could almost feel her hand, gentle and soft, touching him. He thrust his chin out, embarrassed by his longing. He'd outgrown all that, and besides, she was gone now.

Angry at his weakness, Shane swung down from the cab and concentrated on each step on the pebbled driveway. He would have stamped past his uncle and gone directly to his room, but Lance stopped him, his voice urgent.

"I want to talk to you." He flipped a sizzling burger, and flames leaped into the air, making a high, hissing sound. He turned sharply and pointed at the patio table set with plastic dishes on a checkered cloth. "Wash up and bring some soda from the fridge. I made plenty for both of us." He flipped another burger with a quick turn of his wrist.

It wasn't an invitation. It was a command performance. Shane squeezed his lips into an amiable expression and shrugged. "Sure," he said and went obediently inside for the drinks.

After the last tongue-lashing, he tried not to miss any more appointments. Lance set great store by his word, including his promise to look out for his sister's little boy. But even blood could wear thin, and Lance knew the conversation was about to turn down a road he didn't want to go. He'd missed the Grant survey Lance had instructed him to do.

When he returned with the drinks, Shane saw that the burgers were already on the plates, surrounded by rings of grilled onions and red and green peppers. Shane flipped a tab on his drink and sat down with studied ease.

His uncle wasted no time. "How'd the Grant survey go?"

He was supposed to review the surveyor's study for potential buyers, but he had gone to the mine instead, where Lair held all his business meetings. Then he'd caught Bea on her way home from the hospital and taken her for ice cream. Uncle Lance would be ticked. "Fine," he lied, taking a large bite of his hamburger.

Lance said nothing at first. They began to eat in uneasy silence to the accompaniment of birdsong and water lapping against the dock. Shane glanced at his uncle. Had he bought his story? But the eyes that held his were steely. "I spoke with Margaret Morris today."

Shane winced. Uncle Lance had been pretty upset about the metal detecting, but Shane had gotten out of it without much trouble. After all, he was working part-time for the copper mine. When he said he had been testing the Morris place on assignment, Uncle Lance had dropped the subject. Now, Shane attempted a casual response. "Nice old lady. Is she all right?"

Lance straightened in his chair and faced Shane squarely. "Matter of fact, no. She's been quite ill." The little lines around his mouth quivered; his face drew uncomfortably close. "I checked on the mine operations. Margaret's place was never on the list. They've suspended all peripheral detecting, so what were you doing on her property?"

Shane swallowed the last of his burger and took a slow, deliberate drink. "So, you've been checking up on me?" he said with forced control.

There was a tense silence between them until Lance set his glass down with a heavy hand. "You were supposed to be surveying at Perry Grant's today. You never showed."

Shane got to his feet.

"Sit down," Lance ordered. His eyes were blue steel, and the muscles in his jaw rippled. "I'm not through yet."

Shane felt blood rush to his face; he'd been caught. "All right, all right," he said, assuming a nonchalance he didn't feel. "Whatever."

"I asked you what you were doing at the Morris place."

Shane threw up his hands angrily. "Just looking around. What's the big deal?"

"The big deal, young man, is that trespassing is illegal. And I won't have anyone who works for me breaking the law!"

Shane stood up angrily. His uncle got up and came around the table to face him. They were nose to nose—nearly identical in height.

"I know what you're doing. You think Alexei Popov buried something valuable, and you're bent on finding it. Is that why you've been sloughing off on your assignments? Is that why you've been playing up to Beatrice Popov?"

"Who I see is my own business!" Shane sputtered.

"And who works for me and lives in my house is my business!" Lance countered. "Look, I brought you here, gave you a place to live and a job—"

"Sure, sure! You're just all heart. Give me a break!" he said scornfully.

"You—you ... " The look on his uncle's face was a mix of astonishment and accusation.

"Save it, Uncle. I've had it with you anyway. I'll get out of your face." He flicked his uncle's hand off his shoulder, hoisted himself over the deck rail, and beat it across the back lawn. He ran into the stretch of woods beyond his uncle's property without looking back.

Pushing his way to the open road, he jogged angrily for a quarter mile before stopping beneath a tree to rest and collect himself. He had never seen his uncle so angry. There would be no going back now.

He waited under the shelter of a spreading oak until the sun sank low in the purple skies. As the moments passed, he grew more and more restless. Some people got everything handed to them. It was so easy for people like Uncle Lance. They had everything they wanted—houses, cars, boats, property. But he had never gotten a break in his whole life.

Well, he'd make his own breaks. He wasn't going to give up now. He'd invested too much time in this one-horse town. He thought of the days he'd gone along on Alexei Popov's jaunts, hanging around him for weeks and listening to his jabbering.

"It is here, boy. I bury it—long ago. I find now." The old man's eyes had been bright coals in his leathery face, and his lips parted in a toothy grin. "You help me find for my *lapushka*. Is her treasure. I promise her. But my head—no good—no work anymore." Then he'd be lost in watery memory, his voice shaky and weak. Sometimes, he'd double over in a high-pitched, raucous laugh that left him wheezing and clutching his chest. Shane kicked at a tree root. Crazy old man! Where had he put it?

Shane might have dismissed his tale, but something about it all stuck in his craw. Joe Lair had put him onto it. The foreigner had plenty of money. Years earlier, he'd come with plenty of money. It was a matter of public record. Joe Lair said the full treasure had never been recovered, and as long as the Grainger land was unoccupied, it was fair game. Shane cracked his knuckles. With his uncle handling the estate, he had easy access, but it wouldn't be so easy now.

Miss Morris was a long shot, but there was a tie between her and the old man. Shane just knew it! When Popov visited the ailing old schoolteacher, Shane had sometimes trudged along. He was betting she knew something. But searching her land hadn't turned up anything. He kicked hard at the trunk of the oak. He just couldn't give up on that much money!

Then there was that gem Vera Popov wore all the time—probably even to bed at night. It had to be part of the booty—part of something much bigger. The money Alexei had come up with to send Beatrice to school sure didn't come from selling aluminum cans and pop bottles. Shane had pressed Alexei for the truth and kept after him, prodding him to remember where he'd buried the jewels.

"Think, man!" he had said a hundred times. "You buried it! You got to remember."

But always, it was the same. The old man couldn't remember. That day in the woods, though, he had been almost lucid and claimed he was sure this time. Giddy with excitement, Shane had watched Alexei's shoulders heave and roll with each stab of the shovel in the hard ground.

"Here, let me do it!" Shane remembered how he had feverishly shoved the old man out of the way.

"*Nyet!*" Alexei clutched the shovel tighter, objecting in his native Russian. "*Nyet!*"

They had fought over it, and then Shane pushed him hard, and Alexei's head hit the tree. He'd gone down in a crumpled heap.

Horrified but held in the grip of some powerful momentum, Shane kept digging, deeper and deeper, slinging the dirt up and away, hoping the old man wouldn't come to before he discovered the treasure.

But the moments passed with nothing but dirt piling up in a black mound, leaving a gaping, empty hole. And Alexei did not move.

Shane panicked. He had to get out of there. He had dropped the shovel in horror, only to pick it up again and wipe the sweaty handle before thrusting it hard into the mound of dirt. Then he'd run from the woods, his heart flapping wildly in his chest and his knees wobbling like cooked noodles.

Since that day, he had kept his eyes and ears open, concentrated on Beatrice. He was betting she knew more than she was letting on. There were times when he was astonished by her abilities. Poor little deaf girl? Maybe not so poor. He remembered how only that very day she'd told him his radio was too loud, that she could tell by the vibrations. Who would have thought? And the way she could read his lips was amazing.

He rubbed his cheek gingerly. It still stung from the slap she'd given him when he tried to kiss her. He picked up a stone and flung it as hard as he could. Then he got up from under the tree and leaned against it, cracking his knuckles and struggling to formulate a plan. What to do next?

He began walking, aimlessly at first, as though his feet could find their own direction. Then, he moved on toward the house where Beatrice and Vera lived. Little Bea had plenty of time to get home by now. She was probably up in her room crying her eyes out over their little argument. Well, maybe he could still get the truth out of her.

He knew a way to watch her without being observed. He'd done it before. That's how he knew where she kept the locket. While she was at work and Vera was busy with her prize hens, he had sneaked through her bedroom window and taken it. It was like stealing candy from a baby.

He had no idea what he might find now as he quickened his pace to cover the remaining distance to her house. He wished he had the nerve to go back and take the pick-up truck. The key was still in his pocket.

Suddenly, he remembered what else he'd left hidden under the seat— a small caliber handgun and his uncle's Cubs jacket. He'd go back for them, but not until Uncle Lance was asleep. He shivered, wishing he had the jacket now.

He trudged on, trying to think. It was dark when he finally climbed the oak tree outside Bea's bedroom window. It was a large, leafy tree with thick limbs for climbing. He eased his way up, scraping his knees and arms. The wounds were superficial, but they stung like fire.

He was in luck. Her window shade was up, and he could see her sitting on the edge of the bed reading, studying something in her lap with a puzzled frown. Her shiny hair draped the smooth contours of her face. He remembered the softness of her cheek when he'd touched it. God, she was pretty in the lamplight.

She wore a short blue robe—a soft, silky thing tied at her waist with a narrow ribbon cascading over her thigh. One shapely leg crossed over the other moved rhythmically in the muted light.

After a while, she straightened and lay the paper she was reading on the desk by the window. *A letter?* He chewed the inside of his cheek and peered more closely. Her fingers were so close he could reach in and touch them. A light breeze fluttered through the open window, ruffling the curtain and the paper. He held his breath, his heart racing until he felt lightheaded.

The cramped position worsened his leg pain; he'd have to move soon, but something in that paper seemed important. What was it? With his luck, it was probably some sappy love letter or goofy girl talk, but maybe it was more than that. It would be easy to take it. He drew in a measured breath. He'd show her she couldn't brush him off like an annoying fly.

He watched Bea get up and begin pacing the room. A troubled expression was fixed on her face. Twice, she returned to the letter, paced, and read it again. And then she stepped out of the room. He heard water running. Yes, she had turned on the shower. And the letter sat just a couple of yards away. He reached in, took it, and clutched it between his teeth as he shimmied down the tree.

Dropping into the bushes, he grasped the paper in a shaky fist and sped away in breathless triumph. He ran through the woods that skirted Grace Arbor and out to the road. When he felt it was safe, he held the paper close to his eyes and read:

My dear Beatrice,
  You must come to see me very soon. I have something
  that belongs to you. Your Uncle Alexei wanted you to have it.
  You must tell no one except Anne Westin. She will help you.
  Please come soon.
  Your friend, Margaret Morris

Shane felt the power in him growing. Yes! He knew if he waited long enough, he'd find it. The old lady couldn't be talking about anything else. He was sure of it. Trembling with the enticing knowledge that he was nearing his goal, he stuffed the letter in his pocket and sprinted away.

Chapter 19

Anne pulled the last tray of chocolate chip cookies from the oven and set them to cool on the kitchen table. She paused at the window where rain formed an earthy mosaic on the glass panes. Pink and lavender hydrangeas drooped, heavy with the day's constant weeping, and fog rolled over Margaret Morris's distant roof, turning it eerie, like something out of a Gothic novel.

Rainy days usually stimulated her creative energies. She had begun baking early, knowing Peter always looked forward to her cookies and banana bread, but no amount of activity could stop the troubling thoughts that threatened her peace of mind.

Yesterday was a day of surprises and confusion. When she bumped into Lance as she exited the library, she was gripped by the fear that her heart would betray her. She had come to care about him and thought he might feel the same for her. *I wonder if Richard knew how lucky he was.*

She had been prepared to challenge him about trespassing on her property and releasing the deer from her shed. She wanted to confront him about his truck and demand that he explain what he'd been doing at Grace Arbor in the early dawn. But she hadn't done so. Was he about to confess when he blurted out, "It's my fault," and then exclaimed that he should never have sold the property with "that silly cloud over it"?

Silly cloud? Trespassing and threats were hardly minor offenses. The police were taking the whole matter of Alexei's death quite seriously. How dare Lance make light of the things that had happened! They were real, and she'd been threatened. "I'm not leaving, no matter who tries to scare me off," she'd told him.

The phone rang suddenly, startling her.

"You all right, Mom? You sound strange."

"Peter," she breathed, almost giddy at hearing his voice. "I'm fine." She fought the urge to spill out her harbored fears, to let him make everything right as Richard would have done. She covered the mouthpiece with a trembling hand and took a deep breath. "If I sound out of breath, it's because I've been slaving over a hot stove."

"Banana bread?" he queried.

"Yes, and chocolate chip cookies. A ton of them, and I expect you to eat them all, or I'm sending them with you."

"That's a deal I can't refuse. Your cookies could lure me anywhere." There was a brief silence before he asked about Tess.

Anne swallowed. Peter had fallen for her—head over heels, which was really saying something for her level-headed, strong-minded son. Something in Tess must have answered some need that Jennifer or his other girlfriends had been unable to reach.

"She's all right, but…" She hesitated. How was she to tell Steven the deer was gone and that Tess blamed her for its disappearance? There was no good way, so she unfolded the story and, finishing, said, "Tess was upset, as you can imagine."

"But how could that happen?" he asked, incredulous. "Was the door left open?"

Tess might have forgotten to secure the heavy bar holding the door, but it seemed unlikely. "I don't know, Peter. She's usually meticulous about that."

Peter gave a puzzled groan but said nothing.

"I'm sorry. I tried to find the deer, but it was hopeless in those woods. Mackowitz came by and looked too." She stopped, having determined not to mention the official visit.

"The police?"

Of course, Peter would think it strange to involve the police in the disappearance of an animal unless theft had been committed. "He—uh—came by to examine the site, and I told him about the shed door," she finished quickly. "He was good enough to look around for the fawn but didn't find it."

"Tess loves that animal," Peter said huskily. "She'll have to let it go eventually, of course."

"Peter," Anne said, anxious to fill the silence. "I'm so glad you're coming. There's so much I want to—" Now she was unprepared to finish the sentence. Did she sound as desperate as she felt? "When will you get here?"

"I should be pulling in shortly after noon if traffic cooperates." Silence followed as though he was weighing his words. After a moment, he brightened. "I'll take you out to lunch—that great little seafood place in Burketown."

"No, you'll be tired after your trip. I can fix lunch, and we can eat here."

"I won't be tired," he argued gently. "Are you sure you're okay?"

She hesitated, touched by his sensitivity. She longed to tell him everything but didn't want to worry him. She wouldn't mention the uninvited guest in her woods. At least not yet. "Everything's fine," she said. "But I'll have lots to tell you." She broke off, lest he hear the catch in her voice.

After Peter rang off, she held the receiver briefly, praying for calm. She was afraid; there was no denying it. Why did she feel so jangled, so restless?

The phone rang again, interrupting her angst. *Peter's forgotten something.* She picked up on the first ring.

"Anne?" Lance's voice was strained and cautious. "I'm sorry to disturb you; I hope this isn't a bad time."

"No, no," she said, recovering herself. "I was just talking to Peter. He ..."

"I need to talk to you, Anne," he interrupted. "Could we, that is, could I stop by?"

"Tonight?" she stammered. "I'm expecting Peter, and there's still a lot to do."

"Ah." He seemed hurt by her refusal, but he didn't press, didn't say anything right away, and seconds ticked by uncomfortably. Then he cleared his throat and asked agitatedly, "When do you expect him?"

"Tomorrow," Anne replied.

"I see," he said tentatively. "Look, I don't want to alarm you, but I don't think it's a good idea for you to be there alone."

A coldness swept through her, dislodging her fear. She might be inexperienced, still learning how to live independently, but she wasn't a weakling and didn't need to be coddled. And she wasn't going to be run off by anyone. "Lance, we've already been through this. I've no intention of leaving."

"I mean just temporarily until this business is over with. I've been thinking about what you told me yesterday."

"I don't understand you," she said levelly. "You're the one who told me neighbors were just curious about all the gossip. I think you said something about a silly cloud. Well, I have an umbrella and a raincoat."

"Anne, I didn't mean ..." His voice rose in frustration. "Please. There are some things you need to know—"

She cut him off. "I appreciate your concern, Lance, but I have work to do. I really can't talk anymore."

She cut the connection but continued to cradle the receiver in her hand. Her emotions had run the gamut from anger to delight where Lance was concerned. He was kind, attentive, even gallant. He had mown the lawn and run errands for Margaret. A man who cared for his neighbors had to be a good man, didn't he? Or was it all a pretense? Why this sudden concern when he'd downplayed her worries yesterday?

She frowned at the telephone and drummed the fingers of her left hand on the table. She'd checked on the blue pickup. It was registered to Lance. So, what was this call about? Was he trying to make amends for yesterday? Or was he warning her? Did he really think she was in danger? And if so, from whom?

She turned away from the phone, determined to put her nerves on hold until Peter arrived. She'd do something physically demanding that left no time for speculation. Pulling up the hall runner, she headed for the back door. The floor needed polishing, and there was vacuuming to do, as well as the guest room to prepare.

She worked through the early afternoon, and when shadows began to lengthen, she took the shears out to the garden, intending to cut some fresh flowers. White daisies would be nice, or perhaps some purple calendula. She unlocked the back door, pushing Lance's veiled warning aside, and stepped out.

The rain had washed the world, leaving the foliage shining and the grass fragrant as a spring evening. A bank of dark clouds hovered on the pale horizon like brooding mountains. The sun would set soon, but now it tinged the cloud bank with faint pink ribbons.

Anne pulled the sleeves of her sweatshirt down and breathed in the freshness. She left the deck and walked around to the front garden. As soon as she turned the corner, she saw Tess sitting under the silver maple, knees drawn up, her arms clasped over them. She was peering beyond the garden to the bank of bruised clouds but dropped her arms when she saw Anne. She stood quickly, her bright hair touching a low-hanging branch. Her eyes held fear and something else—a question? Need?

Anne half expected her to turn and run, but the young woman made no move. "Tess? Are you all right?"

She nodded but said nothing, her shoulders rising as though to breathe deeply.

"I was just going to cut some flowers for the table," Anne said, holding up the scissors." When there was no reply, she continued. "The garden is beautiful, and I know I have you to thank for it."

Tess shifted her feet and drew another breath—as though calming herself. "I like to work in the garden," she said, fingers moving at her sides.

She mispronounced garden, and Anne remembered that Tess found "r's" difficult. It must be uncommonly hard to speak when you never heard how words sound.

Tess weaved a longer string of words as though thinking with her hands. "I don't know why I like it so much."

Poor child, Anne thought. *Did only her heart remember that Grace Arbor had once been her home as a baby?* Margaret's strange reference to the Romanov Dynasty and a revolution played in her mind. Was Tess aware of it, and was there a real connection to her grandmother?

Tess looked at Anne squarely, her eyes troubled. The shadows beneath them contrasted darkly against her ivory cheeks. "I was—waiting for you."

Waiting for her? Did she want to talk about the deer? Question her again, level another accusation? Or did it have something to do with Margaret Morris's letter? *She must come*, the elderly teacher had whispered urgently, pressing the letter into her hands.

"I'm glad. You're always welcome here," Anne said. She'd said this more than once before, but it didn't make her less sorry for how things had turned out. Under other circumstances, Grace Arbor might have belonged to this young woman.

Tess glanced around nervously, then took a few steps toward Anne. She brushed her hair back from her face with both hands as though the gesture gave her courage. "Could we—walk?"

"Of course." Anne set the scissors and wicker basket beneath the tree and followed Tess. She tried to trace the girl's profile, aware that something important was on her mind. Something important enough to conquer her shyness or suspicion.

They walked to the road in silence and turned east to skirt the edge of the private wood, avoiding the strip of forest outlined by a pale moon. Presently, Tess stopped and looked at her. "You said there were other letters from Miss Morris. Beside the one you gave me."

"Yes," Anne said, "Margaret said she wrote many that you never answered. Why didn't you?" Anne asked gently.

"I never knew about them," she responded wearily, adding with emphasis in sign language. "Never."

Anne looked at her in astonishment.

"I think I may have found one once." She looked past her and began to speak rapidly, her fingers dancing in the waning light. "I found scraps in the trash." She raised finely sculpted brows. "I saw my name."

"Was it from Margaret?" Anne asked.

She shrugged her shoulders, and a lock of copper-colored hair fell over her left eye. "I don't know," she said so softly that Anne could barely make out the words. "I asked Aunt Vera, but she won't tell me."

Anne wanted to reach out and touch her pale cheek. "Tess..."

"Miss Morris says I can trust you," she said quickly. "She says she has something that belongs to me and that I shouldn't trust anyone but you." Her fingers moved erratically; agitation garbled her words.

Was Tess willing to trust her now? Had she forgiven her for the lost deer? For being the owner of Grace Arbor—the place she

loved? "Margaret wouldn't ask you to come if it weren't important," Anne said. "You must go see her soon."

"Will you go with me?" Tess tugged absently at a button on
her shirt and waited.

Was she afraid of the answer? "Of course. I'll drive you. Let's
go tomorrow morning. How about ten o'clock? That will give
me time to get back before Peter comes in the afternoon." She
gauged the girl's reaction and didn't miss the quick pleasure that
leaped into her eyes. She trusted Peter. And perhaps that was
why she had also decided to trust his mother.

Tess began to move again along the road they had come, her
step quick as though driven by decision or relief. But suddenly,
she stopped again and looked up at Anne anxiously.

"What is it, Tess?"

"The letter…" She put a hand to her hair, and Anne could
see her fingers shaking.

"Tess? What is it?" She put her arm across her shoulder.

"The letter is gone."

"Margaret's letter? The one I gave you?" Anne asked
incredulously.

Tess nodded. "I put it on my desk. But when I came back
from taking a shower, it was gone!"

"Are you sure? Maybe it fell on the floor or behind the desk,"
Anne suggested.

"I looked everywhere. It's gone."

What could have happened? If Vera had kept Margaret's letters
from her before, perhaps she had found this one and taken it too.
As they approached the cottage's front door, Anne felt her anger
rising. What was wrong with the woman?

Suddenly, Vera Popov appeared in the doorway carrying
a chipped enamel bowl. She cast them both a dark look and
stretched the bowl to Tess. "You are supposed to feed chickens
today," she said stridently.

"I have to go," Tess said. She grasped the bowl and fled to the chicken coop.

"Mrs. Popov. Vera—" Anne began, startled.

But Vera stepped back, her lower lip fixed in a childish pout, and closed the door, leaving Anne on the porch step.

Had Vera destroyed Margaret's letter? Why? *I'm getting paranoid*, Anne thought as she traced her steps back to her own house. Cicadas chanted their rasping melodies, and an owl hooted a forlorn warning. She dug her hands into her pockets and hurried to the sheltering deck of Grace Arbor. Maybe she should listen to the advice she was getting from various sources and leave this place.

But she wasn't the only one involved now. Something was going on that affected a young woman who needed her help. "Dear Lord," she whispered in the approaching darkness, "help us all." Borrowing a prayer from an Old Testament king, she added, "We don't know what to do, but our eyes are upon you."

Chapter 20

It was raining again—for the second day in a row—pounding the roof like angry fists. Anne woke to the crash of thunder and a heaviness bearing down on the landscape—external and internal.

Sleep hadn't come easily after meeting with Tess, the culmination of a day characterized by vague warnings and startling revelations. In the night, she had heard a thousand creaks and groans—branches scraping the siding, squirrels skittering across the roof like threatening footfalls.

Lance's warning that she could be in danger lingered in her mind. She had been too angry to take it seriously, but in the darkness waiting for sleep, she could not dismiss it. Now, Saturday had dawned; Peter was coming, but she must first fulfill her promise to take Tess to visit Margaret Morris.

Could Margaret be the key to solving the riddles and ending the speculation and gossip that clouded Grace Arbor? What did the disappearance of her letter mean? Tess wouldn't make up such a story, would she?

Anne finished her breakfast and set dough in the old-fashioned way to rise on the counter. When she and Tess returned, There would be enough time to bake cinnamon rolls fresh for Peter's coffee. She grabbed a jacket and umbrella and drove around the rural blocks to Tess's house. It was amazing how much longer it took to drive than to cut through the lilac hedge.

When she stepped from the car, she saw Vera, untidy black hair wisping below her head scarf, hunched over a stack of egg crates. Quick disapproval darkened her features.

"Good morning, Vera!" Anne called brightly, stopping at the base of the porch steps. There must be some way to convince her she wasn't her enemy. The weather was always a safe subject. "Quite a storm we had overnight, wasn't it?"

"What you want?" Vera asked. Her brows were knit in a furry chain, and her eyes were shadowed and fearful like a child expecting to be punished. The hand that had rested on her hip groped for the lapel of her housedress, where a large brooch sparkled like green fire.

"Tess is expecting me," Anne said quietly. "Our errand won't take too long."

"She got things to do," Vera said peevishly. "No time to go with you."

Did she always treat Tess like a child, saying where she could go and when? Perhaps old habits died hard, or Alexei's absence made Vera assume increased responsibility for Tess's care.

Suddenly, Tess flung the door open. She stepped onto the porch in a long yellow raincoat over dark olive jeans. Her hair, pulled back into a ponytail and secured with a green ribbon, made her look like a child ready to play in a puddle. Her expression, however, was serious and determined.

"It's all right, Aunt Vera," she said, weaving the words rapidly. "We will be back soon." She continued to sign until Vera returned inside with a lower lip thrust.

Tess turned to Anne with a shy smile. "I'm ready. I'm sorry you have to go out in this weather." Her fingers cascaded delicately, mimicking rain.

"It's no problem," Anne said. "And the garden will love a good soak."

They set off together as the wipers drummed a steady rhythm. Anne concentrated on the slick road while Tess stared through the window, looking preoccupied and troubled.

Arriving at Margaret's home, Anne pulled the parking brake and turned to her young companion. "Did you find the letter?" she asked softly.

Tess looked down at her hands and shook her head sadly. "Gone," she said quietly. "Like Alexei. Gone." After a few seconds, she added, "Everything goes away."

Anne touched her arm lightly, and Tess did not recoil. She wanted to tell her that there would be happy days again, that she wasn't alone. But would these words ring true to this confused girl who had experienced such loss? She put her hand over Tess's pale one and met her eyes. Their violet depths seemed to hold something different, something Anne hadn't seen before. Hope? Perhaps an inkling of trust?

Arriving at Margaret's house, Anne headed to the porch to retrieve a sopping newspaper abandoned on the step. She exchanged a glance with Tess and knocked firmly on the screen door.

A tremulous voice responded after the second knock. "Yes?"

"It's Anne Westin … I've brought someone to see you."

"Come in, please." The words came from far away—no doubt from the back bedroom. Was Margaret not feeling well enough to be up and about?

Anne led Tess through the quiet house with its faintly musty smell. She gave Tess a reassuring smile at the bedroom door, and they stepped inside.

Dressed in a blue and white floral housecoat, Margaret lay in bed with a crocheted throw flung over her. Around her head was a ribbon like a crimson halo. Her eyes narrowed in the dim light.

"You shouldn't leave your door unlocked," Anne scolded mildly and gave Tess's shoulder a little prod.

Margaret pushed herself up on the bed, quick recognition brightening her pale complexion. "You've come," she said huskily and stretched a blue-veined hand to Tess. "It's been such a long time; I've prayed you would come." She studied the girl from head to foot, and her voice seemed to take on new strength. "Are you all right?"

Tess stepped closer and signed a hesitant response.

"I'm so sorry about your uncle, dear," Margaret said. "Alexei loved you very much." For a moment, she seemed to lose herself in thought. Presently, she continued. "You look like your grandmother, you know. I knew her only a short time, but I know she loved you too."

Tess's eyes were a mask of confusion as she studied Margaret's lips.

"She couldn't have done better than ask your Uncle Alexei to take care of you all those years ago." Margaret drew herself up higher against the pillows. "And your grandmother and Alexei both wanted you to have what belongs to you."

She raised her eyes, suddenly noticing Anne. "Come, please. Close to the bed." She was sitting upright now, and the crocheted coverlet fell away. Her cheeks brightened with renewed color, and her voice took on strength. "Reach under the mattress."

The mattress moved easily under Margaret's weight, and Anne felt something. She drew out a small brown envelope and handed it to Margaret.

"Give it to Beatrice," Margaret said. "It belongs to her."

Tess turned it over in her hand, and something fell out and dropped on the floor with a light click.

"It's a key to a safety deposit box at the bank," Margaret said. "The box contains the inheritance from your grandmother."

"Inheritance?" Tess signed, eyes wide with astonishment. She bent to pick up the key and studied it with trembling fingers.

"I'll explain, and you must try to understand, my dear." Margaret folded her hands over the bedclothes and began, her voice growing steadier as her story unfolded. "Your grandmother left her homeland as a young girl at a terrible time in history. She was a servant in the royal house of Romanov that the Bolsheviks overthrew." Margaret paused, coughed, and then steadied herself. "She was just a little girl when the revolution came, but she escaped, along with some of the family jewels sewn into a cloak that had been her mother's."

Anne listened, recalling the chilling story she had read so recently, how members of the Romanov family, along with their servants, had been lured to their deaths. Family jewels, sewn into the women's clothes, at first delayed their deaths. Perhaps it was in those intervening seconds of chaos that the child, Tess's grandmother, had incredibly escaped with the jewels belonging to her mistress sewn into her coat.

"When she grew up, your grandmother brought Alexei into her household as an apprentice to her cabinet maker. When the opportunity came, she immigrated to America with the help of your uncle, a young man at the time.

"Your mother died very shortly after giving birth to you, Tess. Your grandmother came to Ladystone with you and bought the house Mrs. Westin now owns. She made the down payment with the last of the money she'd brought."

Tess shot Anne an astonished glance and returned her attention to Margaret, who paused only a second or two to breathe.

"When she became ill, she asked your Uncle Alexei to care for you. Of course, you know he isn't your blood uncle, but he couldn't love you more if he had been. Your grandmother turned over her possessions—those ancient jewels—to Alexei."

"But..." Anne interrupted, "how did the house come to be sold?" She stared at Margaret, amazed by her changed manner and voice that had lost its strained quality.

Margaret shook her head briefly as though to clear loose threads of memory. "She was old and couldn't speak English. She didn't make her payments or take care of her taxes while she lived at Grace Arbor. When she died, the house was turned over to the city and sold at auction." Margaret reached for a tissue from the box near her bed and dabbed at her nose. "It was too late for Alexei to do anything about it—even if he could."

"But the inheritance..." Anne questioned. Tess's eyes widened.

Margaret's voice became passionate, almost frantic. "Three uncut diamonds and an emerald necklace tucked away in a little cloth bag. Very old. Very valuable." She looked at Tess. "Your grandmother buried it herself. She told your uncle about the jewels, but she died before she could tell him where to find them.

"He searched for two years—never told anyone. Vera was no help; Alexei knew it was up to him. And then, the terrible accident happened." Margaret's breath caught here, and she fell silent for a few seconds, swallowing.

"After the accident, Alexei wasn't himself anymore. He began to talk about buried treasure and to dig up ground everywhere in search of it. He was still looking for it when he died." Margaret swallowed hard, and her eyes misted over with tears.

"But, Margaret," Anne prodded. "What does this mean?" Anne pointed to the key visible in Tess's open palm.

"The bag with the jewels is in a safety deposit box in my bank." She hesitated, maybe to let the full force of her words sink in. "We found it—Alexei and I—buried less than two feet deep among the gladiola bulbs. Alexei told me to take care of it for Beatrice and that if she ever needed anything..." She broke off, her voice wavering. "By that time, Alexei wasn't able to handle things.

"He promised to keep it a secret from Vera but gave her one of the gems—a valuable brooch that she always wears. She has no idea of its value." Margaret shook her head as though perplexed. "She parades around with it like a child with a favorite toy."

Margaret looked beyond them to the apple tree outside the window. "If things had been different, Alexei and I might have married. We loved each other." She reached for another tissue and wiggled her fingers in the air to ward off sympathy or signal that she wasn't yet finished.

"Alexei kept on looking. He thought the jewels were still buried, even though I repeatedly reminded him that they were safe. I had them appraised and stored in the bank. So, you see, Alexei has been digging all over the area for the last two years, thinking the jewels were still there."

Tears rolled down the old cheeks, and Margaret did not attempt to dry them. "If he had stopped digging, he might not have died."

"Margaret, I'm so sorry," Anne said gently.

Margaret swallowed and directed her watery blue gaze at Tess. "Two years ago, when Alexei wanted to send you to school, I sold one of the diamonds—twenty thousand dollars, the amount needed for the tuition." Her eyes were bright with triumph now or fever. She reached out a hand to Tess. "The rest of it is there, and now you are old enough to handle it yourself." She closed the girl's fingers over the key.

The three of them sat close together, Tess on one side of the bed and Anne on the other. The strange saga left a heavy pathos in the room with its quaint sideboard and old-fashioned wall hangings—remembrances of times past. Poor Margaret. She'd had to keep the jewels a secret, or there would have been people from all over the globe descending on Tess.

Suddenly, the bedroom door swung open and slammed against the wall. Shane Eldridge stood on the threshold, hair and clothes dripping with rain. His jacket flagged open, revealing a silver medallion on a chain.

"I'll trouble you for that key, ladies," he said calmly.

Margaret clutched the bedclothes, and Tess stared, her eyes wide with fright. Anne jumped up from the chair by the bed but froze when she saw the small caliber pistol in his hand.

"Just hand it over nicely, Bea," Shane said, exaggerating the syllables. His eyes took on a fierce gleam as he waved the pistol dangerously.

Tess whirled around, fingers flying in alarm. "Shane! What are you doing?"

"Who would have thought?" he continued in the same high-pitched fervor. He turned the gun toward Margaret, his expression dark with scorn. "The old under-the-mattress trick! I searched everywhere and all the time you had it!"

The sweet-sour odor of liquor mingled with Shane's after-shave lotion made Anne briefly nauseous. She steadied herself against Margaret's bed as though she could shield her from whatever dark plan seethed in the young man's mind. "You followed us here," she said, stunned and angry. "And you've been drinking."

He gave a little smile of self-enjoyment. "Been watching you all real close," he said, giving Anne a cold glance. "You and little Bea here." He took a step closer and waved the gun at Margaret, who was pressed against the pillows. "Like the letter said, you have something to give us, don't you?"

Anne swallowed. *It was the letter she had entrusted to her. Shane must have sneaked into Tess's room somehow and found it.*

Shane grabbed Tess's wrist, and the key flew onto the floor. Shane bent to retrieve it, gun still leveled on his quarry, and placed it in his pocket.

Margaret found her voice. "So you, Mr. Eldridge, I wager that you are why Alexei was digging up the ground everywhere."

"The old coot! Pretending it was buried when all the time he knew you had it tucked away under your mattress!"

Margaret leaned forward. "You goaded him, knowing he wasn't right in his head. You forced him … " She began to cough, grasping the covers with shaking fingers.

Anne placed a steadying hand on the fragile shoulder, but Margaret pressed on through a paroxysm of coughing. "Maybe Alexei was smarter than any of us thought. He steered greedy people like you away to keep the inheritance safe for Beatrice."

Anne reached for the telephone as the reality of what likely happened sank in, but Shane grabbed it away and pulled the cord from the wall in one violent yank. He glared at her as Tess hovered over Margaret, violet eyes registering shock and fear.

"So, Mr. Eldridge," Anne said. "You've got the key. Now what? You don't really think you'll get away with this, do you? What will your uncle do when he finds out?" She dreaded the answer that might seal her suspicion that Lance was in on the conspiracy.

"My uncle," Shane said scornfully. "Ah, yes, my uncle! Shane, do this; Shane, don't do that," he mimicked. "You're late to work. That's not what your mother taught you." He held the key up in one hand and waved the gun with the other.

"Why don't you put that down before someone gets hurt," Anne said boldly, surprising herself.

He shot her a look that could melt steel.

"You know," she continued, "there's nothing you can do with that key. Safety deposit boxes can't be opened by just anybody, whether they have a key or not. Only Margaret has power of attorney and must sign—" Too late, she regretted her words.

Shane seemed momentarily bewildered. If he'd been drinking, maybe it would play in their favor. Or work against them, she realized with troubling clarity.

"No sweat," he said, "bank's open for another hour. Get up!" he ordered, towering over Margaret. To Anne, he added, "Get her dressed. We're all going to take a ride."

Tess glared at him, her expression fierce. Her fingers gestured wildly. "You can't do this. Miss Morris is sick!"

Pausing only for a second, Shane grabbed Tess and pulled her against him like a human shield. He stroked her cheek with the point of his gun slowly, dangerously. "Little Bea and I are going to wait in the car. If you aren't dressed and out in five minutes..."

"Please!" Margaret whispered as she struggled to rise. "Help me up, Anne. Please."

"Don't do this, Shane," Anne said, using his given name for the first time. "Think about what you're doing. You know how wrong it is."

Shane pulled Tess's arm backward, inching toward the door. "Don't preach at me!" he said through clenched teeth. "I've had enough of that. Now, you're going to do exactly as I say!" He drew in a breath and assumed his suave air. "Five minutes, ladies. Don't disappoint us."

Anne watched in horror as he pulled Tess out the door. Margaret, coughing from the exertion and trauma, struggled to get up. Anne put an arm behind her shoulders and lifted her to her feet as her pulse pounded in her ears. Silently, she prayed for God's help.

Chapter 21

Thunder rumbled over the hills, and lightning flashed distant warnings as Peter drew nearer to Ladystone. He should have gotten an earlier start, he realized. With all his mother had on her mind, she didn't need to worry about him being late and driving too fast on slick roads. Like as not, though, she'd do more than worry, he realized. She would pray, as she always did.

He glanced at the package containing a Mary Cassatt print he knew his mother wanted. The American impressionist, whose subjects were often mothers and children, had long been a favorite artist. For Tess, he'd brought a box of chocolates, gift-wrapped and tied with a silver ribbon.

Tanner's Falls lay awash with mist and rain. He recalled how Tess's red-gold hair flew like a silken kite in the wind. She had been as light as air when he held her as she wept over Alexei Popov, the only person she believed had cared about her. But she was wrong about that.

Since that day, he'd thought about little else. Something singularly innocent and genuine in her attracted and astonished him all at once. Life had been hard on her. She deserved so much better; she deserved to be happy. Would Shane Eldridge bring her happiness? He felt a keen dislike. Or was he merely jealous?

He rounded the corner, bringing Grace Arbor into view at the crest of Ringold Way. Oaks and maples, just beginning to hint of waning summer, framed the brick exterior with its white cupola. The meadow surrounding the yard teemed with goldenrod; crimson sumac leaped upward like tongues of fire in the gray light. Such beauty never failed to surprise him. He knew the scientific explanations for these natural changes, but he had never been able to dismiss the argument for a Designer. That the world could have resulted from mere chance defied logical thinking. Yet a heavy curtain hung over his heart. Could he trust a God who sometimes seemed capricious and, at other times, a disinterested tyrant who abandoned his creation?

He pulled up Grace Arbor's driveway and stopped near the back door. He wanted to arrive in time to take Mom for lunch, but he'd been delayed at work. It wasn't the first time he'd been late, but she would forgive him.

He left everything in the car and approached the porch, where a squirrel ran the length of the rail, twitching its tail rapidly before leaping to the ground and darting away.

He rapped on the door, unnerved by an unnatural stillness, an almost eerie pall in the air. He heard no footsteps and saw no fluttering of drapes. Peering in the kitchen window, he saw the well-ordered room with its mahogany table and chairs precisely placed, a bowl of purple and yellow pansies in a silver bowl.

Her car was gone. Perhaps she'd run out to the store for some last-minute grocery item. He climbed back into his car to wait, ignoring an impulse that something might be wrong. It was unlike his mother not to be on hand to greet a guest or family member, late or not. But she was no longer tied to the clock; she had a right to some leisurely habits and eccentricities.

He shrugged and pulled the *Tribune* from the back seat. But when she still hadn't come home after thirty minutes, his worry escalated into nagging anxiety. Maybe Tess would know where she was. Scooping up the chocolates, he sloshed through the grass.

At his knock, Vera Popov appeared, her boxy figure filling the doorway. A hint of recognition flashed in her eyes, but no welcome accompanied it. Struck by the odor of onions and some other substance he couldn't name, Peter asked if Tess was at home.

Vera shook her head emphatically, arms folded across her chest, which seemed massive in a dress of mauve and brown horizontal stripes. A gaudy brooch glinted just below her right collarbone.

"When do you think she'll be back?" he persisted.

She shrugged heavy shoulders and was quiet for a few seconds as though pondering her response. "She go out with her," she said in a rush, pointing in the general direction of Grace Arbor. "She don't say when she come back." Then she stepped back in dismissal, strands of dark hair escaping the bun at the base of her neck.

He pressed forward, his hand on the doorframe. "My mother was expecting me. Do you know where she and your niece went?"

"No," she said with a thrust of her chin and reached for the screen door handle. "I got work to do now." She closed the door abruptly, leaving Peter on the steps.

He considered knocking again—demanding to know more, but something in the steely eyes and furrowed brow told him it would be useless. He stepped down and returned to Grace Arbor, worry building with each step. He tried the door and was surprised to find it open. Had she not listened to him about locking doors? Surely her years in the city had taught her the importance of security.

He switched on the light. Bread dough and baking utensils were laid out on the table. Everything looked polished and ready, and the house was tidy and beautiful, as he had expected. But where was she?

He went to the telephone table in the hall and leafed through his mother's address book. When he came upon "Crane Realty," he picked up the phone, even though it was Saturday and unlikely for anyone to be in the office. But to Peter's surprise, Lance's voice responded to the second ring.

"Peter Westin here," he began. "I'm at my mother's house; we'd planned to have lunch together, but she isn't here. Do you happen to know where she might have gone?" He paused, feeling odd about discussing family plans with a man virtually a stranger to him, though apparently not to his mother. "I've waited nearly an hour, but she hasn't shown up. Tess isn't home either." He broke off uncomfortably.

After a momentary silence, Lance said, "I'll be there right away."

That was all. No questions. No explanations. "But..."

The connection ended.

Why did Crane act so strangely? Why was he dropping everything and heading there? If he knew something, why not simply talk to him? Why had he rung off with such urgency? Peter ticked off the minutes in the ominous quiet of the kitchen. At the window, he watched rain drench the trees and beat on the shed where he and Tess had tended the injured fawn.

Their last moments together had been strained at best. He had disappointed her, though for the life of him, he couldn't understand what he had said to upset her. After the idyllic afternoon, she had run from his car when they watched the water trickle over the rocks like a thousand crystal shards. Today, she had gone somewhere with his mother—but where and why?

Precisely eleven and a half minutes after his call, a dark sedan made a rapid ascent up the driveway. Lance Crane climbed out, his features solemn. Peter threw open the kitchen door and stepped out. "Sorry to drag you out in this storm—"

"You've gone next door?" Lance broke in anxiously. He appeared strained and pale, his face shadowed by the beginnings of a salt-and-pepper beard.

Peter ran a hand through his hair, alert to the man's anxiety. "I thought Tess might know … but her aunt just said she and Tess went somewhere together. She said she didn't know where. It's not like my mother. She knew I was coming; she would have left a note or something."

Lance gripped the porch rail, and the muscles in his jaw flexed.

Exasperated and perplexed, Peter waited for some response, but the man stood looking at him, jingling his car keys in his pockets. "I suppose she just got delayed in town—or her car broke down," he added.

Lance swept a hand over his jaw. "I think we better look for her," he said, backing down the stairs. He headed for his car. "We'll start at the Morris place."

Peter followed, his lips dry as sandpaper. "What's going on?"

Lance gestured for him to get in and began moving down the driveway, his knuckles white on the steering wheel. "There's been some trouble … " he began as they sped to the main road. "Alexei Popov's death is still under investigation, and your mother told me some strange things have been happening. A deer she's been keeping at her place disappeared, and—"

Peter glanced across sharply to engage Lance's rigid profile. "The deer we rescued in Tanner's Wood?"

"At first, I didn't think much about it," Lance ruminated darkly. "I thought she might have just left the door unlocked, and it got away, but … "

A deer was hardly sufficient cause for the panic he sensed in the man. "But what?" Peter urged.

"When your mother told me that someone was watching the house, I tried to convince her to move into town for a while. But she refused to leave."

Peter drew in his breath. "She didn't say anything to me about a prowler or ... " He stared at Lance's profile. "Why didn't someone tell me?"

Lance squealed around a corner, his face pale behind his tan. "The thing is," he began through clenched teeth, "I'm afraid my nephew may have done something stupid."

Peter blanched. Shane Eldridge. From the moment he'd laid eyes on him, he hadn't liked him. "What the devil are you talking about!" he demanded.

Lance braked at an old frame house only a quarter mile from Grace Arbor and flipped the buckle on his seat belt. "Come on!" He clambered out and ran to the house's front door before Peter could release the belt on the passenger side.

Together, they raced up to a weather-beaten porch surrounded by tall hollyhock spears. An old swing hung from rusted chains. Peter forced himself to wait while Lance knocked, then began banging on the door. He wanted to spin the man around and demand an explanation but waited, speechless and tense. When there was no response, Lance pushed against the door, which gave way easily, thrusting them inside.

"Margaret?" Crane's voice echoed strangely in the house, and Peter knew immediately that no one was inside. He followed the man into a back room and found a rumpled bed, a table containing medicine bottles, and a blue gown discarded in a heap. A chair was overturned on the dusty hardwood floor.

"Margaret was too ill to go anywhere on her own," Lance said, grasping the edges of the bedside table. "And look at this mess!" Simultaneously, they saw the telephone ripped from the wall. Near it was a small brown envelope on the floor.

"What's going on?" Peter demanded, "And what does this have to do with my mother?"

Lance said nothing but held the envelope close to his eyes. Peter struggled to read over his shoulder, but the print was tiny and faded. "We've got to phone the police," Lance said, rushing to the door and pulling a cell phone from his pocket. Over his shoulder, he shouted to Peter. "Come on!"

"Where are we going?" Peter demanded when they were once again speeding away. His voice had risen to a fevered pitch he could not control. "Crane, in heaven's name, what's going on?"

"I don't know!" Lance seemed to struggle to keep his voice calm. His sharp eyes roved as though the answer could be detected in the atmosphere. "It may have something to do with that infernal gossip about a treasure. And I think Shane's involved in it." He paused as though trying to work out a sticky problem in his mind. "I think he believed Alexei's ravings. That's why he was snooping around Margaret's place! And I've been too stupid to see it."

They swerved around a car, and Peter had to grip the dashboard to avoid being thrown against it. "See what?" he asked angrily. "And where are we going?"

But Lance only stared ahead, his body hunched over the wheel. He flipped open his cell phone and punched in a number. "Lance Crane here, Chief. Something's wrong at Margaret Morris' place." Briefly, he gave the sketchy details, adding, "I think she's in trouble." He scrubbed his hand over his face. "Anne Westin may be with her. Neither of them carries a cell phone."

Peter winced, remembering how he had urged his mother to get a mobile phone, but she could be stubborn. *I don't want to be available to annoying callers every moment of the day.*

Lance turned sharply onto a deeply rutted road. Thunder rolled, lightning flashed, and the rain beat down on the car as it careened down a steep grade. Dense foliage scraped against its sides.

"Where are you going?" Peter demanded again.

"The mine office," Lance said through gritted teeth. "If Shane is hiding out, he might be there. He's been spending a lot of time there. Blast that Joe Lair!" His tight, short sentences shot like bullets from a machine gun as he bore down on the accelerator, his mouth a grim line.

Peter felt a hard pit in his stomach and knew he was helpless to do anything but sit and wait while this acquaintance, who could be either friend or foe, headed them straight into who knew what. Nothing made any sense. And who was Joe Lair? The road narrowed even further as they passed a verdant forest encroaching on the road like tentacles.

Suddenly, Peter spotted someone ahead waving both arms in a sweeping motion like a human searchlight. Lance slammed on the brakes, nearly sending them flying.

It was Tess, Peter realized. She was waving furiously, her white face streaked with rain or tears. He sprang from the car, ran to her, and caught her in his arms. "Tess, what is it?"

She shivered as she clung to him, then pushed violently away, hands flying to her mouth. Her face was a mask of anguish. "Miss Morris! We've got to help."

Peter grasped her shoulders. "Where is my mother?"

She grabbed Peter's hand and began to pull him. "This way," she stammered, tugging him away from the road.

With Lance close behind him, Peter raced after Tess into a heavy canopy of trees. They hadn't run far when Peter caught sight of something yellow under a tree. A woman covered in Tess's raincoat, head pillowed on what looked like a black handbag. Margaret Morris? He stared in astonishment. *What on earth?*

Lance peeled off his sweater and bundled it under the woman's head. "Are you all right?" he asked gently. "Are you hurt?"

The woman tried to rise but sank again. "About time you got here," she said through chattering teeth. But relief shone in her rheumy eyes. "I'm all right." She reached a hand toward Tess and cast an anxious glance toward Peter.

"It's all right, Margaret," Lance whispered soothingly. "We'll get you out of here." He put his hands under her arms and helped her sit up.

"Your nephew," Margaret began hesitantly, her eyes wide. "He's got the jewels. And he has Anne."

Peter's heart thudded. "Where is she?" he demanded, his voice tight with anger.

Margaret's body convulsed with coughing, and Tess bent closer to comfort her. The struggling lady looked up at Peter, eyes wide and frightened. "Shane left us here and took off with the key to my safety deposit box." She shook her head, and tears rolled down her cheeks. "He has a gun," she stammered.

"I know my nephew," Lance said firmly, grasping Peter's arm. "He'll listen to me." He flipped open his cell phone. "I'm calling for an ambulance. Stay here until it comes. I will find your mother; I promise!"

Peter glared at Lance. Someone had to stay with the struggling woman and Tess. Could this Lance Crane he knew so little about find his mother? Keep her safe? Something in the Crane's voice and the fierce determination on his face made Peter believe him. He searched the flashing blue eyes, trying to gauge what lay behind their penetrating depths. Like it or not, his mother's life was now in the man's hands.

"I've got a flare in my trunk. I'll post it by the road," Lance said and raced away without a backward look.

Peter sat wooden as Lance's engine faded into silence. He should never have left his mother alone in this town without Dad and her family. He should have made her come back with him, at least until the investigation was over. But even as these thoughts ran through his mind, he knew he could never have changed her mind. She loved Grace Arbor, and she wouldn't have left it. He gritted his teeth and struggled for calm.

"Peter?" Tess broke in. "Your mother…" She gave the sign for mother—arms cradled as though holding a baby. "God will help her."

Peter couldn't speak for the anguish that gripped him like a vise. He longed to believe there was help from some higher power, too. Could he believe it after all these years? His father's voice seemed to whisper from some far-away place, "Son, you are loved. Don't forget that."

The words repeated themselves like an epiphany. If his father could love him despite his rebellion, maybe God could forgive him for refusing to acknowledge Him as God. Even as the thoughts tumbled around in his mind, the truths he'd been taught as a little child echoed in his mind. If you could believe in the sun when it wasn't shining, you could believe in God even when He was silent.

But somewhere out there with his mother was a desperate young man with a gun. Could Lance and the local police find them before something terrible happened? He didn't allow his mind to probe the awful possibilities. The wail of a siren penetrated the poignant silence, and his heart sent up a wordless appeal for the help of the Almighty.

Chapter 22

"You can't just leave them out in the woods," Anne shouted as the pick-up truck bounced over the rutted road and tossed her against the door. "Margaret's sick, and Tess is … " A loud bolt of thunder cut off her plea mid-sentence.

Having forced her into Lance's truck, which he had either borrowed or stolen, they were speeding away from the site where Tess and Margaret had been abandoned. She appealed to Shane Eldridge, whose eyes were squeezed in concentration, the rock-hard jaw bearing half an inch of dark stubble.

"It's pouring rain!" she pleaded. "How can you do this? Please, can't we call someone to come and get them?"

"Quiet!" Shane muttered, taking one hand from the steering wheel to run it through his unruly black hair. A vein in his right temple throbbed. "It's hard enough to see in this storm without you talking all the time. Besides, someone will come along."

Rain slashed against the windshield, and the truck bumped and skidded as it coursed over the wet road. Fog hung heavily in the growing dark and wrapped around tree trunks, giving them an odd, disembodied look. She shuddered and coiled her arms around herself to keep them from trembling. Where was he taking her? What would happen to Margaret and Tess? *Someone would come along.* But when?

It had taken only a few moments for the bank officer to release the contents of the safety deposit box to Margaret Morris. At the same time, Shane threatened his hostages with bodily harm if she didn't come back with the contents of the box. Margaret had coped with the crisis, but when she returned, she was shaking with cold and exertion.

Anne faced straight ahead, her fear turning to anger. She spoke into the windshield. "You know, taking something that doesn't belong to you is one thing. That's theft, but if Margaret should die in the woods..."

Shane swerved again, throwing Anne against the protruding door handle on the passenger side. Pain shot through her right shoulder, and her ear stung where it had connected with the window's cold glass.

Shane righted the truck and veered down a narrow road full of deep ruts. She crouched against the door and prayed for someone to help Margaret and Tess. She didn't want to think about what Shane might plan to do with his now sole hostage.

They bounced once more onto a road that had not benefitted from taxpayers' money. She was jolted roughly from side to side while lightning flashed, revealing piles of rock and earthmoving machines abandoned in a littered field. A shack materialized in the uncertain light, and Shane drew up next to it and thrust the truck into parking gear.

"Get out!" he demanded.

Was he going to let her go in this desolate place? Just dump her off as he had Tess and Margaret? She stared at the lump in the pocket of Shane's coat—the blue Cubs jacket—Lance's jacket.

"Get out!" he repeated.

Anne obeyed, and once her feet touched the ground, Shane leaped out and swung around to her side, pulling the gun from his pocket and waving it at her. He motioned for her to walk ahead as thunder unleashed another angry torrent.

"In there," he shouted, waving the gun toward the shack, which Anne realized was part of the fledgling mine owned by Joe Lair. The company office probably, but it looked abandoned. Was it one more failed venture in the shady entrepreneur's bag of tricks? Shane pulled out a key and unlocked the door. He grabbed her arm and pushed her over the threshold.

She saw a battered desk, a computer, and four rough chairs in the muted light. One was missing the bottom rung. A coffee machine and several dirty cups lay on a scarred table. She glanced around, adjusting her eyes to the dimness. A closed door at the end of the room might be a bathroom or a storage area.

"We're going to hole up here until the storm stops," Shane said nervously. Black stubble stood out on his cheeks, and dark circles shadowed his eyes. She wasn't the only one experiencing emotional strain. He stepped away from the door and tossed the truck key onto a nearby shelf. Anne pretended not to notice and willed Shane to forget he had put it there instead of tucking it into his pocket.

She looked around, half expecting Joe Lair to pop out from some dark corner, but all was still inside the tawdry room. She picked up some paper towels from the table to blot her wet hair. The office was cold and damp as a mine. "Can't we turn on some light?" she asked in a small voice.

"No!" he shouted. "Not that anyone could see it. This place is miles from nowhere!" He jerked his head toward the table with the unwashed percolator. "Fix us some coffee; it's in that box under the table."

Anne wiped out the stale coffee grounds and put in a clean filter. She poured water into the grimy top, feeling foolishly happy for the tiny brilliance of the machine's red on/off switch.

Shane pulled a chair near the shack's lone window and sat backward, his muddy boots dripping onto the floor. He leaned his arms over the backrest and set the gun at his feet on the floor, watching her intently as he did so. The click of metal meeting the floor sent a dull shudder through her, as Shane had no doubt intended.

He picked up the telephone receiver and jabbed some numbers into the keypad. She busied herself with the coffee but listened closely.

"It's me," Shane muttered. "I got it."

There was a long silence while whoever was on the other end responded. When Shane picked up the conversation again, his tone was altered, heightened like a child defending himself. "No, the old lady had it ... Well, I had to ... "

Silence again. If only she could hear who was on the other end and what he was saying!

Shane's chair squeaked as he lurched forward in agitation. "I had to hole up here. The storm—couldn't see anything."

Was he talking to Joe Lair? Anne's fingers trembled on the coffee pot. It shouldn't come as any surprise. She'd heard Lair's name in the context of questionable business deals. But had he gotten involved in something as juvenile and unpracticed as what Shane was attempting? She strained to catch Shane's muffled voice.

"They didn't make trouble. The old lady had it in her safety deposit box, but I got it now. I dumped them in the woods, but I got that Westin woman here with me ... "

Judging by the raised voice on the other end, Lair was not happy with his cohort's handling of things.

"What do you mean get out? I can't leave now. I got my old man's truck. Someone will recognize it!" Shane was standing now, one arm rigid at his side. "You gotta' come. You ... "

Seconds elapsed as Shane stared mutely at the phone, his face blanched and angry. Anne could hear his heavy breathing and then the slam of the receiver. Lair must have ordered him out of the office; he'd not want his name tied to kidnapping and stealing a woman's safety deposit box, though he had probably encouraged Shane to find the treasure—maybe promised him something for cutting him in. But Lair was too smart to be tied to kidnapping and theft.

She turned toward Shane, coffee cup in hand, and waited. He remained rigid near the shelf where he had flung the key when they entered. It was just over her left shoulder. She could reach out and touch it. "So, you're on your own," she said after a few moments of strained silence. "What are you going to do now?"

He grabbed the cup, sloshing part of its contents on the desk. "Sit down over there and shut up!"

She moved to the chair opposite the desk and folded her arms, gauging the distance to the shelf. "How long are you going to keep me here?"

"Until I say different!" he shouted. He paced the perimeter of the tiny office, his mouth a tight line. Presently, his features changed as though a plan had occurred to him. A cocky glint sparked in the pale eyes.

"You work for Joe Lair, don't you?" she asked quietly.

His mouth curved in a kind of sneer, and his eyes roved around the interior of the mine office. "I worked my tail off for him, and he promised…" He broke off, as though suddenly aware of his audience. He uttered a curse under his breath and continued. "This could have been a gold mine! But it'll be the next century before they get anything out of this rock the way they go about it! They got no imagination like everybody else in this hick town!"

Anne studied him as he gulped his coffee. How did he plan to get out of the spot he was in now that Lair was leaving him high and dry? Shane wasn't stupid, but he had clearly bungled things in a scheme destined for failure from the beginning. How could he have possibly thought it would succeed? And what would Lance do when everything came tumbling down?

"Didn't your uncle take you in, give you a job and place to live?" she began, regretting the patronizing tone of her voice.

"Yeah, yeah, good old Uncle Lance. He'd have kicked me out long ago if it weren't for my mother." He stopped, suddenly aware he'd said something he hadn't planned to say. His cold eyes flickered at the word "mother" like a Venetian blind opening and closing. And Anne saw a surprising sadness in them. His dangerous ploy must be about more than money.

"And what would your mother think of you now?" Anne asked quietly, leveling her gaze to meet his.

The icy glare returned. "Maybe she'd think I'll finally get what's owed me. Maybe it doesn't matter what anybody thinks." His voice rose to a threat on the final syllable. "Maybe you better get me some more coffee and stay out of my business!" He kicked the chair next to him, sending it slamming against the desk.

Anne lifted the coffeepot and refilled his cup. She waited for him to drink and then addressed him again, keeping her voice level and low. "What really happened to Alexei?"

She wasn't sure he had heard her, but he looked out the smeared window after a long silence. He addressed his words to the air. "Fool! Leading me on like that when all the time he knew his old girlfriend had these." He fingered the little sack in the breast pocket of his shirt. "I listened to his crazy story day after day. I helped him dig up half the county. He had no right to trick me that way." He clutched his cup, and the muscles in his jaw worked in agitation.

"I'd have shared 'em with him and little Bea. Well now, I've decided little Bea don't need 'em, and the old Rusky sure don't."

"Shane," Anne asked again, "What happened to Alexei?"

After a long, noisy swallow, he wiped his mouth. "He really had me going that night. Said he'd finally remembered. He had me crazy. We kept digging deeper and deeper. He was sure that was the spot. I shoved him out of the way to dig faster."

An owl hooted in the distance, and Anne wondered if Shane had said all he was going to say on the subject. But he continued in a kind of dreamy recitation. "The old fool hit his head on the tree. I was sure he'd come to. I kept on digging, but there was nothing there! Nothing but a mound of black dirt!" Shane flung his coffee cup across the room, and it shattered on the rough floorboard.

Anne cringed against the desk, feeling her knees go weak. Was she going to faint? Did anybody know she was in trouble? Was Peter waiting patiently in the calm haven of her house, expecting she would return soon?

And where was Lance? Was he blissfully going about his real estate business? He hadn't believed her about someone watching the house or releasing the fawn. Still, he had pressed her to get away from Grace Arbor as recently as yesterday when she'd hung up on him. Did he know what was going on here? What Shane was up to?

"You sent that letter, didn't you?" she said. "You wanted me to think..." She stopped, suddenly infuriated by Shane's humorless laugh and the way he rocked back and forth on two legs of the chair with his arms folded across his chest. "It was you! You broke into my shed and let the fawn go. And it was you in the woods wearing your uncle's coat."

She peered at her captor, recognizing the similarity to Lance's square jaw and high curving forehead. Did Lance know what his sister's son was doing? The thought flashed through her mind: Or was he part of it? Had he hoped Shane would find the treasure while it was still up for grabs?

It was a strange time to recall the idyllic pleasure of sailing in Lance's boat, how his voice had lulled her in the sun-drenched afternoon as willows wept along the bank and clouds floated listlessly overhead. She remembered the warm clasp of his hand and the tenderness in his voice.

Shane's laugh broke in on her reverie. He cracked his knuckles, and sweat stood out on his forehead, even though the temperature in the mine office was cold. Anne drew a deep breath. Shane was desperate, and desperate men could be pushed too far. She had to be careful.

She said in a flash of inspiration, "Your mother wouldn't blame you. She knows you didn't mean to kill Alexei. It was an accident. An accident, Shane. You can stop all this now. You can give Tess's jewels back."

"Shut up! Shut up!" he shouted, clamping both hands over his ears. A crack of lightning flashed across the room like a judgment from heaven, and Shane leaped from his chair. He gripped Anne's arms in clammy hands and shoved her backward against the wall. She felt his hot breath against her face and smelled the pungent after-shave lotion.

"Please!" she gasped.

Suddenly, he released her as though the exertion had worn him out and sat down again. Anne rubbed her arms where his fingers had dug into her flesh and breathed another desperate prayer.

"Alexei was stupid!" Shane said under his breath. "But I didn't mean for him to die." A flash of vulnerability crept into his features, turning arrogance into boyish fear. He seemed detached, the cold cabin and the gun at his feet part of a scene in a play upon which the curtain had fallen.

He patted the black bag again and then absently tucked it inside his jacket—the Cubs jacket she'd seen in the woods. Why was Shane wearing it? Anne felt her knees tremble, but she fixed them firmly on the floor and clutched the corner of the desk. She studied him as he sat backward in the greasy chair not more than six feet away.

"Your mother," Anne said, trying to bring him back to the subject. She would understand that you didn't mean to hurt Alexei. She wouldn't blame—"

"No, Ma can't blame anyone—for anything," he growled. He began to rock on two legs of the stool again. "She's dead." His voice drifted into a foggy reverie. "She can't see. She can't know anything. She's buried under that black dirt and never coming back."

Anne moved back soundlessly, carefully, as Shane's half-angry, half-sorrowful harangue continued. She closed her fingers around the key and stepped closer to the door. Heart pounding, she bolted and ran to the pickup with the key grasped tightly in her fist, cutting into her palm. As she reached the truck, she heard him behind her.

He had covered the short distance from the shack in seconds. Realizing that there was no way she could get in and start the engine before he yanked her away, Anne threw the key as far as she could and sprang away along the unpaved road they'd traveled only moments before. As she ran, tangled weeds and sharp sticks slashed against her ankles, and her chest heaved with fear and exertion.

Over her shoulder, she could see Shane kneeling in the dirt, scrambling for the key. Finding it would be an almost impossible feat in the darkness. She ran on, knowing he had to be sprinting after her. And when he caught her, what then?

Chapter 23

Anne tore through the brush. Shane was young and strong, but she was still quick and light on her feet. *Dear Lord, help me!* If she could only reach the road before Shane caught up with her. Maybe a passing motorist would stop.

She glanced down at her canvas shoes covered with mud and soaked through to her socks. Thankfully, she hadn't worn sandals or high heels. But why hadn't she worn something other than light tan slacks and a white sweater? The full moon probably lit her up like New York neon.

Not having combed her hair since morning, she could tell it was frizzy from the damp air. She imagined how she would look to someone driving along—a wild half-century apparition coming out of the woods like a crazy woman.

She paused to listen. Was Shane thrashing through the woods in pursuit? Or had he chosen to continue searching for the key? Maybe he'd found it and was coming after her in the truck. She gasped and ran on, unsure if the whooshing sound she heard was her frenzied passage through the woods or Shane's footsteps closing in.

Please, let someone come to help me find Margaret and Tess. The irony of it, she thought. She wanted to make a difference for good in her adopted town. Instead, she was plunged into deception and chaos, into a dark mystery driven by the greed of an angry young man. Others had been drawn into the drama with devastating results.

She had to get help. Where exactly had Shane left Tess and Margaret? It couldn't be far. It had taken only minutes to get from the woods to the shack. The startlingly brilliant moon lit a clear path for her erratic strides, revealing ruts and tree roots before she could stumble over them, but it also made her a lighted target.

Suppose she had misinterpreted the one-way conversation Shane had with Joe? What if Lair was on his way to the mine office, worried that Shane had involved him in a plot that would leave him vulnerable?

"I am with you always, even to the end of the world." She repeated the Scriptural promise over and over as she ran. How often she had pondered those words but never before clung to them with such desperate need! She had longed to make Grace Arbor a place of welcome and grace. Was the bright dream about to end in a lonely wood?

Suddenly, headlights filtered through the leafy network. Someone was coming! With renewed vigor, she raced toward the open road, fleeing the cover of woods to make herself visible. She zigzagged through the trees that bordered the road and flung her arms in wide, furious circles. Help was coming!

Or was she heading straight into the path of Joe Lair? She had never thought of him as truly dangerous. Underhanded, clever, but treacherous?

Suddenly, she stumbled over something—a tree root or a branch broken off in the storm. As she fell, she scraped the palms of her hands on the tangled brush, and blood oozed wet and warm from her left leg. Seconds later, she felt the painful throbbing. The car was almost there. Going too fast. "Stop! Please!" she shouted breathlessly.

But the car passed, continuing steadily down the road away from her.

Tears of desperation rose in her throat. She struggled to her feet, wiped her stinging hands, and fought the rising panic. She must stay focused. She must keep one foot moving after the other.

Was she heading toward town or away from it? Ever since childhood, when she took a wrong turn in a tiny town, she'd feared losing her way. She was grown now, but the warrior was still a child, she thought ruefully. Heavy foliage protected her from the full impact of the rain, but the forest floor, with its hundred hidden hazards, was slippery. She ran on, keeping under the cover of trees but staying close to the road so she could quickly leap out and wave for help. If one car had come along, surely another would. *Lord, let it not be a familiar battered pickup!*

Where was Peter? She'd have left him a note before going to Margaret's but planned to return well before his arrival. What if Peter should lose both Richard *and* her? No. She mustn't allow the thought. Not when her son was beginning to find his way back with the help of a gentle deaf woman and a God who heard and saw everything.

A bird cry pierced the air like the scream of the blue jay on the night Alexei had died. She envisioned him lying stiff in the wood, eyes burned out fuses in his sunken face. Shane had said it was an accident, but he hadn't done anything to help until it was too late. Was she to become a second victim of avarice?

She had to rest—just for a moment. Her leg continued to throb. She longed to lie down, to pillow her head on the bed of pine needles. Richard's soft gray eyes seemed to beckon her. It would be so lovely.

Suddenly, the sound of an engine forced the dream away. She shook herself. Someone was coming. She ran to the edge of the road, leaving the protection of the pines. Feeling the last bit of strength draining from her, she raised an arm and waved, or at least thought she was waving. Why were her arms so heavy?

The car slowed, then stopped. Anne flung herself at the door. As she pulled the handle, the driver raced to the passenger side and reached for her.

"Anne," Lance murmured. He helped her inside the car and wrapped something around her—a coat or a blanket. His hands were warm through the thick cloth, and she drank in the comfort of his arms. He was kissing the top of her head and saying her name over and over. Her heart pounded with such relief that she thought she might lose consciousness.

As quickly as relief spread over her, a vivid picture pierced her consciousness—Margaret, pale and trembling, and Tess being shoved out of the truck. She drew away from Lance and tried to speak through her chattering teeth. "Margaret—Tess! We've got to find them."

"They're safe, Anne. We found them over an hour ago. They're all right." Lance spoke softly but insistently as though she were a child. "Margaret and Tess are all right. They're safe. Just lean back and rest."

Anne gave herself up to the comfort of his voice and relaxed against him, hypnotized by the rapid beating of his heart blending with hers. How long she sat braced against him as he drove, she didn't know. Where was he going? Maybe she had slept or even briefly lost consciousness. She struggled to line up the events of the past hours.

When city lights appeared just ahead, she bolted up in the seat. She was no longer running through winding countryside and sinister woods. She was safe inside Lance's jeep. But was she safe? Were Margaret and Tess all right, as Lance said? She tried to clear her throat. She had to find Peter. Everything was such a mixed-up jumble.

"Just rest now, Anne," Lance said. "We'll be there soon."

She leaned back and felt sleep drawing her in again until she heard Lance speaking quietly into his cell phone. She struggled to make out the words. "I've got her." A chill raced up her spine. Was Lance in on everything with Shane? Perhaps with Joe Lair, too? Was she now caught in their trap? She listened, her mind reeling.

There was a note of restrained triumph in his voice. "I'm bringing her in."

No. As the car lurched around a corner, a building came into view—a building with windows and gleaming glass doors. The hospital! Lance slowed, but before he could come to a complete stop, she flung herself out and ran toward it. He was calling her name, but she didn't look back. And suddenly, someone was bursting through the hospital door.

It was Peter, haggard and disheveled, hair flying about his face. His rumpled shirt streamed out like laundry on a line as he drew her into his embrace. Inside, he hovered over her with grave eyes. "You've been through a terrible time, Mom. We need to get you checked out here at the hospital."

"I'm all right," she tried to say, pulling out of his embrace and trying to smile through quivering lips. "Peter, it's so good to see you!" She wanted to say how much she loved him and that he was the best son in the world, but the words wouldn't come out.

He must have asked someone to bring a cup of coffee, for one magically appeared in his hand. "Here, Mom, drink this."

She pressed it to her lips. "So glad ... so glad you're here," she stammered. "But how did you ... how did you know?"

"We've been so worried. When you weren't home, I didn't know what to do. I called your realtor friend."

Lance?

"He found you. He was out of his mind with worry and kept blaming himself. We didn't know where you were, but he remembered your neighbor, the Morris woman." Peter's dark brows drew together. "When we got to her house, she was gone, and her room had been ransacked."

Anne tried to follow Peter's account, willing her muddled mind to sort itself out. Where was Lance? Had he joined his nephew to find the inheritance Shane coveted?

She pushed against the confusion in her mind, recalling how Shane had yanked Margaret out of the Jeep. She could have fallen and broken something despite Tess supporting her. Anne tried to shake the image of them stumbling through the woods with the rain beating down on them. Lance had told her that they'd been found. They were safe.

She searched Peter's face. "Margaret…and Tess?"

"They're fine, Mom, and now you're safe too." He broke off and pushed his glasses up with the back of his hand. In a hushed voice, he added, "Our prayers have been answered."

Chapter 24

*L*ance watched Anne disappear through the double glass doors of the hospital.

When he'd found her along the road, she had been so traumatized that she couldn't speak. Gradually, she had settled down enough to tell him that Shane had stolen the jewels from Margaret's bank deposit box and left her with Tess in the woods. He shook his head. He couldn't believe it. Yet, he could. He should have known and acted before Shane did something so stupid, so dangerous.

He had tried to make Anne understand that it would be all right, and she had settled against him, wrapped in the blanket he tucked around her. He told her Peter was waiting for her at the hospital and that Tess and Margaret were there too. They were all safe.

He phoned the sheriff and briefed him on what was happening as Anne slept from exhaustion. After a few moments, she woke and shifted away from him, pressing against the passenger door with an inscrutable expression. When they pulled up to the hospital, she leaped out without a word to him. Run from him as though the devil himself were after her.

What was she thinking? It struck him to the heart as he watched the closed door she had passed through. Why hadn't he guessed what his nephew was up to? He wanted to go to reassure her again, but he had to find Shane before he could do any more damage to anyone—or himself. He put the jeep in gear. Anne was with Peter. She would be all right. She had to be all right!

He retraced his path to the outskirts of town where the copper diggings were located. Signs once advertised the location, but as hopes for a real find had diminished, few people ventured down the abandoned road that led to the mine.

Shane, what happened to you? How could you endanger the lives of Anne and Margaret—and the young woman you said you cared about?

How little he knew his own sister's son. When they'd been children, Jane had talked endlessly about the family she'd have one day—a girl with curly dark hair like her own and a boy who'd grow up to do heroic deeds. She used to invent roles for her son to play that showed his strength and bravery. How devastated she would be if she knew the role he was playing now on this dark day at summer's end.

Lance nearly missed the dirt road hidden among scrub trees and brush. The tangled path led upward in hairpin turns and ended in a clumsily cleared field where ravished stalks poked up from the ground as though in shock. A great pit yawned on one side of the field, surrounded by fencing to keep a curious public away. Abandoned trucks and rusty machine parts lay scattered about the yard.

A dilapidated shack, sinister-looking in the moonlight, appeared at the bottom of the hill. What had happened inside? Thank God Anne had escaped—and that he had found her. She had outlined her breathless escape. *I threw the keys into the brush and ran.* Had Shane set off on foot or found another set of wheels? He wouldn't still be here in this desolate place, would he?

Lance got out of his Jeep and approached the shack. The ground soaked through his shoes, and he felt the little hairs on his arms stand up on end. In the deathly quiet, he headed for the little cabin. Did Joe Lair still conduct business here? He wondered if the old diggings were part of the sheriff's usual rounds and how long it would be before Shane's connection with what was happening here would be discovered. Was there a chance he could get to the boy first?

"Joe Lair is no friend to you," he had cautioned Shane only days before. But he had stared at him, anger in his eyes, and stalked away, sputtering that his friends were his own business.

"And who works for me and lives in my house is my business!" he had countered.

At that, Shane had hoisted himself over the deck rail and beat it across the back lawn. Lance kicked at a stone, remembering how angry they were.

As he approached the mine office, something in Lance melted. Jane's husband had never accepted Shane. He had never loved him and left when his son was a child. Jane had left him too—not by choice, but she had left him all the same. Life had failed Shane. His only family had failed him, too. Lance ducked under an overhanging branch. He should have gone after him when he'd stormed angrily away, but he hadn't. Caring hurt, and he didn't want to hurt anymore.

He leaned into the rough-hewn door, but it didn't give way. He thumped it with his fists and waited, but only the drone of insects answered. "Shane! You in there?" His voice reverberated in the still air as he shoved his weight against the door. "Open up, Shane."

"Get out of here!"

The voice startled him. Shane was still here! "Open up, Shane."

"I'm warning you. Leave me alone."

"Please, let's talk about this. I can help you."

"Go away!"

But Lance detected a faint, almost imperceptible tremor. Why hadn't Shane run? Why had he remained inside the cabin like a deer in the blind, waiting to be captured?

He pushed against the door again and heard the wood creak. "Come on, Shane. We've got to talk. Open up." Anne said that Shane had a gun. Would he use it? His nephew was behind the door—his sister's son, not some mafia henchman. Still, his mouth went dry.

"Leave me alone!" came the voice again, but there was no mistaking the plaintive tone this time.

Lance gave the door a mighty shove, and the old wood cracked. He stumbled inside.

It was pitch black in the cabin, but Shane couldn't be far away. Lance thought he could hear Shane breathing. He groped in the silence, willing his eyes to grow accustomed to the darkness. He made out a vague square of light through the gloom—a window backlit by the moon—and then an overturned chair.

"Shane," he said quietly. "Where are you? I want to help you."

Something like a groan came from behind him. Lance fumbled in his pocket for his phone. It afforded enough light to see Shane sitting backward in a chair, head down, hands between his knees. A gun lay on the floor at his feet.

This was not the cocky Shane Eldridge who had scoffed at work and, in every other way, tried his patience since coming to stay with him. Here was a dejected boy crouched in a dingy backwoods hole with nowhere to turn. "Shane?"

"I couldn't even do this right," he muttered without looking up. "You might as well call in the posse." Shane kicked at the gun and sent it clattering across the wood floor. "The thing ain't got bullets. Screwed that up too."

Seconds passed. Lance flicked a switch on a nearby wall, and light flooded the grimy room, revealing hastily affixed, unpainted wallboard. Old newspapers yellowed under the desk, and a pile of dirty cups cluttered a scarred table. A mound of papers that might have been blueprints or assayers' charts made a haphazard pyramid.

Shane was slumped in the chair, untidy hair obscuring his face. He rubbed his hands together with small rhythmic movements like a tired, old man recollecting his past.

Lance righted the overturned chair and pulled it close to his nephew. Several minutes passed without a sound. Presently, Shane straightened and spread his feet out in front of him. "What? No posse?"

"I'm alone," Lance said quietly. "I was looking for you."

Shane cracked his knuckles and folded his arms across his chest. "Yeah, well, you found me." He looked away, but Lance could see his pulse pounding in his temple.

What could he have been thinking to force three women into a truck, steal from one, and hold the others captive? Lance shuddered. Had Alexei been one of his victims, too? He worked to control his anger and the sorrow that engulfed him. "Why, Shane?"

"Why? Why? Who cares why anyway?"

"The why matters," Lance said firmly, commanding his nephew's eyes. "You're guilty of kidnapping and theft. You've screwed up royally—all for nothing!"

Shane pulled something from inside his shirt—a black bag with a drawstring that had come untied. He clutched it, then dropped it in his lap as though it were hot. "That's not nothing!" he shouted. "It's a fortune. I never had nothing before, but now I got it." He thrust the bag back inside his shirt.

Lance gasped at the sight of the bag. Was it possible that the rumors were true? Had there really been buried jewels? Treasures carried away from a dank cellar where a dynasty had been destroyed?

Lance had heard the rumors that spawned a rush of curiosity, then faded as interest waned. Reporters and history buffs who occasionally visited their small town came and went. Gradually, everyone believed Alexei was just a troubled man who had internalized the events of his country's trauma so many years ago.

"That old man didn't need it. And that old woman didn't do nothing with it. It was up for grabs!"

"You stole it from Miss Morris. She's in the hospital right now," Lance said. "You left her by the side of the road, and if it hadn't been for Tess and Anne Westin, she could have died."

At this, Shane's head jerked up. Surprise that the three of them had been found? Maybe relief? The little veins in his temple twitched. After a moment, he said, "The jewels weren't hers. Weren't that old man's either."

"Shane, what happened to Alexei?"

Shane pursed his mouth like a spoiled toddler's. "It wasn't my fault. He fell. I thought he'd come to, but he didn't."

"You've got to tell the truth to the police," Lance said quietly. "The truth—all of it." He leaned forward. "You can give the jewels back, Shane. It won't change what you've done, but it will go easier for you."

"Nothing goes easy for me. Nothing ever will. Mom and me had to scrounge for every penny, and she—" He stared at Lance as though he saw something startling or terrible in his uncle's face.

"And just what do you think your Mother would say now if she knew?" Lance asked. "She loved you."

"Shut up! Shut up!" Shane clamped his hands over his ears. "Why does everybody have to bring her into it?"

"Your mother always expected you to do the brave thing, the right thing. She believed in you." Lance left his chair and took a step nearer. "Why don't you tell Chief Mackowitz you want to return the jewels?" He pulled out his cell phone. "Why don't we call him now?"

He looked down at the bowed head with its glossy young hair. Shane nervously rubbed his hands, the blunt fingernails bitten to the quick. Lance was seized with longing and regret.

The silence lay long and heavy. For all his bravado and cynicism, maybe Shane wanted it to be over. Had he stayed in the cabin instead of running, hoping someone would stop him?

Lance sat down again quietly, cell phone open in his palm. "They'll be all right—Miss Morris and Tess. Anne, too," Lance said quietly. "You did a terrible thing, but it doesn't have to get worse. You can return what you stole and face up to things." He paused, watching Shane with an aching heart. "I'll be here for you," he added. Keeping his eyes on his nephew's downcast face, he punched in the numbers and heard Mackowitz's voice.

"Lance Crane here. I'm with my nephew at the old mine shack off Cooper's Road. He has something to tell you."

Shane made no move to run or even to move. Lance closed the phone, aware that his hand was trembling. Something of great importance was happening. There was something greater than greed, stronger than loss, more profound than the death of a dream. Something that could turn the course of a young man bent on his own destruction.

Grace could change the trajectory of his life, too, Lance realized. He had lived with little passion and purpose since Rose died. But God had heard him, though he had not known how to plead for that grace. He pocketed the phone and placed his hand on Shane's shoulder, aware of an uncommon peace.

Chapter 25

Anne exchanged a glance with Peter before stepping hesitantly into the room. She had been assured that everything was being done for Margaret and that she was lucky. But luck had nothing to do with it, Anne knew, and her heart surged in gratitude.

Margaret looked up as Anne and Peter entered, and a smile teased her lips. The hospital gown hung loosely at her neck and shoulders as she fluttered the fingers of one hand toward the apparatus by her bed. "Don't be put off by all this."

Anne looked away from the saline drip and the tube carrying oxygen into the frail nostrils. "I'm so sorry," she whispered. "Are you all right?"

Margaret's eyes lit with an unmistakable twinkle. "I'm all right—thanks to Beatrice. She watched over me until your Peter came along." She smiled at Tess and Peter by the side of her bed and looked back at Anne. "Your son was like a knight in shining armor."

Peter colored at Margaret's words and scratched his left ear, the perennial sign that he was embarrassed. "We're so glad you're all right," he said. He touched Tess's shoulder, smiling fondly. "But she's the one who deserves the credit. She flagged us down, or we would never have found you."

Tess tucked a hand shyly into the crook of Peter's arm. Stray tendrils of her ponytail fringed the creamy oval of her face as she smiled up at him. His old college sweater hung almost to her knees and could have gone around her twice.

"She found her way out of the woods," Peter continued. "And yelled until we heard her. Crane and I were trying to find you, Mom," he added. "We were so worried."

Anne swallowed. It seemed days rather than hours since she and Tess had driven off together under Vera's disapproving gaze. "Does your aunt know you're all right?" she asked, forming the words carefully to ensure that Tess understood.

"We sent word as soon as we got here," Peter answered for her. "Shane put all kinds of ideas into her mind, and she was pretty confused. Actually, I'm still confused myself." Shaking his head had dislodged his glasses. He pushed them up with the back of his hand.

Anne knew they were waiting for her to tell them how she had gotten away after Shane left Tess and Margaret in the woods. But she was puzzling over what Peter had said a moment ago: *Crane and I.* They had been together and gone looking for her. "How—"

"When I got to the house and you were gone, I didn't know what to do," Peter continued. "Vera said Tess went off with you, but she didn't know where. That's when I called Crane. He came over right away, figured it had something to do with his nephew." Peter broke off, watching his mother with a puzzled expression.

"Shane kept me in that abandoned mine shack," Anne said quietly. "The storm was bad, but he knew the authorities would be looking for him."

When Anne saw Peter's fists clenching at his sides, she added, "He didn't hurt me, just bossed me around and made me fix coffee. He finally confessed that he had tried to get Vera to show him where the jewels were buried."

"I was afraid that's what he was after," Margaret said huskily. "When Alexei kept digging up all over town, Shane must have believed the story of buried treasure. He searched my place, too. He never guessed that the jewels were safely stored at the bank."

Anne drew in her breath. Where was Shane now? Had he found the truck key and made his getaway? Had Lance been party to it, at least in the beginning? Was his tenderness and kindness a ploy at best and a sham at worst? Like Shane's overtures to Tess—pretending to care about her so he could get his hands on the treasure. Anne swallowed. "I managed to grab the truck key, and when he came after me, I threw it into the bushes and ran."

"Thank God you're all right," Peter said, eyes soft with concern. "Lance and I kept in touch on our cell phones. I was so relieved when he phoned to say he had found you."

Anne caught her lower lip in her teeth, recalling Lance's breath in her ear and later his furtive message over the phone: *I've got her. I'm bringing her in.* She thought he had been conspiring with an accomplice, but he'd been talking to Peter at the hospital.

"I don't think we would have found you without him," Peter said. He took off his glasses and rubbed a hand over his jaw. "It's tough on him, Shane being his nephew. He feels responsible for it all."

Anne swallowed. The suspicions, misunderstandings, and veiled phrases spun around in her mind. He had tried to warn her. He'd been afraid for her.

Watching them with a furrowed brow, Tess moved away from Peter and came around the bed to touch Anne's arm. "You were kind to me from the very first day," she said, signing as she spoke. "And I was … I thought you … " She stopped, her lips quivering.

Anne put her arms around her, feeling Tess's pulsing warmth through Peter's sweater. "I'm just glad you're safe, and Margaret is too." She paused. "I'm so sorry about Shane."

Tess lowered her head, and her jaw trembled visibly. "I thought he was my friend. Alexei did, too."

"Sometimes it's hard to know who people really are," Anne said wistfully, thinking not only of Shane but of Lance. "We've all come a long way. We have a lot to be thankful for. *I* have a lot to be thankful for," she amended. She glanced across to Peter. "There's something I have to do. All right if I meet you at home later?"

She found Lance looking out the window at the end of the lobby, his back to her. He had flung his suit coat over his left shoulder, where it hung like a flag of surrender. Slightly too long hair strayed over the collar of his shirt.

She paused. The moments they had shared played in her mind like accelerated film footage. She recalled his silver head bent over the stern of his boat, eyes alert to the water's moods. She remembered the way his arms felt around her when he had bundled her tenderly in a blanket and driven her to the hospital. She remembered the shocked look on his face when she had flung herself out and run from him.

How could she apologize for her suspicious fears? She stopped a few feet behind him, feeling time suspended.

Perhaps sensing her presence, he turned. "Are you all right?" His voice was husky, as though it had been a long time since he'd used it. A muscle in his jaw rippled.

She came alongside him and touched the fingers of his right hand that rested on the window frame. "I'm fine—thanks to you."

Surprise and confusion shone in his eyes, and something inside her melted. "I'm sorry—about thinking…" Overcome, she tucked her hand into the crook of his elbow. "I want to go home," she said softly. "Will you take me home?"

They moved out of the hospital and into his Jeep, neither speaking until they had traveled a few miles to the intermittent clacking of the windshield wipers. Then Lance broke the silence. "I never thought he would go so far," he said, keeping his eyes on the road. "I knew he was messed up, but I never thought he would…"

His words trailed off, and Anne felt his shoulder tense beside her, felt the enormity of his regret. "Shane didn't mean to kill Alexei," she said softly, seeing in her mind's eye the old man zealously guarding Tess's inheritance. She imagined him digging furiously until Shane had shoved him, and he had fallen, hitting his head on the rock. She imagined the silence that ensued, and she couldn't stop the shiver that passed through her.

"My nephew put you all in danger. I'm so sorry."

"I know," she whispered.

Grace Arbor appeared, enveloped in the mist that lies over the land between moonlight and dawn. Anne drew in her breath sharply, feeling a bittersweet ache. "Home." She wasn't sure she could ever feel at home again with Richard gone. But now…

"Home." The word embodied all that was good and meaningful, all that endured, all that was love. Misunderstandings, sorrows, and fears were mere shadows that vanished in its embrace.

"I'm afraid I've been a real coward," Lance said softly. "I couldn't even talk to God anymore. Then you came. I saw how your loss didn't turn you away from him and other people. How strong you were."

They had driven the length of the driveway and stopped a few feet from Grace Arbor. The trees cast dancing shadows on the beautiful old house in the moon's glow. Tess's well-tended bushes and flowers bore their fragrance on the dawning day as the wind chimes played softly.

"Shane will need all the help I can give him now," he said quietly, drawing her close and stroking her hand gently.

"I know," she whispered. Shane had gone quietly with Mackowitz and confessed to everything. The days ahead would be anything but easy for him—for any of them. Reporters eager for a story would descend on the small town again. Tess would need help handling the sudden appearance of a fabled treasure and all that a country's sad history had bestowed on her.

How much had Vera known? What had she suffered? Had she who should have been protected been left to flounder in confusion? She had been used and abused, like too many of the world's vulnerable citizens, but there was grace for her, and Anne yearned to help Vera find it.

In the darkness of fear, the light was guiding them to safety. It would continue in the days ahead—for Lance as he supported Shane, for Peter and Tess and Vera. *And for me*, she thought. *How tender is God's grace to us all.*

The rasp of crickets faded with the stars, and light broke through the mist. Lance's shoulder pressed close. His hand covered hers as they watched the sun's relentless climb over Grace Arbor. It was a new day, a day to be glad and rejoice.

About the Author

Marlene Chase is an ordained minister, serving as a Salvation Army officer for 43 years. She retired from her position as editor-in-chief and literary secretary for the Army's publications in the United States, having served in that capacity for 11 years. She traveled extensively in teaching/preaching ministries both in the U.S. and abroad. She holds a Bachelor of Arts degree in English from Mid-America Nazarene College and attended The Salvation Army College for Officer Training in Chicago, Illinois, and the International College for Officers in London. She has published 24 books and a host of articles, poetry, and internationally aired radio scripts. She continues to write both for the popular market and Salvation Army publications from her home in Rockford, Illinois.

More Books by Author

The Other Side of Silence, Barbour, Ulrichsville, O
This Trembling Cup, Barbour, Ulrichsville, O
A Seed in the Wind, The Salvation Army, Chicago, IL
Twenty-Five Years of CMI, The Salvation Army, Chicago, IL.
Our God Comes, Crest Books, Alexandria, VA.
Beside Still Waters, Crest Books, Alexandria, VA
Pictures from the Word, Crest Books, Alexandria, VA.
The Salvation Army, Crest Books, Alexandria, VA.
(Translations in Korean and Spanish)
Forever and a Day, Guideposts
The Greatest of These, Guideposts
Sapphire Secret, Guideposts
The Hidden Gate, Guideposts
Larceny and Old Lace, Annie's Mysteries
A Crime Well Versed, Annie's Mysteries
All That Glimmers, Annie's Mysteries
Deceptive Hearts, Annie's Mysteries

Acknowledgments

This story was my mother's before it was mine. She lived the ideals it purports and throughout her life modeled the sterling characteristics of Anne Westin. She always thought of herself as ordinary, a small part of the network of humanity that graces this planet. But I, who know her well, give tribute to her who always reached—not for the stars—but for their Maker, in whose house of grace she now lives.

To Diane Tolcher, my friend and companion of more than 30 years, thank you for making this story come to fruition through careful critique and artistic support. Her stunning photograph of the "House of Grace" appears on the cover of this book.

I'm grateful to Story Architect and Jill Kemerer at Books and Such, as well as my agent, Wendy Lawton, for making this book possible. And heartfelt thanks to you, Reader, for making the hours of writing worth the effort. I hope your investment of time is rewarded.

www.ingramcontent.com/pod-product-compliance
Lightning Source LLC
Chambersburg PA
CBHW020325200626
46814CB00006BB/2422